New Dimensions

SCIENCE FICTION

NUMBER 5

Edited by ROBERT SILVERBERG

HARPER & ROW, PUBLISHERS

NEW YORK

EVANSTON

SAN FRANCISCO

LONDON

NEW DIMENSIONS SCIENCE FICTION, NUMBER 5. Copyright © 1975 by Robert Silverberg. All rights reserved. Printed in the United States of America. No part of this book may be used or reproduced in any manner whatsoever without written permission except in the case of brief quotations embodied in critical articles and reviews. For information address Harper & Row, Publishers, Inc., 10 East 53rd Street, New York, N.Y. 10022. Published simultaneously in Canada by Fitzhenry & Whiteside Limited, Toronto.

ISBN: 0–06–013870–X

Designed by Sidney Feinberg

75 76 77 78 79 10 9 8 7 6 5 4 3 2

CONTENTS

NEW DIMENSIONS 5

NICHOLAS FISK *was born in 1923, and has written for a living since he was sixteen, with, he says, "excursions into acting, photography, the RAF, playing jazz, journalism, paperback publishing, copywriting, and illustration." Now, living in "what used to be village quite near London," he concentrates on writing, photography, and serving as "creative man" for a well-known British publishing house, diverting himself after working hours with such amusements as "underwater sightseeing, billiards, microscopy, and a late addition to his family of four children." This elegant, playfully malicious short story is, we believe, his first appearance before the American science-fiction audience.*

■

Nicholas Fisk

■

FIND THE LADY

The scarred metal grab reached out and touched the little wooden writing desk. Mitch, feeling the giggles rising in him, clutched Eugene's arm. Eugene glared, but it only made things worse.

"Ooop!—ooo!—ooop!" went Mitch.

"Shut up! Oh, do shut *up!*"

"Ooop! Oh, dearie me, I'll die!"

"Silly pouf! Shut up!"

"Don't call me that name—"

"Shut UP! They'll hear!"

The metal grab protruded a metal claw. It made a tiny puncture in the ginger wood and withdrew. A hundred feet or so away in the grab's parent body, a message was received. There was a lacklustre spurt of messages—a dim buzzing and clicking and whirring echoing up and down the extensible limb.

The metal grab, with surprising delicacy, again protruded its claw and began tracing the outlines and surfaces of the desk. It was what had been known as a Davenport. It had a tooled-leather inclined lid with storage space beneath it, supported on a body containing a multiplicity of drawers, sliding boxes and trite gadgetry. The claw explored.

"God save us," wheezed Eugene, "when it gets to the *legs*..." The giggles were fighting through again. The legs! "The *legs!*" groaned Mitch, clutching himself.

They were too absurd, the legs. Once, the Davenport must

3

have been possessed of two respectable curlicued fretwork legs
—or perhaps two faked wooden pillars with capitals. They had
long gone. Filled with joyous spite, Mitch and Eugene had replaced them with two rusty chromium-plated tubes they had
found in the rubble. The effect was lunatic: the grandiose little
ginger Davenport had somehow become a desk of easy virtue.
They had danced round it, shouting at it.

"Harlot!"

"Strumpet!"

"Wicked thing!"

"Dirty French whore, showing your legs!"

"Soiled dove!"

"Naughty saucy beastly dirty DAVENPORT!"

Then they had staggered in helpless laughter, holding each
other up; two ageing queers, delirious with malice and joy.

"Bet you They buy it!"

"Bet you They don't!"

"Don't be such a sillybilly, you *know* They will! They'll *leap*
on it! They'll *lust* for it! Our dirty Davenport!"

"Just because They bought the telephone and the King
George the Fifth biscuit tin doesn't mean They'll—"

"It does, it must! They'll simply *coo* over it! They've simply
no *taste*—"

"They don't understand *nice* things, *pretty* things—"

"They've no *feelings*—"

"Well, how could They, the poor loves? I mean, just *look* at
Them! *Gaze* upon Them!"

They had both turned their heads and gazed upon Them.
There was nothing much else to look at. What had been a
country town was now a plain of reddish dust. What had been
trees were now fungus-pocked stains on that dust. What had
been railway lines were rusty traces of another red. Even the
sky was tainted with the same glowering, indelible redness. The
dust was everywhere.

Not that They stirred it. For five years They had stood senti-
nel, ringing the area of the town centre. They seldom moved.

The reddened sun glanced off their opaque bodies—fused glass which sometimes emitted winks and rays and subdued noises, but more often not. The metallic legs, 250 feet or so high at full extension, seldom shifted their articulated, raft-like feet, which might be embedded for months on end in the compound of brick dust, vegetable dust and human bonemeal. Lichens and fungi grew over the feet, and once Eugene swore he had seen a rat. But never an insect or a bird. Dead five years.

But now, at this very moment, the claw was tracing the lines and textures of the Davenport and Mitch and Eugene clasped hands, shaken by suppressed and holy glee. The *legs!* The claw solemnly examined them, the clumsy grab moving on hidden articulations of silken perfection.

"OK," said the grab. It spoke in an approximation of the town's mayor—a voice five years silent.

"OK. Will take genuine antique. Genuine. Or kill. OK?"

"OK," whispered Eugene, the giggles suddenly gone.

"OK antique!" said Mitch. "Genuine. No kill. OK. *Hon*estly."

"Ask!" hissed Eugene.

"No, you!"

"It's your turn—"

"Fat pouf! You know it's your turn to ask—"

"Pouf yourself!"

"Bedwetter! Queer! Stinkpants! *Ask* it!"

But Mitch began helplessly to cry, so Eugene had to ask.

"What will you give us? Something good, OK?"

No answer. Messages ran up and down the grab's arm. Then the voice in the grab answered.

"More food. More bricks. More alcohol. More water. More lamp oil. OK."

"Yes, but—*how* much more? *Much* more this time, OK?"

Again a long pause; then, "OK." The grab retracted with a soft whirr, carrying the Davenport as if on a platform. The machine's legs twitched and moved and a great metal foot knocked the top off the humans' hovel, then guiltlessly crushed its way, hayfoot, strawfoot, across the dust to resume station.

"Oh, and *now* look what They've done!" wept Mitch. "Clumsy beasts! I hate Them! I loathe Them! Big silly *cows!*"

"Come and help me put it all *back*—"

"You called me *names,* you're always calling me *names*—"

"I didn't mean it, you know I didn't mean it. Do be a dear and *help.*"

"If I'm what you called me, so are you and worse. Worse! Sometimes I think I hate you, you're so cruel, so mean, you've given me my pain again—"

"Come and *help.*"

"My pain—"

"Oh, do please, please, please SHUT UP."

They put the hovel together and crawled into it. It grew darker. Quite soon, the only light would be the dim blue chain of beams linking Them. You could not pass this chain. Nobody had tried now for four years and eleven months. The powdery marks of disintegrated bodies had of course long since disappeared.

◆

Two hours later, Mitch and Eugene were giggling mad again.

"Do stop!" gasped Mitch. "You're killing me! I'm quite *damp!*"

But Eugene wouldn't stop. "I'm one of THEM!" he chanted. "One of THEM!" He had pulled a broken plastic bucket over his head; the remains of two squeegee floor mops served as Their legs and feet. He jerked and slithered grotesquely. Then, inspired, he picked up an oil lamp and hung it over his backside.

"Deathray!" he shouted. "You can't get past! Oh no, you can't! I've got a deathray in my bottie!"

In the corner, the alcohol dripped from the still. Tonight was a good night. Tomorrow, They would bring more of life's little luxuries. Life was good.

◆

Life was awful. Most of those who had lived past Their coming had died more or less voluntarily. There was nothing to live for.

It had all been very simple. One day, you were a barber or a butcher or a baby or a businessman or a beautician. You said "Good morning" or kept yourself to yourself. You ordered lamb chops, put the cat out, mowed the lawn, tinkered with the car, watched TV, played bingo, distributed leaflets for the council elections.

Next day, They came and you were dead.

The TV was dead, the telephone was dead, the neighbours were dead, the flowers in your garden were dead, the cat was dead, the baby was dead, the municipal county council was dead. All without a whimper. All inside one violet-flashing, flesh-eating, matter-consuming millisecond.

All except those who were actually under and within the areas covered by Them and Their machines. For those, if their hearts did not burst with the shock, there was life of a sort. Not that anyone understood what sort. Consider Eugene and Mitch.

They had been the scandal of the little town. As they walked together, their waved hair and their glittering slave bangles caught the sun. Their staggeringly tight jeans displayed rolling hips and twitching buttocks as they walked. Under the broad straps of their sandals peeped the lacquered toenails, now crimson, now silver-pearl. No hairs showed on their toes; they plucked them out with tweezers.

They touched each other incessantly as they walked. A manicured hand would find a sunlamp-bronzed forearm and rest there to stress a point. They were always stressing points. The waved heads would converge and nod and shake, the sibilant whispers would be exchanged, the eyes would roll and pop; then the heads would be thrown back and shrill whinnying laughter would bounce off the Georgian brickwork of the high street, tinkle against the curved glass of the slenderly framed and elegantly proportioned windows, desecrate the war memorial.

They simply adored the town, it was too utterly winsome and tender.

The town blackly hated them.

♦

They ran the antique shop. Or seemed to do so. For no towns-
man would ever visit it. Perhaps Eugene and Mitch lived on
legacies; perhaps they supplied the big, important antique deal-
ers in the cities; no one knew how they lived or what they lived
on. It was enough of an affront that they lived at all, a disgrace
to the whole community.

Not that they had any part in the community. They lived in
their own little tinkling pagoda of a world, primping their hair
in the sweetly darling Regency mirror by the Adam mantel (but
could one be sure it was really, truly Adam?) and pouting
naughtily when it was their turn to make the Lapsang Sou-
chong, or pursing lips in concentration when trying out new
drapes *(not* the voile, Mitchie love, something more *floating*
and *ethereal)* to hang on the great fourposter they were said to
share . . . They needed no one but each other.

◆

It was on one of those ordinary, halcyon days that Mitch said,
"Oh, but Eugene, do *listen!"*

"I won't, I simply won't. I'm stopping my ears. There!"

"But Eugene, hear you must, hear you shall! It's a com*plete*ly
genuine and *quite* ridiculous earthenware water filter thing,
something from the Crimean *war,* I dare promise, and it's lying
in a *field* not a mile from here and we could fill it with pot-
pourri—"

"I despise the very sound of it."

"But if only you'd come with me and look at it with me
and help me carry it, you'd make me the happiest boy in the
world—"

"Really, Mitch, how camp can you get! 'The happiest boy in
the world'!"

"Well, *will* you or *won't* you help me carry it?"

That evening, they had minced briskly down the main street
and were soon out in the fields. The water filter, a great ceramic
thing bespattered with relief plaques saying NONPAREIL and

PATENTED and so on, lay in a ditch. As they bent over to lift it, the strange shadows darkened the ground. It was Them, one of Their machines, directly overhead.

A second later, the world ended.

◆

"But did it?" Eugene asked. "I mean, who are They? I mean, is it the machines—"

"H. G. Wells hardware, that's all the machines are!"

"Well, what and where are They?"

"Grotty little *insect* men, with colds in their heads. Or delicious hairy, bug-eyed monsters. *Do* you remember that *blissful* horror film, with that too utterly *ghoulish*—"

"Oh, do make an *effort*. I mean, at *most* fifty people survived in our town. We're probably the last people alive. And They took the mayor, do you remember . . . Why the mayor? Did They *know* he was the mayor? They can't have done, such a *plebeian* little man, you could never have told—"

"I can't see why They bothered to let *anyone* survive. I suppose we're merely specimens, and They keep us alive just to *gloat.*"

"But the darlings do fancy our antiques."

"Oh, yes, we've always got that. Well, for a few weeks, anyhow."

"Anyhow, we're obviously not the last people alive, there's Adam and Madam and Crazy Annie. Oh, no, she's dead now, isn't she? *Poor* old faggot."

◆

In a hovel some hundreds of feet from theirs had lived a crazy old woman called Annie. She had been crazed enough, God knows, before They came. Latterly she had rooted in the dust like a hen, scratching at nothing in particular with horny fingers and mouthing filth when Their machines came with supplies. Mitch and Eugene had been afraid of her. Not for what she *was*, but for what she represented: themselves, later . . .

Farther away, there was Adam something-or-other. He was dark, unpleasant, disgruntled and musical. He shared his hovel with a girl who had worked in the greengrocer's shop when there had been a greengrocer's shop. Then, she had been a nice little miniskirted, pony-tailed, blond piece. Now she was a nasty, gross, sacking-skirted virago and the blond had grown out. Her name was Lucy. This was the couple that Mitch and Eugene called Madam and Adam. But the two couples had seldom spoken to each other. Burying crazy old Annie had brought the four of them together.

Adam and Madam made musical instruments out of bits of tubing, and played and sang. They played very softly, for they were afraid of Them. They might hear and take away the instruments.

Possibly there were other people here or there, but there were reasons for not finding out. As Eugene and Mitch agreed, "We might seem a little odd, but we're used to being thought odd, aren't we? And we've got each other, while all Adam and Madam have got is a hatchet to *kill* you with, or a kinky tin whistle to *bore* you with . . . I mean, they're not really people any more. They've nothing to live for."

But then, only too often Eugene and Mitch would have a little spat and say things they didn't mean—or worse, things they did mean—and see each other as they really were. They would weep and accuse and even slap and scratch, and end by sobbing, "What are we living for? Why do we go on?"

◆

One reason was the cellars. The Davenport had come from a cellar. Shortly, the Davenport would be transmuted into food, warmth and comfort. They knew this from experience. They had already offered Them oddments from various cellars and each time had been rewarded. It was rather like the old days when they ran the antique shop. Only now it was a matter of survival.

That was why they were so pleased with the pickaxe. Mitch

had found it in the Davenport cellar; with it, they could open up more cellars. The pickaxe was their key to capitalism.

Almost immediately, it opened up a treasure-trove.

In a freshly opened cellar they found a birdcage, a settee covered in brown plush and a wind-up gramophone.

As they were about to dig up more treasure, they heard the noise they should have anticipated: Their machine. It was shuffling about in the near distance outside their hovel. It was saying, "OK. Come out. OK. Bricks, lamp oil, food, alcohol, water. OK. OK, come out."

"Jesus H. *Christ,*" whispered Mitch. "If They knew we were here—"

"Oh, do be *quiet!* Walk, do not run, to your nearest hovel—"

"If it ever suspected—"

"Well, let's take it something. Distract it."

"Not the birdcage, it's *too* precious—"

"The gramophone, then. Quickly!"

The two of them slid through the hole in the cellar wall, Eugene carrying the gramophone. In seconds they were back in the hovel.

"Where you were?" said the grab.

"Call of nature, dear. OK?"

"Not OK," said the grab. "Perhaps kill."

"You don't have them, calls of nature, do you? Lucky old you!"

"Perhaps kill."

"Got its needle stuck, poor love," whispered Mitch.

"Oo, what a good idea! Show it the gramophone!" said Eugene.

"Look, dear!" said Mitch to the grab. "Lovely gramophone! *Ever* so genuine antique, worth goodness *knows* how much!"

"How much?" said the grab. Its messages had started up.

"Oh, lots and lots of *everything.* You see, gramophones are *quite priceless*—"

"Better even than Davenports with chromium-plated legs—"

"What is for?" said the grab.

"Ah," said Mitch, "I'm glad you asked me that. Well, no, I'm not. You see, it's ever so—complicated . . . Particularly," he added aside, "when you've got no bleeding records to play."

"What is for?" said the grab's voice, dourly.

"Like I said, dear, it's a gramophone—"

Messages started going back and forth within the grab's arm.

"Do be careful, Mitch, They take it all down and look it up in something," whispered Eugene.

"Gramophone OK," said the grab.

"OK? It's simply *fabulous*. Particularly these very super-delicious ones with the *doggies* on them—"

"Gramophone," said the grab. "What is for?"

"Well, as I was saying, this is a *round-and-rounder* type gramophone. You wind it up like this"—Eugene wound the dismally creaking handle—"and you turn the lever *so*, and there you are! Round and round! *Too* enchanting!"

"Not OK," said the grab. "Perhaps kill. Incomplete. Not OK. Perhaps take away oil, water, food—"

"Don't let's be hasty!" said Eugene, horrified. "Mitch, for heaven's sake get back down there and look for *records.*"

"Don't be so *crass*. They mustn't find out about the *cellar*—"

"Oh, dear. Listen, love," said Eugene brightly to the grab. "My friend and I will just riffle through our little treasures while you trot off and have a lovely rest. Your poor *feet . . .*"

"And come back before it's dark and perhaps we'll have a *surprise* for you!" said Mitch.

More messages; then the machine lumbered away.

"Cheeribye!" cried Mitch.

"Drop dead! Turn blue! Perhaps kill!" added Eugene, quietly.

It was gone, back in station with the others.

"Please God," sighed Eugene, "we'll find some records."

◆

They found them. Old 78s in a sort of hatbox.

"Deanna Durbin!" breathed Mitch. "How too *utt*erly, in*toxi*-catingly, de*lir*iously mirth-provoking!"

" 'I love to climb an apple tree, but apples disagree with me—' "

" 'And I'll be sick as sick can be—' "

"Perhaps kill, OK?"

They pranced with joy and put the record on. For a moment, the voice from the past clutched at some soft and vulnerable and half-forgotten soft centre inside them. But they were tougher than they knew. Soon their mocking falsettos blended with the scratchy soprano from the gramophone. They sorted through the records.

"Duke Ellington! 'The Mooche'! Whatever happens, we'll keep that, and *bother* Them!"

"Nothing *really* my style here, except one Peggy Lee."

"What's the good of records if we give Them the gramophone—"

"Oh, do *look*, I can't believe it. A Benny Goodman quintet! 'Seven Come—' "

"Not 'Seven Come Eleven'! Utter bliss! Throw darling Deanna away and let's get *in the groove*, as one said!"

They were dancing together, Eugene leading, to the strains of "I'll be loving you, always" when suddenly they became aware that Their machine was standing looming over them. They broke apart and Mitch made to switch off the gramophone.

"OK," said the grab. "Continue. Don't stop."

"Well, actually, dear" said Mitch, "that was the last waltz and Mummy will be furious if I'm not home by midnight." He switched the gramophone off.

"Don't stop!" said the grab, loudly and instantly.

"In a *trice*, all our lovely clothes turn into *rags*—"

"Again," said the grab.

"—And Prince Charming will do his *lot!*"

"Again," said the grab, menacingly. The messages thrummed.

"Give him Deanna," said Mitch. "Don't waste Peggy Lee on old Tin-ear."

" 'Ave Maria'!" announced Eugene. *"Wholly* holy." Deanna

Durbin's voice warbled. The grab was still. The needle went "Grrk" at the end of the track. There was silence.

Then messages started running up and down, furiously.

"Again!" said the grab.

"That's all for now, there isn't any more," said Mitch.

"If you liked us, tell your friends," added Eugene. "If you don't like us, turn blue."

"Again!" said the grab.

"Goodies," said Eugene, blandly. *"Lots* of goodies. Oil, water, alcohol, everything—*lots* of everything. Then we play it again, OK?"

Messages percolated. "OK!" said the grab. "Again. Now."

"Okay, toots. One more time, Deanna baby—and make it *swing."*

"Aaaaaaaaah . . . vay . . . MaREEEEE–EEEEE–aaah . . ." began the record. The music poured over the derelict landscape like treacle over iron filings.

"Too grotesque!" murmured Eugene. *"Too* puke-provoking."

"Look!" whispered Mitch.

"What? Where?"

"The *grab! Look* at it!"

Eugene looked. His eyes and mouth made Os of amazement. The grab was swaying in time with the music.

◆

Mitch swilled the Médoc round his teeth, swallowed, considered, and said, "No. Positively and irrevocably NO."

"Well, I think it's very fair for a 1962. And it must have been utter *agony* for them to find anything at *all—"*

"Not a nice wine. Not nice *at all.* If they can find that very acceptable Riesling, they can find something better in Médocs. I will *not* be put off with this dis*gus*ting, *spec*ious, hydrochloric-acid Médoc. Not after all the music we've played them."

"I suppose we'll have to pass the Médoc on to Adam and Madam. Though they couldn't care *less* what they drink . . ."

"They wouldn't notice the difference between python's pee

and Piesporter. All I'm saying is, up with this I will not put. I shall tell our little metal chum when he comes: *could do better if tried harder.* I shall tell him, go and find some better red wines—*preferably* château-bottled—or it's *Smackbottomsville.*"

"And no Golden Hour of Melody tonight."

◆

But of course there was a Golden Hour of Melody. There had to be. It was the GHM that bought the rugs, the unlimited lamp oil, the bottled chicken breasts, the sprung mattress. It was the GHM that had turned the hovel into what Eugene and Mitch called the Mixed Blessing—a home filled with extraordinarily assorted furniture and fittings, but a home for all that.

For music had, to put it mildly, caught on with Them. It had infected Them, almost enslaved Them. They had to have their music. They had to pay for it with untold diggings and burrowings, by uncovering God knows what mounds of rotting horrors. The grabs would thrust and gouge through shreds of decaying scalp, through pavements and pelvises, through Old Masters or a stockpile of suppositories . . . The spoils would be laid before Eugene and Mitch: a doll's head, a belly dancer's nipple cover, a pack of cards, a garnet brooch, a German dictionary, a set of dentures—nearly, but not all, broken, decayed, crushed, torn, mouldering, useless, horrible; grist to the music mill, grist to the Mixed Blessing.

Adam and Madam arrived, dour, half-drunk, bickering, stupid, smelly and uncouth.

"Darlings!" said Mitch, advancing on them, then recoiling from their stench. "All tuned up, are we? Ready to play?"

"Ur."

"How *very* fetching that sacking looks, Lucy. But now I *insist* you wet your little whistles with some of this too-scrumptious Médoc—the wine of France, the very latest consignment from our shippers, specially for *you.* Eugene, foaming beakers, *if* you please."

"With beaded bubbles winking at the *brim*, loves. Ladies first."

"Ur."

"The true, the blushful Hippocrene."

"Grr."

On the whole, though, the party was going very well. Adam and Madam tuned their by no means unsophisticated instruments—the grabs had worked overtime to find guitar strings, tuning heads, pieces of wind instruments, even a flute in working order—and, whatever their social failings, Adam and Madam played and sang rather well. Even more important, both had an excellent ear. Between the four of them, they could produce an almost endless anthology of words and music, containing anything from "Greensleeves" and harmonised fragments of operatic arias to soldiers' songs of unspeakable filthiness.

"Tonight, I *ra*ther thought," said Mitch, "we could oblige with a *soupçon* of the hey-nonny-no stuff. 'There was a lover and his lass,' perhaps. Then a nice slow rendition of 'Danny Boy,' very *pathetic*. Then—but do let's agree on the words— that rather *malodorous* song of yours, Adam, 'I've got a bulldog called Big Ben.' "

"Ur."

" 'Eats like nine and'—oh dear!—*'defecates* like ten.' I *can't* bring myself to utter it. But They seem *so* to enjoy it—"

"They're coming," said Eugene. "Now, are we all in tune? *Goodness*, at least a quarter tone flat. How one *longs* for something that doesn't need tuning with a *spanner . . .*"

"They're here."

And there They were (three of them!) with grabs extended. "Like Oliver Twists," murmured Eugene, preparing to enjoy himself. He was Master of Ceremonies and as such felt himself licensed to be amusing at Their expense.

"Ladies, Gentlemen, and assorted Hardware," he began. "This evening, we celebrate the *umpteenth* Golden Hour of Melody—an occasion of *particular* significance, as you will readily agree—with the rendition of a deliriously auspicious conglomeration of polyphonic exuberances—in short, something for everyone. Something old, something new, something borrowed—yes, and something *blue* to set those turgid old circuits tingling—"

"Hurry *up.*"

"Don't *pull* at me. But before commencing our programme —which will begin with that stirring and ever-popular anthem in praise of our staunch four-footed friend, the bulldog—I will ask you to show your appreciation for the artistes in the accustomed manner. In short, *clap,* you bleeders! Rattle your puddies!"

"Good and *loud!*" muttered Mitch, leaning forward expectantly. This was the only part of the concert he really enjoyed —Their obligatory applause beforehand, the grating, rattling noise that the grabs had been taught to make. Applause! Well, after all, it represented some small victory or other . . .

"Let's hear it for the melody makers!" said Mitch in his DJ voice.

But there was no applause. No applause! The grabs were motionless. Mitch and Eugene looked at each other. Adam and Madam grumbled an uneasy "Ur." Eugene faced Them.

"The *usual* thing, the *polite* thing, before a concert is a nice cosy round of *applause*—" he began.

A grab moved, ominously. It came toward them. *"Sing!"* shouted Eugene. They sang. The grab kept moving forward and lifted to the height of their heads. Then higher. The song tailed off.

The grab kept moving. Now it was poised above the Mixed Blessing.

"Don't you *dare*—" yelled Mitch.

The grab slammed down. The Mixed Blessing bulged, leaked, crumpled, puffed red dust and flattened. Then the grab went up and down, slowly and rhythmically and deafeningly pounding the Mixed Blessing into the ground.

Mitch had stopped yelling and started blubbering. Eugene

just looked, wide-eyed and expressionless. Adam and Madam
formed a pyramid, leaning against each other. They looked
merely bovinely interested, but tears trickled down the girl's
face.

"They'll 'ave our place next," she snivelled.

She was right. The grab, leaking red silt, snaked away on its
apparently infinite flexible arm, reached the hovel, smashed it
at a blow, and turned over the debris as if with a spade. Madam
began to howl *"Ooooooo!"* and Adam growled.

Shattered, the little party stood there. The grab snaked back.
An almost visible question mark hovered over the bowed human heads.

The question was answered.

"Your music," announced a grab, "no good. We kill."

"Natch," said Eugene, bravely flippant.

"Not OK music," said the grab. "We learn all you know.
More. Listen."

There was a click, and it started. Their music. The music of
Them. Music vast in amplitude—

> *A mother was bathing her baby one night,*
> *'Twas the youngest of ten and a delicate mite,*

They sang. The massed choir was so loud that dust trembled. The
hooting orchestra was so sweet that teeth ached.

> *The mother was poor and the baby was thin,*
> *'Twas only a skellington wrapped up in skin...*

"Skellington . . ." murmured Mitch. "How bleeding, bloody
funny."

> *The mother looked round for the soap on the rack,*
> *'Twas only a moment, but when she looked back—*

Divine harmonies fluttered and swooped, twittered and
burped. *"Crinoline* ladies, can't you *see* them!" said Mitch.
"And we taught them. *We* taught them *this . . ."*

My baby has gorn down the plug 'ole!
My baby has fell down the plug!

bellowed the grab, in a maelstrom of bathos.

The pore little thing
Was so skinny and thin
It oughter been washed in a jug—

("—in a jug," echoed a million metal voices through a million metal noses.)

My baby has gone down the plug 'ole,
It won't need a bath any more,
My baby has gone down the plug 'ole—
Not lost—but gone—beeeefore.

("Oh, gone, be–fore!" echoed the choir, its vibrato a whole tone wide, its pathos as wide as the ocean and as deep as an ink stain.)

The song ended. The silence was deafening. The game was up.

"You poor, silly, po-faced, stinking, bleeding, boneless, gutless, soulless, mindless *tin turds,*" said Eugene at last, and began to laugh. Soon the four of them were laughing. They laughed until they cried, cried until they hiccupped, hiccupped till they choked. Then were silent again.

"Now kill," said the grab.

"OK, kill," said Eugene. "Big deal."

"And so, as the sun sinks in the west, we bid a reluctant 'Farewell' to lovable old Mother Earth and her dirty denizens," recited Mitch, shakily.

"Kill," said the grab. The other two machines had already plodded back and resumed station. The blue beams were linked.

"Not with a bang, but a whimper," said Eugene. "We could be the *very last four left!* On this whole planet! It gives one *furiously* to think." He began to weep, quietly.

"—— Them!" said Adam, indistinctly.

"Oh, *don't* do that for God's sake, I do *beseech.* There's enough of Them already," said Eugene, hysterically.

"Kill now," said the grab.

"How are you going to do it? Smash us flat?"

"Through the beams," said the grab. "Walk. Kill now."

"Bags, I not go first!" said Mitch, flightily.

"Cut," said Adam. He bent down and picked up their pack of cards out of the dust.

They cut, cut again, and cut again. But it could not last.

"Now! Kill now!" said the grab. "Walk."

It lithely glided behind them, shepherding them. They walked.

"So ri*dic*ulous!" said Mitch. "The last! The very last! We could be the very last people in all the world! I mean, there was Jesus Christ and Fabergé and Socrates and the Unknown Soldier and poor Oscar and Queen Victoria and that boy in Corfu, and George Washington—everyone—"

"—and the pyramids and spacecraft and men on the moon and Cleopatra on the Nile and soldiers dying from phosgene gas . . . Then us. Pitiful us. Oh, Mitch, pitiful, pitiful, *pitiful!*"

"First you see it, now you don't," said Adam unexpectedly. "The bloody end. Like this!" He spat in the red dust. They were very close now to the blue rays and death.

"First you see it, now you don't!" said Mitch. He was sniffling and at the same time doing a card trick. "First you see it"—and there was the card between two fingers—"now you don't." A flick of the wrist, a turn of the fingers.

They were at the perimeter. They stopped.

"Walk," said the grab. "Walk."

Eugene crumpled at the knees and sat down, legs straight out like a doll's. "It's no good, I just *can't!*" he sobbed. "Not like *this* . . . I'm *me, me!* It's not *fitting*, it's not *seemly*, it's too *hideous*—"

The girl sat down too. "I bleeding won't!" she said.

The grab sidled up and scooped them to their feet. "Kill now," it remarked. "Walk."

She began to run, away from the perimeter. She ran and ran,

stumbled and fell, got up and ran again. The grab smoothly
wove its way after her but when she stumbled, overshot. Mitch
sniggered hysterically. "Find the lady!" he shouted. "Now you
see her, now you don't!"

In the end she was shepherded back by the grab. No one
could bear to look at her face; no one could keep their eyes from
it. Desperately, Mitch shouted, "Come on then, you lucky lads!
Find the lady, win a fiver! I place three cards, so!—Acey-deucy,
King, and last *but* not least, the lady—the Queen! *Face* down
on the ground, positively no deception! You want a second look,
lady? Right you are—Ace, King, Queen. Positively no deception! Now, keep your peepers on the *Queen*, that's all you've got
to do! On the Queen! On the lady!"

His hands swept over the three cards, fluttering and magical.
Yet it was easy enough to see through the trick. There was the
Queen! Now there! Still there! Now over there, on the left!
Child's play.

"All right!" shouted Mitch. "Now—*find the lady!*"

Adam spat disgustedly. Lucy looked at nothing through her
swamped, defeated eyes. Eugene— But the grab pushed him
aside, hovered over the three cards, extended its metal claw,
and said, "Lady."

"Do I hear you aright, sir? *Here*, sir? *This* card, sir? You're
quite *sure*, my dear sir?"

"Lady!" The metal claw tapped.

Mitch turned over the card: the King.

Messages tinkled, swelled, hummed.

"Again," said the grab.

The sun was lower, lower still.

"Again," said the grab.

The lamps, Their lamps, blazed under the night sky.

"Take a card. Any card! That is your choice? Excellent. Com-
mit it to memory . . ." Mitch shuffled gaudily and kept up the
patter. "Now, you, sir, as I instantly discerned, are no mere
acolyte at the shrine of prestidigitation, but a veritable *adept*.

So when I ask you once again to select a card—"

Dawn.

"Again," said the grab.

"Again," said the grabs.

DOROTHY GILBERT *is a medievalist who teaches at the Davis campus of the University of California and whose published work—poetry and translations from Old English —has appeared in* The New Yorker, the Nation, Fantasy & Science Fiction, the California Quarterly, *and other distinguished periodicals. Now she makes her debut as a science-fiction writer with a witty, graceful variation on the classic theme of communication with extraterrestrial intelligences.*

■

Dorothy Gilbert

■

A SOLFY DRINK,
A SAFFEL FRAGRANCE

> If a lion could talk, we could not understand him.
> —LUDWIG WITTGENSTEIN,
> *Philosophical Investigations*

Author's Note: This article was planned as a discussion presented in the usual critical and scholarly format. In attempting to deal with the unique problems of Musæan literature, the writer decided that it was desirable to alter the format slightly and give a somewhat personal and conjectural account, in addition to recording the progress of research. The study of extraterrestrial literature is such a new field, so full of unprecedented experiences and problems, that it seems useful to record as much as possible of the great adventure; not only the discoveries themselves, but the reactions of the investigators, their intellectual and emotional adjustments, even their mistakes. This article, then, is intended as a kind of log; an account of the staggering discovery that we are, indeed, not alone in the universe, that the planet Musæus sustains not only life but a unique literature. I have tried to describe our attempts to understand that literature, and I have attempted to make a few scraps of it comprehensible to readers of English in the translations below. Translations into other languages will, we hope, soon follow.

PART I

Some readers may remember that a little over thirty years ago, in 1960, the U.S. Navy conducted the experiment known as Project Ozma, at Green Bank, West Virginia. At that time scientists spent a month listening to radiation emissions from two stars, Tau Ceti and Epsilon Eridiani, which are between ten and eleven light-years away from the earth. There had been some question in the minds of these scientists that "artificial"—i.e., intentional—radiation signals were being sent out from these stars or their vicinities, and that these signals might be evidence of conscious life in that region of the universe. The naval scientists found no evidence of artificial radiation emissions, however, and the project was temporarily given up.

In July of 1989, this writer (then working in New York as a translator) received a letter from J. R. Lollius, a college acquaintance, and a then unknown astrophysicist working at the radio-telescope observatory at Lynx Mountain in Labrador. The letter read, in part, as follows:

We had been hearing these curious rhythmical sounds for three or four months before we had any idea what they were. Mostly they were so infrequent that we had little chance to investigate them. We checked all the equipment carefully, and we made careful note of any object close enough to us, on land or in the atmosphere, to cause disrupting noises. Nothing gave us a clue. The problem fascinated and annoyed us, because these sounds, when they did occur, were so rhythmical; they had very definite repetitive patterns. When we heard them in the midst of the usual hissing noise made by the telescope, they gave us an eerie feeling. We would be sitting in the lab, listening to the faint continuous hissing, and suddenly there would be a sound, something like "soo-wit, soo-wit," an intensified whisper. Sometimes it was a heavier, more shushing sound—maybe like solids moving slowly against each other. At times the same rhythm would be repeated again and again, then, after the sixth or seventh time, it would vary, and lines would be a little shorter and then go back to the former length. I wish I could describe to you what it is like, sitting here in this observatory, in an isolated Canadian community, listening to these strange, soughing, playful sounds. If you have ever heard recordings of whale songs, these are like that, except that the range is often much deeper, there is a predominantly whispery quality, and the rhythms are extremely complex. We called these sounds "the fish sounds" at first; then we began calling the assumed makers of the sounds "They" and "Them," at first partly in joke. We discovered that they came from the general area of Tau Ceti; we finally traced them to a hitherto unknown (or at least unrecorded) body slightly larger than Earth, a satellite of Tau Ceti. At this point we gave the body a name. After some discussion we named it Musæus, after a poet-singer somewhat like Orpheus, associated with Orpheus, in Greek mythology.

Then, in January of this year, the Amissy Code was perfected and some of the material on it declassified. Do you know about it? It is the code which makes it possible for us to decipher electrical messages from outer space—certain kinds of messages, that is, that are not too complex and do not come from too far away. Luckily, Musæus is near us. We tried the A-Code on our "fish sounds," with astounding results. We had begun to suppose seriously that the noises—if they were artificial radiation—were electrical signals of some sort, or the rhythmical "songs" of some creatures of outer space. This they turned out to be, but they turned out to have a meaning to which their rhythm and tone had given us no clue at first. They were, in fact, *poems*, words being pronounced in rhythmical patterns.

We have set down some of the songs, but we should like very much to have your assistance in completing this work, in making a comprehensible translation for the public, and in interpreting the poems. Could we interest you in the job—could we urge you to take it? You will be working in absolute secrecy, you understand; this is work of the most highly classified nature, and I'm afraid we can't pay you nearly what we would wish. I hope the salary I've mentioned is feasible. Your work will be tremendously frustrating at times—but I promise you gratitude! Your wants will be few in this community; it is a pleasant place, if howling wilderness appeals to you; and you will, of course, be in on an extraordinarily exciting development of the Space Age.

Please let us know as soon as you conveniently can. We do hope you will join us.

Cordially,
Jim Lollius

I left for Lynx Mountain within the month. A desk was set up for me in the observatory, where I could watch the radio-telescope graphs and hear any irregular sounds as they occurred. It was as Jim Lollius had described: the eternal soft hissing of the telescope, with occasional tiny ripples and underlying hisses, which usually vanished just as one's curiosity was aroused; the flickering screen with its graphs. I have had no training in astrophysics or electronics, and at first the station, with its several miles of intricate equipment, totally confused me. I was shown the fragments of messages which Jim had described in his letter. Then they seemed very mysterious; now I am familiar with their varieties and genres. I will discuss these in more detail in the second part of this article.

Eventually I heard the sounds myself. It was late one evening, about eleven o'clock. We had made ourselves large mugs of very strong coffee, and Jim, George Perry (Jim's assistant) and I were all quietly working at our desks. There was a pleasant, comradely atmosphere in the place; there always was. I suppose this was caused by the knowledge that we were working with something momentous; though it was mysterious and intricate, there was constant evidence of its presence, and it often seemed to me, at least, as if Something—something incredibly vast—was listening to *us*, or perhaps reading us on some remote screen. None of us ever said this, but I think we felt, at least when we were sitting in there by ourselves at night, that if we said anything petty or stupid, or if we quarreled, we would seem unbearably, cosmically ludicrous to some vaguely sensed audience listening in. Our belief in what we were doing, and the secrecy of it, was a great bond between us.

That evening I may have heard the sounds first. A deep, low noise, which rose to a whisper; it took a second or two for me to recognize it from Jim's description. I was struck by the lowness and resonance of the initial note. At the same time, the graph began to register. A series of tiny, jagged peaks appeared on it. The rhythm was something like

or

but not so exact; the sounds glided too much, they were too fluid.

"Turn on the A-machine, quick!" Jim said.

The sounds continued. They went on for a long time. Every so often, just as Jim had said, there would be a variation in their rhythm. As the noises continued on and on, suspense began to build up; we felt that we could hardly bear our excitement and curiosity. Then, after thirty-five minutes, the sounds suddenly stopped. A moment later, Jim went over to the Amissy recorder.

"An odd rhythm," I said. "If it were in human words, it might sound something like *Beowulf.*"

"Really?" Jim said. I doubt if he actually heard me. He was bent over the Amissy machine, concentrating totally on it. I didn't distract him. George Perry and I watched him; we were stiff with suspense.

"God damn it!" Lollius said suddenly. "God damn it to hell!"

"What is it?"

"The machine ran out of charge fluid. The tapes are almost all blank. I didn't check them before. Oh, God! Oh, GOD!"

He picked up a book and threw it on the floor. Lollius is a gentle, cerebral person, the kind of man who seems restrained and courteous out of reflection and kindness, and genuine choice. George and I had almost never seen him angry before.

"We were taken by surprise," I said into the silence.

"There's a little bit of tape that was processed. We'll put it in the transformer and see what happens."

Very little, of course, was salvaged. The tape was put into the transformer, run through the first computer, assembled on the data processor, and recorded on another tape before it was transposed on the Amissy screen and sorted out by the linguistic codifying mechanism. A few lines of the original song were deciphered; they are quoted in Part II of this essay. They are all the evidence we have, after listening for over half an hour to a song from outer space. Lollius has never recovered from this incident. I include this account of it, and the description of the lost signals, at his insistence.

◆

Later, with other works, we were more successful. In the five months that I worked at Lynx Mountain we recorded nineteen complete poems of what appear to be five different genres, and fragments of what seem like others. Examples of some of these, with my own translations and a critical discussion, are given in Part II below. I wish that it were possible to convey the emotions I felt during the time I was engaged in this work. I have mentioned the feeling of accord that we all shared, the sense of participating in something momentous, the occasional feeling of shame at human impatience and pettiness, as if a great Ear were listening to us and judging us. Each of us had a somewhat different reaction to the actual sounds made by the Musæan messages. These sounds, we think, after great efforts to check and investigate them, are probably something like what human ears, or terrestrial animal ears, would hear on Musæus. (We are satisfied that the noises are not made by the mischievous clanking of our own instruments, or by some other factor in our atmosphere or in outer space.) The rhythms and stresses must certainly sound similar, and perhaps the pitches as well. (This is the sort of dismaying problem, of course, that we have run into again and again.)

At first, following Lollius's suggestion, I thought the sounds reminded me of whale songs. There is the same deep resonant quality, with notes gliding up to a whisper. But the Musæan noises do not have the glassy, icy, at times terrifying coldness that the whale sounds have for my landbound sensibility. They seem more like noises of earth than of water, as if bubbles of earth were rising slowly toward the ground's surface, or burrowing animals were surfacing with a kind of swimming motion. These sounds have a powerful insistence. To George Perry their urgency and physicality suggest pain, and seem to express pain. He knows his feelings must be anthropomorphic (or at least terrestrially conditioned) to some extent, but he accepts them as an impression; he thinks the noises *seem as if* they express distress of some kind, or anxiety, or incompleteness. Once he said cautiously, "I know you'll laugh; sometimes the sounds strike me as being painful and sexual, like mating or wooing noises." I don't share those impressions; perhaps I am overcautious about attributing terrestrial emotions and instincts to the Musæans. To me the noises themselves do not suggest pain of any kind. Lollius, who is older and a more reserved, noncommittal personality, has said very little about his speculations or emotional reactions. He shares with us the feeling of listening to a vast consciousness of some sort, and he agrees about the *physicality* of the sounds, thinks they express something affective, that they sound urgent and intelligent. This is all impressionistic, of course. One question that has always vexed us is whether the Musæans are sending us their poems on purpose, or whether this extraordinary event, the communication of personal experience and of art between inhabitants of different planets, has resulted from some kind of electrical accident. "We have *no* idea who the Musæans are," Jim Lollius kept saying to us. "We have no idea what sort of organisms they are, what sort of minds they have, if indeed they have what we would call minds. We have no way of telling whether the creators of these poems, or the reciters of them, are still alive. All we have are these songs, and we must be terribly careful—as careful as we have ever been or can be— that we see the songs *for what is in them*, and project nothing of our own to obscure them and take their place."

This last is what I would like to urge, above all, in this essay. It has been suggested frequently that there must, in all probability, be physiological resemblances between organisms throughout the universe. We almost certainly have something in common, chemically and biologically, with the Musæans. But are the writers of these songs living now? Do they come from one nation or one locality? (The poems we have are all in the same language, but it may be that there are dialect differences that we have not picked up.) Is the poetry from a tradition thousands of years old—was it created hundreds or thousands of years ago?—or is it scraps from here and there, still organizing itself? What place has it in Musæan civilization? And are the singers who sent the songs living now, or have the last eleven years put them forever beyond our reach?

These questions are unanswerable at the moment. *All we know for certain* is that the poets and singers *have* existed, that they have created these messages, and that they seem capable of certain thoughts and feelings that we can comprehend. Always the danger exists that we will interpret their work so much in terms of our own experience that the Musæan poems will lose their uniqueness. I think that, up to a point, it would be possible for us to understand Wittgenstein's speaking lion; where that point lies is the staggering problem. It is, of course, impossible to translate Musæan poetry adequately. I hope that, in this paper generally and in the following attempts at translation, I have given some idea of our discovery, of what it was like when a small piece of another world, its thoughts and feelings comprehensibly stated, burst from eleven light-years of outer space and through several miles of terrestrial machinery, into our ken.

PART II

I will pass over the scientific details of our research; they, and their attendant problems and vexations, are discussed in the technical journals by those trained for such work.[1] The poem

1. F. R. Tullius, "Psycholinguistics in Outer Space," *New Astrophysical Quarterly*, 9 (April, 1990), 17–36; Helmut Morgenbesser, "Musæus: Was ist den geschehen?" *Sprachwissenschaftliche Probleme*, 7 (January, 1991), 167–206; Jonas Farrell, "Thoughts on the Nature of Insult," ψυχη, 21 (October, 1990), 18–32.

mentioned in Part I, most of which is lost, appears to be a long history or narrative; perhaps it is some kind of official record composed in rhythm to aid the memory (as was done in the earliest stages of our own literature). Here is the translation I have made of what we were able to decipher:

> After some days   [he?] came to the ice-fields
> where the torb dead   are kept forever.
> Slabs, up-ended, huge   flat pieces of ice
> where bodies are shelved;   each slab contains one,
> bodies look out,   beings long gone.
> Each slab with its own   long-preserved face,
> . . . . storehouse
> a country's memory . .
>
>   the end
> of the icy field.

The word "torb" seems to mean either "criminal" or "evil person" or else "unfortunate person," this last possibly with connotations of foolishness or helplessness. I think that the two former meanings are the dominant ones in this instance, but I can't be sure, and so I have used the word itself and supplied this explanation. Otherwise I have made fairly direct use of the transliterated material our instruments provided.

I will mention another venture which has been only partly successful. We have recorded six poems, of thirty to thirty-eight lines in length, that have a short, bouncing rhythm and that appear to be a type of ritual insult, or insult contest, between two opponents. Try as I may, I cannot always decipher what is being said. Either the insults are descriptions of an adversary's anatomy, its lacks and excesses, or they are comments on the deeds and behavior of the adversary. It is often impossible to tell which. The emotional quality of these poems is derisive and (to us) coarse; it is hard to tell whether the poems are meant as brutish joking, earnest battle, or some combination of the two. They all begin with the line "Something to listen to," and each speaker in the poem begins his diatribe with this formulaic phrase. Other Musæan poems which appear to have no connotations of insult also occasionally begin this way; it may be that the custom has an origin that makes its use in the diatribe poems especially ironic. Here is a sample passage, clearer than many:

> Something to listen to. Torb, what sippels
> clasp and crissel you, fessel your brain!
> Fangel, you siff
> at the stib of a kloovagunion, you croff,
> rissop, at its flast; it flasts you, you are fotted.
> Rissopol! Fangel! Torb!
> Take that!
>
> Something to listen to. Rissopol, you raise
> your slow clup, subbering,
> and lobbeling. You siff
> at the stimbs, and fail. You droop, lool,
> flasted . . .

And so on.

One of the genres we have most of, and which translates most successfully, is that of the cook-song. The cook-song is a short poem which appears to be half incantation, half recipe. It begins with a declaration—a kind of heroic boast—of what the cook intends to accomplish. Then the speaker describes in detail what he is including in his creation. What he describes is almost certainly food, since the Amissy machine records words that can be translated "brew," "stew," "cook," "drink," etc. None of the items recorded in these poems appears to be known on this planet. I have used their Musæan names, and made as faithful a translation as possible. At the end of the poem the speaker sums up the boast, claiming to have fulfilled it.

Here are some examples of the cook-song:

> Ho, I am going to brew
> a sweet stew; you will like it.
> First I will take green simmels
> and peel their yellow pips. Then I will brost them,
> add winey lippas with their rosy hulls.

Then seebs; when you cut them open
what a sweet smell of sith! Dried herbs are next,
libbet and sath, the yellow flowers of teth;
the kitchen smells like a field of simmel-flowers.
I will wait half a day.
Ho, I have done it.

◆

Ho, I am going to soof
some damber-beer; you will enjoy it.
I will take lippas, not quite ripe,
so that their juice is still sweet-smelling and pungent
even at a little distance, and a deep red.
Then I will braff the blue and brown seeds of damber
as fine as possible. I will add them, and pong-berries,
and stew the juice for a day. Ho,
I have done it.

◆

Ho, I am going to make
something you will like, a solfy drink.
I will take callups, and braff them to a pulp,
yellow and brown and red, with a saffel fragrance,
and let them sit in a barrel made of stip
until fermented. Then I distill them,
adding thester. This is a sweet drink, silky,
it clears the vision, and brings the good hearing
needed so in the colder months. Ho,
I have done it.

We have made endless conjectures about the origin and development of the cook-song, and about its ceremonial character. Terrestrial parallels inevitably present themselves. Are
there cooking contests, perhaps huge fairs where acknowl-
edged masters of the art gather and perform these boasting
rituals? Or is the cook-song a more frequent celebration, say, a
ceremony that takes place before small feasts or before every
meal? I for one would give a great deal to know whether it is
ordinary life that is being celebrated, or some kind of special
occasion.

There is another kind of poem we have seen which makes me think of a terrestrial child's song, or perhaps a riddle:

> kep   little kep
> you surprise me
> coming from corners   my shadow
> with your own thoughts
> your fur is so soft
> it is a gift   kep
>
> little joke

We have had other messages, short scraps of verse that we don't know what to do with, because we can't tell whether they are fragments of something long of whether they are some variety of epigram. One of these snatches says, almost literally:

> and like liquid
> and the soft sounds of flying.

Some of the messages are so short that it is almost impossible to tell their significance: e.g., "this part of the year," "something to listen to," or even, simply, "a barrel." On one occasion when we were all particularly exhausted and frustrated, we received several of these scraps: "standing," "going," "something to listen to," "the day," "something to listen to." George Perry, exasperated and hysterical with fatigue, went to the front of the Amissy machine, placed himself against it, and before anyone could stop him, leaned into the sensitive mechanism and screamed as loudly as he could, "ARE YOU KIDDING US?" There was, of course, no immediate response. If there is to be one (if indeed a message was transmitted), perhaps we will know what it is in twenty-two years.

This is the record of our work with Musæan literature so far. We have made a few wary speculations based on our discoveries. Occasionally it has seemed to us that the Musæans mentioned experiences and memories that the speaker of the poem could not possibly have had. There is a theory that the Musæans may have another memory sense in addition to the kind that we have, that if these beings reproduce by division, it may be that they inherit their ancestors' memories and have, in a more direct way than we can imagine, both a race memory and individual memories.[2] Since we know so little about the Musæans' concept of time, and nothing of their sexual or reproductive life, we can make only the most tentative guesses about such matters. We do have a little astronomical evidence about life on that planet, facts that our very specialized instruments have given us. We know that the Musæan day is longer than ours and that the year is longer, by about eighty of our days. The gravitational pull is stronger there, and the weather is probably colder if atmospheric conditions are at all similar. One gets the feeling that life there may be something like life here, but lived in longer units of time, and in all probability at a slower pace.

Our technical equipment has often seemed to us to be infuriatingly quirky. The Amissy machine in particular seems often to have crotchets and limitations, like a person's mind, but it is even more intransigent. It will think in the subjunctive only after some wheedling and bullying, and it will not combine certain rhythms and units of time. At times, for me, the old translator's problem of selection has been almost unbearably intensified. Always, to choose a word is to limit what one is saying; language *defines* experience, it selects, chooses, and assigns. Language can petrify memory and experience; in my work I have had the feeling that I must, at all costs, keep alive the small organisms I was discovering, and not obliterate them by some clumsy inadvertent mental gesture, like so many plant or animal tissues killed by a careless lab assistant. I have learned that all of us are captive investigators; our senses and intellects are as much shields and envelopes as they are instruments of perception. But we have found and interpreted these poems;

2. Morgenbesser, *op. cit.*, pp. 174ff.

we hope that, gradually and with patience, we and others will learn thoroughly at least a few pockets and corners of this immense new field. Not long ago we believed that our Earth alone supported sentient, intelligent beings. Now we have discovered our insularity and arrogance; we have begun to discover the universe where we have always lived. Sometime, perhaps, we can hope that the Musæans know of our existence.

I will close by quoting one more poem from our neighbors in space. Here it is:

> listen   listen
>
> the lights burn blue and red over the doors
> in the country you have never seen
>
> listen
>
> a country   listen   I can only describe
> and fail to describe   listen   you will
>
> never see it
>
> if only
> you could see it
>
> listen   it is unbelievably beautiful
> when it is dark the doors are sprinkled with simmel-dust
>
> to make them fragrant   listen
>
> the dark itself appears to
> listen   be full of simmel-dust
>
> it is very wonderful
>
> the air is full
> of things to smell and hear
>
> if only
> you could hear
>
> listen

THIS VIVID AND VIGOROUS STORY *is the second s-f piece Marta Randall has sold; an earlier one appeared in the British experimental quarterly* New Worlds *in 1973, and as this is written she is working on her first novel, due to see publication late in 1975. Ms. Randall was born in Mexico but has spent most of her life in California. Currently she lives in Berkeley and is employed as an assistant to a Bay Area patent attorney, processing other people's inventions during the day and looking after her own literary ones after dark.*

■

Marta Randall

■

A SCARAB IN THE CITY OF TIME

I skulk in a forgotten alley while they scurry by outside, search-
ing for me. Whippety-whip, they dive around corners with
unaccustomed haste, and they have all donned worried faces
for the occasion. Even the robo-cops look worried, and look
well; were there stones in this City they would turn them all.
But they won't find me, not me, no. When their programmed
darkness falls I move from the alley, slyly insert myself in their
streets and avenues, slink through the park to the City Offices
and scrawl "I am a scarab in the City of Time" over the windows
of the mayor's office. I use a spray of heat-sensitive liquid crys-
tals; my graffito will be pretty tomorrow as the wind and fake
sunlight shift it through the spectrum. Then I sneak to an outly-
ing residential section where I've not been before, eluding
robo-cops on my way, and steal food from an unlocked house for
my night's meals. I wouldn't steal from citizens if I could help
it, but my thumbprint isn't registered, isn't legal tender in the
City of Time. So I burgle and the Association of Merchants
grows rich because of me, as locks and bars appear on doors and
windows throughout the City. I'm good for the economy of the
City of Time, I am.

I'm a sociologist. I'm not supposed to be doing any of this.

When morning comes they cluster before the City Offices, gesticulating, muttering, shifting, frightened. I watch them from a tree in the park, am tempted to mingle with them, sip the sweet nectar of their dismay. No, no, not yet. I remain hidden as the mayor appears on the steps of the building, glares at my beautiful sign. Workers are trying to remove it, but there's a bonding agent in my paint and the colors shift mockingly under their clumsy hands. The mayor reassures the people, calming them with the dignity of her silver hair and smooth hands, and they begin to disperse. I'm tired. The pseudo-sun is far too bright today, a faint wind rustles the leaves around me. When noon comes I slip from my perch, move easily under the eaves and edges of bushes to the Repairs Center, sneak into a storage room and curl down on a pile of cables to sleep.

◆

The City is hard on the eyes, from the outside. Its hemisphere rises from a lush plain, catches the light of the sun and reflects it back harshly at the resurrected earth. Time has silted soil high around the City, but it's probable that the City doesn't know, or care to know. When we returned to colonize Terra we tried to make contact with the City, sent waves of everything we could manage at the impervious dome, received nothing in reply. Years passed and we built our own cities, clean and open to the fresh winds; sailed our ships and floated through the skies, tilled the soil, farmed the seas. Occasionally threw more junk at the City and argued about it. Some held that the City was dead, a gigantic mausoleum; some that it was inhabited by inbred freaks and monsters; some that it was merely the same City our ancestors had left behind as they fled from a poisoned planet. But no one knew, until I dug down beyond the City's deepest foundations, through the bedrock and up into the City. And I can't get out again.

◆

I awaken at nightfall, as the dome of the City turns dark and the stars come on, and spend some time on the roof of the Repairs Center watching the sky and plotting new mischief. Those stars, those stars—no one has seen the original of these dome-printed constellations in two thousand years, yet here they shine in mimicry of the true sky. I tighten the straps of my pack, slip from the building, through the dim streets. The robo-cops hunt for me while the good citizens of the City sleep. And the bad citizens? There are none in the City of Time, none except me, me, and I only by default. Tiers of buildings loom over my head, tapering to the arch of the dome; cascades of plants spill over the walls and display fragrant, flagrant blossoms; most of the doors are locked, the windows closed tight, the citizenry unquiet in their quiet beds. I move to the museum and inside, pad softly through the dark to the echoing Hall of Animals. Hundreds, thousands of them here, some preserved carcasses, some simply statues of those beasts that were extinct by the time the City locked its dome against the poisoned world. I holograph each exhibit carefully, setting the receptors with delicacy, with art, and when I am finished I move through the hall and append notes in liquid script to the signboards: "This animal survives, outside." "This animal is now twice as big and looks like an elephant (see Exhibit 4659)." "This animal now flies." "This animal now breathes air." And, in huge block letters on the face of the museum, "HERE THERE BE DRAGONS." As I finish, the street explodes into a commotion of light and noise, scores of robo-cops and citizens pour from the cross streets and buildings. Have I tripped an alarm? Possibly, probably, someone has monkeyed with the wiring, created an alarm in this uneventful City. The scarab is the mother of invention. Someone sees me clinging to the face of the museum and sets up a cry in counterpoint to the larger one. In my initial surprise I almost drop the paint, then finish the last swing of the "S" before swinging myself down to the roof of the portico, scamper along the protruding tops of the columns and slither down to an open window. I run through the museum, not stopping to stuff the paint into my pack, up one shaft and down another, followed by the hue and cry behind me. I halt for a bare moment to pop the cube from a holojector and stuff another in its place, flick on the machine, and when I am two corridors away I hear the howling populace come to a sudden halt as they face the new projection. And so they should. I took it just before invading their sealed city, setting my receptors about the rim of the hills surrounding the plain on which the City sits. They are seeing their City from the wrong side, from Out, and as it is now. Perhaps they do not know what it is, but the surprise of its presence gives me time to flee through another corridor, out into a dawn-lit empty street and away.

◆

"When meeting a strange animal, stay quiet until you know where the teeth are," they had told me; when I entered the belly of the City of Time I remembered, moved through shadows. Watched from vantage points as the citizens lived their lives before me, whispered notes into my 'corder, took holographs, invaded their library at night with my screens and read their journals and books, lists and agglomerations. Snuck into their City Offices and recorded their records and records of records until my cubes were filled and most of my food gone, and then I tried to go home. But the robo-techs had found and filled my miniature hell-mouth, sealed it over and sealed my digging tools in it. I searched the City for another way home, delved in corners and edges and ragged remnants, and found nothing. Not a crack nor a leak, door nor window. Nothing. How large a City is, when you search for one small scarab-hole. Nothing. I looked about me at the strange, pale people, I opened my ears to the archaic rhythms of their speech, I sniffed the ancient odors of their air and I wept, homesick, from the tops of trees in the park by the City Offices. When they came looking for me I fled. Stole my food from unlocked houses, stole my sleep in small snatches in small places, lived miserably, yearning for the fresh sweet scents of home. Until it came to me that the only way I could go home was if everyone went home, if the City grated open its rusted doors and let the clean air blow in. I considered this, lurking in odd nooks and corners. I couldn't walk into the mayor's office and say, "Hey, listen, lady. The world's all fresh and clean and lovely outside, and it's time to take a walk in sunlight." People who say that are heretics. They dispose of them. It says so in their books, it is recorded in the records of their courts, their preachers bellow it from the pulpits of their temples. I don't want to die, I don't want to be a martyr. I simply want to go home again, to my children, my husband, the stones and rafters of my home, the voices of my students. So I pound in the night on the gates of the City, and hope that those behind me will hear.

◆

I'm hungry. No food on tonight's expedition, just some water I poured into my wetpouch on the run, from a fountain by the Wheel of Fate. The streets around the Repairs Center are swarming with people up and about, in full hue and cry, and I search for a new place. Here, a church, deserted and dim. I scuttle inside, up to the lofts, through undisturbed dust beneath the eaves, and curl myself into a tight ball behind a filthy window. Feed my hungry belly on nightmares and wait for another dusk. Sleep. Sleep.

Dirty windows? Are their purifiers breaking down, their life supports whimpering to a halt after all this time? Dust?

How pale these people are! Fair pink skins and light brown or yellow hair, light eyes; they look like illustrations from a history book. When they locked themselves up in their unhatched egg there were still races in the world, people simplistically divided into preposterous colors; the people of the City were "white" ones, fair of skin, straight of nose and hair, lords of the globe for a time until they grew frightened and hid. The rest of humanity poured out into the galaxy and soon the ridiculous distinctions were lost, for in space and on new worlds people are people are people, valued for their simple humanity amid environments alien beyond description. The books of the City tell of the battles fought, of the expulsion of the black vermin and yellow lice. If I showed my brown face and epicanthic eyes, my bush of light brown hair, they would stopper my mouth with death before I had a chance to speak. I peer at them from the grimed church window, shake my head, tiptoe to the vestry to steal bread and wine from sacramental silver.

How long does it take for a two-thousand-year-old egg to rot?

They hold a service below me for the expulsion of the demon. A wise conclusion: I obviously could not have come from Out, and I am not one of them. They've checked themselves, most carefully; they are, each of them, finger-printed, foot-printed, voice-printed, retina-printed, lip-printed, brainwave-printed, holographed, measured and metered from the moment of their metered births. They're all present and accounted for, and so I am a demon, a ghost amok in the City of Time. I make a note to add that to the sign on the City Offices, and watch the archaic stars appear. Stars. Floating through ancient skies.

When the prank comes to me it is so obvious, so clear, so simple that I laugh aloud, and the congregation below me freezes in fear. I laugh again, pure joy, and hide in a forgotten closet until they stop looking and flee superstitiously from the building. I follow them out, across the City to the vault of controls. I've picked the locks here before and I do it again now, slip inside, lock the door behind me and consider the panels on the wall. Here, and here, linked to this, and here the main nexus, here the central time control. Then I sit and open my mind to memories, recall the clearest, purest night of resurrected Terra I have seen, and I program the skies of the City of Time, jumping their heavens two thousand years forward in the space of half an hour. I add to the moon the smudge of Jump I, I put our latest comet in the sky. What else? Of course, the weather satellites, all five in stately, if not entirely accurate, orbit through the heavens. The computer is not programmed to let me add a starship, or I would do that too. There. There must be stargazers in the City of Time, people who will look above them and see my altered cosmos, will wonder, speculate, go take a look. They will. They *must.* I lock the door behind me and go to write graffiti on the walls of the static City.

Why has their birthrate declined? The City was built to accommodate twice as many as it now encloses—such an empty City now!

Someone finally noticed the report from the robo-tech that found and sealed my way home, and someone else decided that the hole might have some connection with the haunting of their sealed City. A large group of them has come down to inspect it, while I inspect them. Hope springs eternal, yes, and perhaps one of them will come to the right conclusion. But no, they inspect the sealed hole, they argue at great length about it, stamping their feet on the plasteel floor. Perhaps they think that some small animal with laser teeth has sawed its way around their citadel, or that some anomalous tremor has produced this round aperture with fused sides. Whatever, whatever; they decide finally that the hell-mouth couldn't possibly have been made from the outside; no one lives out there, no one could live out there. They are very certain. After a while they leave and I emerge, howl in rage, kick at the floors and walls, tear at the impervious sides of the machines. The echoes of my disappointment rampage through the vault, activate some electronic curiosity in the robo-techs, and they come to investigate.

But I am long gone, following the course of my despair up into the nub of the City.

◆

They argue about it now. I listen to the mayor berate the police system over my unapprehended state, yet there is hesitation in her voice. I hear my pranks and myself denounced from pulpits while the congregation sits oddly silent. Young ones at the schools explode with oratory, wave their urgent hands skyward. I listen, strain my ears, want to rush to them yelling, "Yes, yes, you are almost right! Come, show me the doors, I'll take you Out into clarity! Come!" But I remain hidden, eager, awake, hope boiling within me. Come, hurry, let me go home again!

◆

They still argue, endlessly. I am impatient. It's harvest time Out, the schools and shops are closed and the population pours forth to reap and celebrate. Home! Home! I program their night skies to blink at them, I paint pictures on fountain lips of harvests under round moons, of large cats prowling the yards of houses, calling to be fed and stroked; of giant lilies floating in the calm air of forests. Home! I consider poisoning their water, rerouting their waste system, flooding their streets, giving them twenty-hour nights and two-minute days. I could do it all, easily, from the depths of the service cores, from the corners of the control rooms, but I refrain. The City is unbearable enough to me by itself, without my self-made catastrophes. Home! Jora will be seven by now, Karleen twelve, my corn ripens on the hill and my students wait in classrooms, Petrel stalks the hillside and awaits my return. Home! I huddle in a corner of the park, weeping, until the universe shrinks to accommodate only my soul pain and nothing more. Then, angered, I waken the rusting voice of the call system above the City Offices and bellow through the streets, "For God's sake, walk into the light! The sun shines Out, there are trees and birds and water sweet as spring! Come Out! Come Out and home again!"

◆

They're opening the door. They found it, buried in a forgotten service area, behind piles of wire and cable, guarded by an ancient robo-cop. I watch, amazed, through the shards of plastiglass in an abandoned storage room, my fingers at my mouth, teeth to nails, reverting to primitivism as the young people overpower the robo-cop by the airlock. They do it quite simply. Five of them lunge at the robot, grab, twist the paneled head until it pops off and rolls down the alley, trailing multicolored wires. The body, relieved of its burden, wanders in a melancholy way down the blind alley and stands bleeping aimlessly at the end of it, uncertain of where to turn. The young ones ignore the distressed machine, turn their attention to the great wheels and plates of the airlock door. Have they . . . yes, they've brought meters, and one of them applies the leads to a small, unobtrusive control box, reads the meter, shakes her head, shakes the meter, tries again, shrugs. More uncertainty, more discussion, then the robot-slayers grasp the great wheel of the door and strain at it. Two others join in, the last one watches uneasily at the entrance to the alley. Why didn't they completely dismantle the robo-cop? Where's the transmitter in the damned thing, anyway? It's likely, possible, probable, certain that the mutilated beast is sending silent, roaring distress signals throughout the City, calling cops and more cops, bringing them rushing to the door to freedom. I watch the young ones as they wrench and twist at the wheel, frightened, excited, defiant, sweaty, the age of my students. The wheel groans, turns, suddenly spins free, spilling the young ones over the polymer pavement. Quickly then, yes, they gather at the door, pry it open slowly, swinging it on its ancient hinges. Hurry! Hurry! From my higher vantage point I can see scurries in the distance, fast approaching, hurry! And the door stands open, they cluster at its mouth, waver, enter one after another. My God, the door's closing! Of course, an airlock, of course. I scramble from my perch, tear through the empty storage center, down to the alley. My pack falls to the floor behind me, my torn tunic catches on something and tears completely from me but I can't stop, mustn't, run, *run*, watching in agony as the door closes, closes, closes and suddenly I am inside, braking the force of my flight on their soft bodies, slumping against the far wall, panting, while they stand gaping at me. The door swings shut, clicks into place. Safe. Safe.

I catch my breath, gesture toward the next door. "Out," I gasp. "S'okay, clean, open."

But they're frightened of me, hair, skin, eyes, semi-nakedness. They huddle together, shivering slightly. I force the beating of my heart down, take a deep breath, tell them of my journey, my trials, my homesickness. Do they believe me? They cluster together, wide-eyed, silent. I've not bathed properly in five months, my hair bushes in lumps around my sun-starved face, my eyes are rimmed with weariness. Why should they believe this horrific apparition? I shrug, reach for the great wheel, yank. It does not budge to my pulling. I grasp it more tightly, desperately, pull again, sob, and then there are two hands, four, ten, sixteen pulling at the wheel with me. It groans, shivers, turns ponderously, clicks free. Together we pry the great door open.

And, over the piled dirt of centuries, the sunlight pours in.

Ex-NEWSPAPERMAN, EX-SOLDIER, *ex–college professor, ex–bookstore manager Robert Thurston first came to the notice of science-fiction readers in 1971, when his short story "Wheels" won a prize as the best work to come out of the previous year's Clarion SF Writers' Workshop. As his list of abandoned professions indicates, Thurston is a bit more mature than the average Clarion attendee— he is well along in his thirties at the time this is written —and his prizewinning story and those that have followed it reflect considerable technical skill and hard-won wisdom. He appears now in* New Dimensions *for the first time.*

Robert Thurston

■

THEODORA AND THEODORA

I.   Theodora hated Italy and all Italians. What am I doing here, she thought. "What are we doing here?" she asked her husband, Spencer. Spencer, irritable because of the pain in a black eye he had suffered in Venice the previous day when he had stumbled while getting out of a gondola, ignored his wife's question and hollered at her to do something about Tendra Jane, who was playing cat's cradle with spaghetti strands. The owner of the restaurant, a tall handsome man whose self-confidence made Theodora think of open sores, gently removed the tangled food from the child's grasp. At the same time he whispered something softly in Italian, a language she refused to understand, in Theodora's ear.

◆

II.   Theodora and her husband strolled down an oppressive and narrow Italian street, the squalling Tendra Jane clutched between them. Spencer lightly touched the black eye he had received yesterday from a rude, argumentative cab driver. It seemed to Theodora that distinctively Italian smells were attacking her. They came out onto a wider but crowded street, where an angry mob gestured fiercely, and sometimes obscenely, at a passing ornate carriage. Theodora, Tendra Jane, and Spencer were pushed up some steps and against a wall. Although it felt as if they were being pressed to death by the massive crowd, at least the view was better. They could see right into the carriage. Inside it, dressed elegantly, was a tall handsome self-confident man who, while Theodora gazed at him, leaned out the carriage window. He seemed, even from his vast distance, to stare directly into Theodora's fear-filled eyes. "We must leave this country," she told her husband, who told her to watch the goddamned kid more closely.

◆

III. "Theodora!"

"Theodora dear!"

"And Spencer!"

"Dear, dear Spencer!"

"Hello, old chap."

"Hi, buddy."

"Fancy meeting you two here of all places."

"Just what I was going to say."

"Isn't it the truth? And your Tendra Jane, my, she *has* grown."

"Not to mention your Tendra Jane whom I hardly recognize."

"Except that she still resembles your Tendra Jane."

"That's true, all right."

"What are you folks doing over here of all places?"

"Spencer thought it was time to take a year off from the business. He had a heart attack, you know. Last year, on his forty-third birthday."

"My Spencer also. Fell right into the cake."

"Should have known. I mean, after all."

"Yes, we should keep in touch. For our own stability. My God, wait till everybody hears this one!"

"You think so? I can't get anybody interested in *that* any more, not since both Rovers died under the crunching wheels of identical Pierce-Arrows."

"Now that you mention, I've noticed sudden silences when I've brought up the subject lately."

"There you are."

"How's business, Spencer old chap?"

"Just piling up on the line, buddy."

"Me, too. Backup's terrible this year."

"Couldn't stay good forever."

"Look, we have to run, but we're staying at the Imperial."

"Us, too. Room 343."

"Why, we're in 434. Wouldn't you know? We *must* get together."

"Yes. Soon."

"Ta-ta."

"Bye-bye."

◆

IV.   Theodora found herself in a lush garden. A light breeze fluttered the petals of a hundred varieties of flowers, and also the edges of the purple notepaper she held in her trembling hand. The note said in ornate script: "Follow the map below. Be at X by 9 o'clock this evening. I must see you again. I am being watched. If I am late, please wait, my beautiful one. Love, R." The garden was too mysterious. Theodora longed for the security of Newark.

"Italian moonlight becomes you."

It was him, the man who had sat in the carriage earlier, suddenly standing in front of her. He had stepped into the path from behind a tree. He was dressed in a white and gold operetta suit.

"You speak English."

"I speak English as often as possible. In my own language I am tongue-tied. I mispronounce words, substitute one word for another without logic, stutter, add unnecessary syllables. I shout 'macaroon' when I see a pretty girl."

As he said macaroon, he waved his hand in a very Italian way. Theodora shuddered.

"But in English I am perfect."

◆

V.   Theodora, tired of Spencer and his black eye, found herself walking by the restaurant they had eaten in earlier. The self-confident proprietor happened to be standing in the doorway. He waved his hand and whispered "macaroon" as he saw her.

"I will follow you wherever you lead me," the man said.

"There are already too many Italians in Newark," Theodora said.

♦

VI.   He would not admit to being a nobleman, but in his eyes Theodora could see the lustiness of the student prince, the gentle ironic humor of a dweller at Mayerling, the steely determination of Rupert Count of Hentzau. He talked of his wife Maria and his son Benito in a voice that was both sad and tortured.

"They no longer understand me," he said. "They see me already as a statue in the park, as all virtue preserved in granite and streaked with pigeon droppings. Benito thinks I am now a relic of the past."

"Tendra Jane has always been a loving and loyal child," Theodora said.

"I am so unhappy. Give me a chance to please you."

"Spencer pleases me enough, I'm sure."

"I will abdicate. I will come to America and become a wealthy hoodlum. You will sit beside me as my moll."

Theodora felt dizzy.

"I do not particularly . . . *approve* of Italians. I like some Italians, of course. Enrico Caruso, uh, Garibaldi, uh, Dante Alighieri, Leonardo da Vinci . . ."

"Give me a chance to please you."

"Spencer pleases me. Tendra Jane pleases me. Please, dear, do not try to please me, else I be undone."

He continued to whisper in her ear and, beneath the soft Italian moonlight, Theodora became his.

◆

VII.   The restaurant proprietor took Theodora to his gun room. He showed her at least a dozen weapons whose names she could not pronounce.

"They are nice," she said. "For guns."

"I am so glad you like. My family hates the guns. Not my wife Maria, not even my one son, Benito—nobody likes the guns. Just you and my twin . . ."

"You have a twin brother?"

"He is not really my twin, but we might as well be. We resemble each other physically, we even talk alike, although we come from different families, unrelated in any way. We were born on the same day in the same city—"

"Why, that's amaz—"

"We married our wives on the same day, at the exact same hour. We each were honored with the birth of a son named Benito on the same chilly February day. On the day I opened up my restaurant, he received his title and inheritance. We share characteristics and tastes. Silly, but we are amused by it."

"It is not silly. I must tell you about myself and *my* Theodora. We met in a hospital in New Jersey where we were both having—"

"It is all very fascinating. I wish to kiss you now."

"No! I must tell you now."

"Later. I will follow wherever you lead me."

Theodora felt dizzy.

"You are just a wop pasta cook," she said. "Leave me alone. I am an American tourist and you have no right to press me so."

"I know no other way of life. I always go after what I want."

"And I always submit. But not here, not with your family asleep upstairs. I will meet you tomorrow in front of your restaurant and we will do whatever you like, no matter who leads whom."

◆

VIII.   He rubbed Theodora's tears into the white and gold
fibers of his sleeve. He seemed suddenly aloof.

"Go back to your Spencer," he said. "It is better."

"I don't like Spencer. I have never liked Spencer. I will never
like Spencer. I did not marry him out of choice. Something
compelled me. Suddenly he was standing there in his seer-
sucker suit and his striped Arrow shirt, and he said to me, 'We
will be married,' and I said, 'Yes,' and I was sick to my stomach
because I could not stand either his bulbous face or his squeaky
voice. I pretend that we are a perfect match because I have
always believed there was no other choice, that everything
depended on Spencer and me staying together. He never lets
me do what I want. For once I would like to do something
alone."

"If only that were so. I especially know that one cannot always do what he wants. All my movements are restrained by
duty. All my actions are observed for correctness. There is nothing but destiny for me. I cannot be free."

"I understand."

"Do you?"

"Americans can understand that sort of thing, you know."

"I love you, Theodora. Please do not forget me."

"Don't be silly, my little Italian sausage. You will be in my
memory always."

"You revive my spirits at a time when I thought they were
dead. I must see you once more. Tomorrow be in front of your
hotel and I will ride by in my carriage. If I can be free again in
the evening I will wave to you with my left hand. If duty re-
strains me, I will wave with my right. Will you be there?"

"Yes, my liege."

◆

IX.   In a corner Tendra Jane sobbed meaninglessly. During
the hour before her scheduled rendezvous, Theodora smiled
often at Spencer. She felt peculiarly sentimental towards him,
perhaps because there was so much Newark in his face. He was

so stable, so decisive, so incredibly filled with pep. How could she leave him for a greasy-spoon creep?

There was still a chance for her to renege. After all, she had made no commitments to the restaurateur and she was certainly able to keep the impetuous Latin at a distance. Yet, there had now been so many years of Spencerian predictability, how could she give up her one opportunity for a romantic escapade? It seemed vital to succumb to the single reckless decision of her life. She sneaked out of the hotel room while Spencer busied himself with the current bill. He cursed to himself as he struggled to translate lire into dollars and cents. He must get it right, no Italian tourist trap would swindle him out of a penny.

Theodora shuddered as she struggled to shoulder her way through the unusually large crowd in the streets. She hoped that, whatever her new lover did, he did not surround her with a lot of other Italians.

As she progressed through the streets she noticed that there was something odd about the crowd. In addition to the usual mixture of loungers, shoppers, business people, and tourists, there seemed to be large amounts of less savory creatures— bearded and ferrety types who moved snakelike through the crowd as if they had a shared purpose. In some faces was the look of many secrets, in others fierce hatred. The atmosphere was definitely antisocial. Theodora wondered if there was some sort of jailbreak going on.

The press of the crowd delayed her, and she arrived at the restaurant late for her appointment. She ran the last few steps, pushing those who were obviously natives aside. But her lover was not pacing the front of his eatery. Theodora muttered something to herself about how foreigners perpetually ignored punctuality.

◆

X.   Theodora waited impatiently in front of the hotel. She felt a little perturbed, spending all this time merely to see if he waved with his left or right hand. What if it was his left? Would she scurry to that little garden again, just to play the adulterous American wife out for her second fling? She imagined how he probably saw her—as a silly Daisy Miller type, a stupid night of fun for a bored aristocrat. Yet he had been tender, and there had been such sincerity in his glistening eyes. It was foolish of her to accept morning-after blues for what had, after all, been a pleasant adventure which required no vindictive emotional colorings. She would see him again, or she would not. That she would decide after his wave and an afternoon of restful contemplation. For now she practiced the tender and loving appearance she had planned for their visual exchange as he rode by. It was designed to fit whatever his message might be. She would look tearful, a shy smile playing at the corners of her mouth. His look, she knew, would be secretive. Regretful if he waved right-handed, sly if lefthanded. Whatever happened, today or tonight it would be all over. Then she and Spencer could get out of this damned country and back to decent people.

The street was relatively empty. When she'd first come out, there had been quite a mob, but they had slowly filtered out, most of them heading for the north corner. It was around that corner that her lover would come any moment now. She wondered what was keeping him. If he didn't show up soon, Spencer might solve whatever schedule or financial assessment he was presently at work on, and come out of the hotel.

She jumped, startled at the sound of a sob beside her.

"Why, Theodora! Fancy meeting you here."

"Always the way."

"What *is* the matter? You're crying."

"Yes, I guess so. I've been crying for blocks now. Walking and crying."

"Whatever for? Please tell me. You know you can. Of all people, you can tell *me*. You have to, it would seem."

While speaking the words of consolation, she could not help taking glances at the corner, hoping that she could clear up this incident before he came.

"I know. Where would we be if we didn't always tell each other everything?"

"Insane, I suspect. It's gotten me through many a tight situation, I can testify."

"Me, too. Until I met you in that hospital, everything seemed so . . . so . . ."

"I know, dear. Please tell me everything, but right away. I only have a few minutes."

"Well, it's . . . it's about my lover. He—"

"You have a lover? You have a lover, too! Italian? And you were with him last night?"

"Yes."

"My stars! Me, too, dear—me, too."

"No, no! I won't allow that! It is un—"

"But wait till you hear. Mine is a genuine—"

"I don't want to hear. I don't care about *your* lover. I don't care about him, I don't care about him, I don't care about him . . ."

"Dear, what is the matter? You don't have to get hysterical with me. Just tell me."

"He is dead!"

"Who? Not Spencer. It couldn't be. It couldn't hap—"

"My lover is dead. I was supposed to meet him and he didn't come and I went to his home and there were people out front. They told me he was dead, that apparently he had been cleaning one of his prize guns and, in front of his son and everything, he turned the gun around, pointed it at his chest and fired it. It was as if the gun did it all by itself, his son said. He was my lover. I was going to run off with—"

"Extraordinary. And he killed himself today. Did you say it was today? Tell me! It's important!"

"It happened hardly an hour ago. When I got there, they were carrying out his body."

"Your lover. We must get this straight. *Your* lover!"

"Well, not lover exactly, but he would have been, after we eloped, after we got out of this rotten—"

"Then—then there's a chance. There must be a chance. He wouldn't kill himself, I know. Not *him*, not—"

She stopped, trying to discern if what she heard in the distance was a gunshot. Everything seemed so terribly silent. Then there was a second sound, again it seemed like a gunshot, followed by a loud and sustained cheer from what must have been a massive crowd. In the midst of the cheer she seemed to hear another sound, a crash followed by an upsurge in the cheering. Both women reached a hand out at the same time. They gripped each other tightly. In the doorway of the hotel, both Spencers collided. They nodded simultaneously at each other. The cheering kept increasing in volume. Around the north corner, swaying and teetering as if it followed a drunken path, came an ornate carriage wheel. It continued rolling for an unlikely length of time, then flopped over suddenly and skidded to within inches of the two women's feet.

FELIX GOTSCHALK *is a psychologist from North Carolina who contributed two stories to* New Dimensions 4 *and has been appearing in various other s-f collections lately. His mind is strange and inventive, and his style, a wildly original technology-speak, is maddening to some, delightful to others—with this editor joining the latter camp. Gotschalk is likely to be the most infuriating and controversial s-f writer of the mid-1970s; and, I think, he's going to produce some of the most stimulating and rewarding work.*

■

Felix C. Gotschalk

■

A DAY IN THE SOUTH QUAD

Compared with routine actuarial samplings of early anti-meridian inputs, Cal's day started off near asymptote. Eva awakened him with a softly penetrating personalized kiss, and then skewered herself onto him with lithe and skillful movements of fitting and refitting. She wove a complex pattern of friction vectors into the coitional matrix: gusty heavy downstrokes, excruciating slow withdrawals, light dabbing thrusts, and little dervishes of rotational nuance. She hung like a ripe melon, descended like a velvet pile-driver, and throbbed and pulsed and quivered. Cal lifted ever higher and touched critical mass. A single orange flower bloomed at the base of his spinal column, and stunning plumes of nectar sluiced up into the uterine cosmos. Cal felt oceanic, pinnacular, messianic, at the glowing tip of the exponential cone.

While they slept the brief, delicious sleep of detumescence, the sun edged soddenly above the camphor trees, like a red blister. The thick fleshy grass held wetly infusive dew, the canna lilies hung lush and red, and field larks began their pure tone calls: glistening ethereal messages, vague aching nostalgias, dimly poignant déjà-vu wisps. The air smelled wet and fleetingly sweet.

Cal vaulted softly onto the rug and jogged in slow motion, breathing deeply and carefully, as if he were airing out a favorite room. The temperature and the humidity were coincident at 70, and he missed the nippy dryness of the North Quad. Cal

65

was completing the third month of a year's assignment as an Agriculture Peer in the tidal marshlands of the Southern Gulf Coast Quad of the Continental Synod.

The bulkhead vesicle irised open and two-year-old Rob stood there, smiling, a mini–margay clone in his arms. He dropped the cat and scooted past Cal to the circular discbed and climbed onto Eva, sitting astride her back like an equestrian and blatting her trapezius with soft blows of his little hands. Eva protested sleepily and affectedly, and her empathic vectors flooded Rob with conjugal warmth. He lay his head flat in the smooth concavity between his mother's shoulder blades and flashed a precocious Oedipal wink at Cal. The thrill of fatherhood was still fresh in Cal's mind, and Rob reinforced the joys and all but extinguished the troubles.

Cal sonic-bathed and watched the trivid news: the historical society was trying to prevent the municipal synod from demolishing the Huey Long Bridge. The ten-mile-wide Atchafalaya Spillway from Natchez due south to the gulf had dried up the Mississippi fifty years ago. The channel became a valley of stinking black sludge, drying into a silt trench about one mile wide and 100 feet deep, then bloomed in incredible varieties of hybrid foliage. Cajun squatters moved onto the loamy quilting and fought over tiny arpents of rich soil. The synod allocated arpents 50 feet wide and 100 feet deep, and the valley burgeoned with half a million individual gardens, from Belle Chase north to Oak Alley. The produce-guild members now wanted the ancient bridge vaporized so as to provide additional crop areas. The approaches had been bombed out during the 2520 civil war and a sordid line-up of shantytown hovels spread across the center spans and far down both approaches. The bridge squatters peed and shat onto the girders and the gardens far below, and one or two bodies fell every week, along with assorted detritus. The orchids and the asparagi and the artichokes did their tropistic aversions but received pigeon shit on their tuxedos. Cal palmed another trivid facet and got the traffic patterns: terrestrial auto reprods recommended for pleasure driving, flitters for intracommune travel, and thoracic transport implants for commuting to megalopoli. Rob loved to see Cal put on the projectile-shaped transport helmet, palm the softly glowing force field over his body, and soar off over the cane fields. Flitters were fun, but were governed down to 50 mph and 500 feet maximum altitude. Auto reprods were strictly nostalgic. Cal fluxed on an epithelial toga of soft mesh, clamped on a life-support cumberbund, and stepped into levitation boots. Eva and Rob met him as he walked into the hall. Rob had the margay dialed up to lion size and was hugging the clone-beast in a relaxed quarter nelson.

"What's on your docket today?" Eva asked, dialing breakfast readouts on the trivid screen.

"Supposed to hop down to Lutcher," Cal replied. "Got to check the lading tapes on some perrique arpents. The stuff is growing slow enough to give the mole crickets some real solid nibbles. The last load factored out at about eighty-seven percent good wrapper leaf, but I think we can go to about ninety-three and make everybody a little happier. That perrique makes the best black stogie ever."

"Eva knows full well," she said with a playful wince. "I'm glad you stopped smoking inside the house." Rob had the margay back to lynx size. He sat on a vitaminic charging pod and peered around Eva's head at the menus. He chose carmel nectar and giant wheat germ, inflated collard ringlets and embryo pig flanks. Eva had Hu-Kwa tea, compressed pumpernickel cubes with butter pellets, and grapes. Cal fingered the keyboard lightly, undecided, then punched in a wide-spectrum protein blastula, chilled lime water, and a beautiful parfait of plums and cream.

"How pretty!" sang Rob, and dialed one for himself. "Get something for kitty." Eva dialed some whiting planks and gave them to the margay.

"What are you two going to do today?" Cal said, pulling a striate off the protein cube.

"Rob wants to check his gar rings again this morning. Ever

since that two-hundred-pound one took the bait last week, he keeps taking his flit back in the bayous."

"I go by myself, Cal," Rob said brightly, not fully aware of the safety parameters assured through his own levitational implants and force-field isomorph, plus Eva's teleport implant. She could whisk him back if any real danger coded on her visual monitor or emo-monitor.

"And I am playing topological bridge this afternoon. You know, my contract sphere was pear-shaped last week and I won third prize. Louise got a great sphere, almost round, and was first."

"How did Helen do?" Cal asked playfully.

"Poor girl, she'll never learn the game," Eva sighed. "Her contract sphere looked like a dented pyramidal stack. But then she bids on raw hunch, she horrifies her partners. By the way, the Fli-Mart is due today, if you want anything. I got some good nutria meat from it last week."

"Nothing, thanks," Cal said, getting up. "Oh, unless they've got any new mutant birds. The aviary's top-heavy with finches. Well, good-bye, you two." Cal bent and kissed Eva low on the cheek, his tumescent radiates tingling at the touch. He touched Rob's head lightly and went out through the autoport vesicle.

The house was a West Indies cottage reprod, slightly lowered and elongated. The life-support facilities were modern, but the simulated cypress walls and columns were indigenous to traditional southern-quad culture, and the effect was organic, in the broad architectural sense. The lot was 200 feet wide and 600 feet deep, all matted with thick creeper grasses. Lilies and marigolds grew in small beds in the front, but the entire lot was treeless. The rear property line was marked by a thick row of camphor trees sprouting from a shallow trench and extending far back into the cane fields. Two concrete strips formed a driveway out to an access road of crushed white shells. Cal thumb-printed a panel in the autoport bulkhead, revealing the transport console. He looked at the bright steaming sky and decided to go slow and nostalgic for a while, pushed the auto-reprod bar and scanned the listings, and settled on a Lancia sedan circa 1960. He pressed the selection bar and the car materialized on the driveway, coming by molecular transporter from a station about seven miles down Bayou Lafourche. He swung into the black leather seat and got the heady smell of well-tanned Scottish leather. A huge speedometer and tachometer showed their white-on-black faces through the smallish wheel. Cal backed out onto the shell road, waved at Rob standing by a window, and spun the rear wheels gently in the shells as he pulled off. On what the people called the blacktop, Cal accelerated the car and the silky V-6 sent the tach spinning without protest. He drove past the double row of huge live oaks leading up to the plantation house, past neatly painted pastel geodesics, past rusting iron sheds where tugboats were once fabricated, and past plank roads leading off into the swamps to wildcat oil-rig sites. A small church stood somberly in a grove of gray trees, long trailings of Spanish moss floating from the branches. The ground around the building was dark and smooth and spongy. Cal turned the Lancia onto the drawbridge across the bayou, then turned west, up the old Lafourche blacktop. The bayou was dry and planted in arpents of tomatoes and scallions. Century plants soared unsteadily to thirty-foot heights and elephant ears spread next to Spanish daggers. The road was in poor repair, sword-grass cut bold serrations into the lanes often, and the asphalt turned soft and gummy in the high heat of midafternoon. Cal drove slowly past a large white church with a huge sprawling graveyard surrounding it. The crypts and slabs and drawers looked like hundreds of giant chessmen crowded beyond growth limits onto a board of tidal-marsh sponge. Ecological-demographic lines of village patterns persisted, with dwellings adjacent to the bayou and crop arpents snaking away on both sides. The university lay on Cal's left, long ago abandoned in the face of fiscal woes and lack of students. He entered the town, the Tara reprod of a medical man marking the corporate limits, followed by several mansion reprods, an odd and smelly metal-plate sphere built by the town eccentric, and a remarkable old wooden school building some five stories high. Then the buckling juxtapos of old gas stations, bank ruins, fish + chips stores, frozen custard booths, Laundromats, convenience food stores, and all the dreary artifacts of an earlier time. Cal waved at a girl in a bubble-canopy Messer reprod and ducked away as a flitter buzzed him. He recrossed the bayou trench and turned due north toward the Mississippi. The road was straight as an arrow, flat as a tabletop, and bumpy as a washboard. A few rusting and folded oil rigs lay forlornly on the right, while the left side of the road butted against deep swampy woods. Crayfish scuttled across the road in migratory masses, the clicking mass requiring Cal to sit and wait for the road to clear. He had tried ramming such groups of crayfish before and found himself with genuine control and friction troubles. Thousands of lovebugs moved with strange slowness through the air, quickly flecking auto reprods' windshields with a whitish substance which dried into tough hard spots. The sword-grass barriers were more frequent and the road had a lushly unreal quality. Overhead, the flitters and the people with transport implants seemed to vie for air space, but the clumping was really more playful-ritualistic than purposeful. After some few minutes of driving, Cal saw the levee, an earthen dam some twenty feet above the tidal-marshland levels. Despite its simple role and construction, the levee suggested the "Alps on Alps arise" words in Cal's thinking. Many years ago, people would stand at the foot of the levee and see nothing but the bank and grass and flowers. Climbing to the top, slowly approaching the summit, then feeling the wet breeze and standing on the summit, a visually stunning world pouring into the senses: the vast wide wallowing river, the huge ships boring through the brown water, the wakes lapping the levee, the distant shoreline so clear, so diminutive, promising, yet mirage-like. To see the river at flood stage was to stand on the edge of a world filled to the rim with heavy water. The horizon itself rose up to impart a giddy sense of being awash in a lumbering slow surge of water, with no visual cues to keep the perspective meaningful.

Cal parked the car at the base of the levee, got out and stretched, and looked up and down the old river road, adjusting his vision to ten-power mag. St. John plantation gleamed a dull chalky white through the shimmering heat and sawing insects. The heavy gate was down and the upper gallery sagged gently. He sprinted to the top of the levee and stood in a Colossus of Rhodes stance. Old man river had long ago lumbered off into the central gulf like some ponderous macrocosmic slug, and the wide shallow valley of bright fleshy flowers and vegetables lay before Cal. Calendulas pushed up in twenty-foot-high clusters and the century plants beamed up their ropy shafts once a year. Eglantine and foxglove, harebell and jasmine, lotus and mimosa, ranunculus and snowball, the variety of growth was incredible. Squares of Bengal grasses and bristly foxtail shone like jelly mints in a candy bowl. Millet and mesquite and papyrus grew unabashedly adjacent to each other, strangely robust bedfellows. The salty tomatoes were red as blood blisters and the alligator pears gleamed a wet thick green. On the far side of the valley, beds of giant truffles lay like huge puffballs abandoned by a playful giant. A blue heron flew by on its butterfly-soft wings. Cal resisted the urge to sit down. A dull concussive roar rolled in from down river and a copper-colored Saturn XII lifted into the sky, headed for the polar-cap villa complexes. Cal felt global homeostasis. A conflict input is overdue, he said aloud, as he slid onto the warm seat of the Lancia and headed down the old road toward Lutcher. Two miles away, a milk truck was bouncing toward Cal, the driver dribbling and cursing his black helper.

The road had never been a good one—scenic, yes, nostalgic, time-binding, rich in particulate residues. Now it was lonely, threatening at night, and was impassable from time to time, depending on the whims of the natives, the mutant animals, the foliage that grew as you watched, and the gambols and litter of the air riders. Cal began to wish he had taken a flitter. An armadillo as big as a hog scuttled across the road like a heavy metal toy, and a tower of mosquitoes hummed sharply, moving like a jellied tornado funnel. Cal dodged bottles and boxes and thorny tumbleweeds. A circle of voodoo women cawed obscene curses at the car as it moved tentatively past their hovel-place. Palm trees leaned out over the road and a robber crab skitted out of sight like a squirrel on a tree trunk. Around a curve lined with pyracantha lay a straight clear stretch of road and Cal breathed out a soft sigh and settled back. About half a mile ahead, a car lay halfway off the road on the right. Half a mile more and the milk truck rattled heavily up the corduroy road. Cal saw the truck coming and got a bleep on the radar scope. His force field and impact neutralizer fluxed on automatically. There was plenty of room for the Lancia to clear the truck as they met where the abandoned car lay, but Cal saw that the truck was giving no ground at all. In fact, the truck swayed across the faded center line. Cal figured he had shot the breech of space with maybe one foot on either side, and the truck driver's face had been twisted into a murderous leer. The son of a bitch tried to run me off, Cal said, the words grating in his throat. He activated the provobot monitor and gave a terse report, but the screen showed the nearest provo about ten miles away. Even with robot cops, you never can find one, Cal thought. His galvanic skin response and heart rate increased flaringly and his foot began to shake on the accelerator. His neck flushed red and a sharp respiratory blowing came as an autonomic surprise. Then, as he stopped the car on a spongy arpent shoulder, he felt adrenaline pour over his kidneys like Tabasco sauce on a soft raw potato. "The granny-hopper really did try to get me," Cal said, intent and incredulous. The face of the driver was clear in his mind: large asymmetric head, bald, fleshy, sunken eyes, canine fangs, no eyebrows. Probably subhumanoid, Cal thought, and spuriously programmed, and what the hell is he doing driving an old drayage vehicle? The autonomic fight-or-flight reaction still simmered in Cal's viscera. He suddenly turned the car full lock, spun a gravel-timbre arc across the road, clapped briefly into reverse, and headed back upriver after the truck. He muttered plosive invectives and gripped the wheel tightly. His heart surged again as he rounded a soft curve and saw the truck stopped dead ahead. A hulking figure blocked the adjacent lane, heavily muscled arms placed akimbo. Cal knew that his life-systems pak would keep him safe, but the leaking visceral queasiness nudged him again. For an instant, he felt he would better avoid the confrontation, but a sharp surge of anger supplanted this feeling and he nosed the car up against the back of the truck and stopped, jabbing the brake hard and pulling up on the handbrake noisily. He opened the door like a cop running for cover and fluxed on a neutral physiog mask. The truck driver moved toward him like a down-field blocker setting a tack on a target. "Gladiator!" a voice shouted from the truck. "Don't try to take him, mister." It was the black man and he sounded scared. Cal ducked reflexly into a gunfighter pose as the big man swung a tire chain at his head, the metal links swishing in the hot thick air. The man snarled like a jungle cat and flooded the empathic space with smothering purple hypothalamic gusts. He crashed into Cal's force-field isomorph and brayed raucously at the shock, spinning off quickly into a sumo stance. The black man had climbed onto the top of the truck and shouted down at Cal. "Kill him if you can, mister, he ain't nothin' but a cyborg glad, and mean as a bucket o' snakes." Cal drew his phaser and notched it to stun. He pointed it at the man's head and moved it in a tight circle from a knife-fighter crouch. "You sumbich boy," the glad garbled, "me fight you good, fight good for emperor." He shaped the tire chain into a clinking sphere, like a boy fashioning a prize snow-ball, and threw it at Cal. The sphere became a bolo rope and glanced off the force field at Cal's hip. "Back away, back away," Cal said urgently, "I can immobilize you." His emo-monitor seared with the strength of the glad's hypothalamic spikings, and the semantic monitor gave off a pure-tone nadir note. "He don't know what you're talking about," the black man said. "Go on, put him away—phase him—you the one what got the phaser!" The glad dove at Cal, the force field crackled, and he spun away again, bellowing like metal chunks in a siren. He

seemed to be checking his pulse, then chrome thorns spat out
from his fingertips and he advanced once more. The phaser
hummed and the lumbering form slowed and stopped. Cal
sprayed a force field around the man and began to examine
him, like a hunter walking around a fallen beast. The man was
about seven feet tall and looked like he weighed 300 pounds.
The head looked like a one-sided basketball, laced and stitched
and melded in cross-hatch patterns, and bore a physiog plate aft
of an ear nodule. Cal leaned in to read the plate:

PNEUMOFLUX CYBORG TYP GL
CEREBROMORPH ANTHROPOID TRANSPLANT TYP A 6
PROPERTY OF NEW ORLEANS ATHLETIC SYNOD
RESTRICTED. LETHAL

The form quivered and lurched slightly, like a statue being
toppled by young revolutionaries. Cal started. "Let him fall,"
the black man's voice rang out, and he vaulted onto the levee
bank and strode over to Cal. "You big ugly sacka shit," the man
taunted the glad, "whut you gone do now?" He kicked at the
form tentatively and jumped as a low snarl gutted out of the
sagging mouth.

"How did you happen to get on a truck with a cyborg gladiator?" Cal asked.

Circling the immobilized form, the black man seemed proud
of the catch and sadistic. "He jumped in my truck and 'bout
twisted my neck off. Then he say he want to drive the truck and
I say, man, you doan know how to drive, and he say, me drive,
you black fart."

"How did he get out of the stadium pens?"

"Man, I don't know no way."

Cal pressed the provobot monitor again and got a reply: a
Lafourche Parish bot was two miles away and approaching. But
then a whole airsled full of synod-level provobots came swishing
along just above the levee, hissed to a shuddering stop, and

levitated noisily as the bots jumped off. The sled settled onto the sod and seemed to wallow like a hog in mud. A provomarshal walked up to Cal and gave a careless high-hat salute.

"We'll take him from here," he said. "Thanks for the help."

"How did he get away?" Cal asked.

"Slipped a DNA key-pawl and ratchet from a clone in the next pen, *plus* a teleporter, multilocator, levitator—he really got an entire life-systems minipak."

"And started palming activators randomly?"

"Like a chimp with a time bomb." The bots had the glad spun into a plasti-foam cocoon and were carrying it up to the sled.

"As best we can reconstruct it, he teleported about two miles from the pens, commandeered the truck, and set off on a joy ride. I'll need your retinograph tapes for the records. And there's a reward stipend too."

"Hey, man, what about me?" The black man seemed to want in on the action.

"Where you live, boy?" The provomar asked, turning mean and somehow rural.

"Marseilles Plot, your provo, sir." The man sounded testily deferent. "I was mindin' my own business when this cyborg cat jumps me. Man, I got the backlash and a loose tooth. I need bread, man, I coulda got kilt ver-ry damn easy." The provomarshal waved the man silent.

"We'll take you back on the sled, unless you want to drive the truck." The man ambled into the truck and began to rearrange the crates noisily.

"The damn city is 97 percent black humanoid, 2 percent cyborg and holobot, and about 1 percent Caucasoid human," the provomarshal said quietly to Cal. "It's a tough beat, but I'm due for a switch soon. Where are you from?"

"Northern polar cap," Cal replied. "Doing a stint here, just like you."

The parish provobot sled whistled in over the cypress bog and skidded to a stop. Both groups of provos conferred briefly and left. Cal watched the sleds lumber up in skittering trajectories, then angle away and move off, like giant silver whistles.

Low clouds scudded in, like cotton balls sprayed with india ink—mammalus clouds, that means trouble, Cal thought, as the funnel cloud began to form some miles upriver. An ebony ceiling hung like a wafer-thin monolith, etched against an insipid yellow sky. The funnel fingered down, tapering to a point and gaining in size as it thundered down the valley. Now the sound grew louder, like steam locomotives churning over metal bridges. Detritus flicked out from the funnel and a single tree spun in the vortex like an insane dervish. Cal ellipsed his vision to ten-power and got a 500-foot field view at 1000 yards. He autovectored increased foveal sensitivity so as to get top-quality retinograph slides. Then a vast circular chimney into the stratosphere bloomed into view, and the funnel shot straight up and out of sight. Cal glanced at his chronograph: it had taken the meteorological center about thirty seconds to track the tornado and exhaust it into the high atmosphere. The technology which facilitated this was not clear to Cal, but he knew that it involved the generation of pure vacuums and supracompact molecular masses. Like a suction fan eating oily smoke, he had been told.

The perrique leaves were lush and smooth as gelatin. The overseer showed Cal the deep arpent of tobacco plants, imparting the vaguely defensive aura of the farmer being visited by the government agent. He showed Cal one of the mole crickets, the formidable insect looking like an armored lobster about an inch long. Cal sampled the soil layers, tried some radiational alternates in the underground grids, and expanded the nutritional spectra of the guano pumps. Bat shit, he kept thinking, bat shit. He recommended a slight increase in sonic sweeping and the priming rate of the beds, and a musk extract to distract the voracious mole crickets. A desultory handshake and a Cajun camaraderie good-bye grunt, and Cal left.

The cigar looked odd, even ludicrous, but it represented the pinnacle of the art: nine inches in length and a full inch in diameter, 100 percent perrique filler, and a wrapper of maduro perrique. Cal pulled slowly on the shaft as he drove slowly toward the return road. The amber fire kindled the tiny compressed cubes of baked foliage into glowing prisms, and the particulates formed a smoke of superior gustatory-olfactory stimulus value. Cal lapsed into pleasant reverie. Then a warning aura flashed slowly, a scotoma, and Cal's life systems wavered. He felt faint, a bleeping came through his audio sensors, and then the soothing voice of Synod Energy Dome:

CITIZENS, WE ARE EXPERIENCING AN ENERGY BROWNOUT. THERE IS NO CAUSE FOR ALARM. FULL SATURATE POWER IS EXPECTED MOMENTARILY. IF YOU ARE CURRENTLY IN TRANSIT, LOCK INTO AUTOPILOT AND HOLD POSITION. IF YOU ARE NOT OPERATING A TRANSIT VEHICLE, PLEASE ASSUME A SUPINE POSTURE. YOU MAY FEEL WEIGHTLESSNESS AND THIS IS SPURIOUSLY PLEASURABLE. YOU ARE CAUTIONED NOT TO UNDERTAKE EXPLORATORY PROPRIOCEPTIVE OR KINESTHETIC ACTIONS UNTIL THE ALL CLEAR IS SOUNDED. IF YOU HAVE AN IONIC CHARGING POD, YOU MAY ACTIVATE IT AT THIS TIME OR SET THE RATE AT DOUBLE FOR YOUR NEXT SLEEP PERIOD. BE HAPPY AND QUIESCENT IN YOUR ROLES. GODSPEED.

Cal let the Lancia drift to a stop under a huge live oak. He eased the upright part of the seat into a nearly flat plane, lay back slowly and closed his eyes. Scotoma fluttered across his blackened visual field. Back at his billet quarters, Eva lay perspiring on a shallow couch, and Rob hung in his flitter just above the black bayou water where he had been gar fishing. Eva's emo-monitor read quiescence from Rob and the trivid screen showed no danger, so she had decided not to use teleport energy to get Rob home. She could not get any signals from Cal.

Goddamnit, Cal thought slowly, as if thinking was like jogging at 10,000-feet elevation, this is the second brownout this month. It's bad enough to have powerpak implants—almost like having springs that wind down—but when the geological electromag field gets drained down by consumer load, it's even worse. Most of the time I feel plugged into 220 volts with high amperage. Now I feel like a sick cat. Cal looked at his white hands and dim blood vessels. His auxiliary aortic pump puckered and blipped weakly and the ionic metaboles glowed feebly. He lay still for several minutes until the all-clear tone sounded through his auditory implants. He yawned and stretched and felt the resurgence of hot, rapidly pulsing blood and crackling synaptic junctures. Twenty miles away, Eva got to her feet, like a water nymph on a mossy mound, and Rob blasted for home, his flitter spewing a high roostertail of white dust as he rode along just off the ground.

Cal left the car and activated his thoracic transport implant. He always felt like Lilienthal at times like this, running slowly with an ornithopter strapped to his back, trying to gain enough speed to feel safe in diving flat and hoping for levitation. His body felt feather-light, yet like a projectile cleaving through yielding ethers. He lifted off prone, extending his arms forward, then back slowly, as his speed increased. He angled his head slightly and the cochlear cilia responded to the liquid message by vectoring in a five-degree starboard bank. He raised the angle of his head and soared upward. He drew in a long swelling draught of the whistling sulfurous air and his air speed increased proportionately. A shapely copulatress in a silver-mesh sheath angled in close to him, flashing a zircon sensor mounted in her pubic hair. She slipped supine under Cal and locked herself to him. God, these cruising hookers are getting brasher every day, Cal thought, worse than bees after the queen. The girl had a fine oval face and a warm humid mouth. She encapsulated her body in a force-field teardrop with Cal and whispered, "I'm programmed for Grien replays." The famous flying fuck, Cal mused, usually done with a rocking chair and a chinning bar. Cal drew the girl to him as the rain forest flowed past beneath them and held her briefly. "You're a lovely jewel," he said, "but not now." Before the girl could give the predicted emasculatory reaction, Cal pressed a Locus I barter medallion into her hand, overrode the force-field vectors, and broke away and up into a chandelle that carried him to 10,000 feet.

The tidal marshlands lay below him like soft green moss, the filigrees of dark water like beadings on velvet sachet bags. He arced up to about 15,000 feet and began a series of relaxing falling-leaf patterns before easing into a placid shallow glide for home. He was about 500 feet over Lake Boeuf when Rob drifted up to meet him, steering a flitter made up as a Spad reprod and waving over the top of the fabric wing. Cal cut speed and flew beside Rob. They came in low over the camphor trees and used the entire 1000 feet of arpent behind the house to simulate the Spad's landing. They left the craft near the road and walked through the ankle-high clover toward the house.

"Did you lose power here today?" Cal asked lightly.

"Yes, it was fun, a little scary though. I had a big gar caught in the noose and was going to use some of the flitter powerpak to get him up on the bridge, when I started to feel funny and sleepy. The flitter hung still for a while and I felt tired. Then Eva told me to get back to the house."

"How is your mother?"

"Fine. She's making you something good."

"What?"

"She told me not to tell you."

Cal and Rob walked through the irising vesicle into the food preparation area, where Eva was appraising a roast pig with an intent look on her face. She adjusted an apple under the glistening snout and fluffed up the mint leaves all around. "A surprise for lunch," she said gaily. They carved the pig with careful ritualistic strokes of a large knife, and ate. The trivid deck undulated with willowy dancers and the stereo played Mozart sonatas. The sun beat down in steaming yellow cataracts and the land seemed to swell like baking bread. In the 70-degree cool and 40 percent humidity of the house, Cal and Eva and Rob moved about in another world. Yet there was a mantle of depressed mood tones evident in their small talk. Even Rob seemed controlled and adult-like. Cal's emo-monitor picked up something like pathos in a matrix of whistling-in-the-dark environmental control. The central isochronon read one hour postmeridian. Cal and Eva locked in brief eye contact and seemed to exchange sad little messages.

"What's wrong?" Rob asked in a small earnest voice.

Cal got up and spread his hand over Rob's soft blond hair. "Nothing to worry about, Rob," he said softly. "Just the usual energy-level troubles at this time of the year. The sun is so hot and so close that it keeps the power deep under us when we need it close to the surface."

"I feel so much better on cloudy days," Eva said cheerily. "Sometimes the power level is so strong that the basement grids seem to glow and even crackle."

"Why do we have a sun, then?" Rob asked.

"We used to have four," Cal answered, "and they gave our planetoid a great and strong core of electromag power. Now, three of the suns are off in different orbits, and the one we have left is beginning to move off. It's still charging the core, but not well enough, so that we're getting weaker fields of the power we need to run our implants and paks." Cal fell depressed as he thought of the dozens of prostheses in their bodies: fulcrum energizers for physical strength, plasticized striate ribbings in the muscles, vascular pumps, peristalsers, synaptic jumper— and the ever-present household charging pods beneath the floor.

"Well, let's get it done, you all—we're supposed to doze an hour on the charger."

"I won't be able to sleep," Rob protested.

Cal handed him a sedative bonbon. "Here, eat this, it tastes good and will help you sleep. Are you ready?"

"Okay. Can I take the kitty?"

"Dial her small enough so she can sleep on your stomach."

Eva drained her wineglass and dabbed lightly at her mouth with a linen napkin. She got up and followed Cal and Rob through the center hall to the charging area.

The ionic charging pods lay in a shallow cryptlike area just below the cypress floors in the center of the house. To get recharged was to do the Dracula bit, Cal had often told Eva. He palmed a toggle and the floor receded to reveal the three padded chaises, separated by annealed metallic shields. The similarity to plush coffins was striking. Cal lowered Rob into a chaise and fitted the skullcap plate on gently. "Sleep tight," he said softly, and energized the pod. Rob sank flaccid into the padding. The margay mewed deeply and stretched out on Rob's stomach. Eva lay supine in the center chaise, smoothed the folds of her sheath, and felt for the cap. She adjusted it, blew a light kiss to Cal, closed her eyes and flicked the charge toggle. She seemed to stiffen just slightly, then relax, as if pneumo-plasted and deflated. Cal stepped down into his chaise, dropped to his knees, and clipped on his charging cap. He lay prone and looked up at the small control panel. He set the timer for one hour, lay his head down, and activated the mechanism. He blotted into deep unconsciousness.

About ten feet below the house, buried in the warm alluvial mud, the grids warmed and gave off their life-sustaining flows of electromag kilovolt amperes, innervating the cells and tablets and platings of precious alloys melded into the bodies of the small sleeping family.

Outside, the mutant animals felt their tropisms vacillate in the geological energy surge. The landscape was as still as a painting. Fifty million miles away, the fourth ancillary sun spun at 10 mps and orbited at about 1000 mph. It sank to a fourth post-meridian azimuth, though the isochronons read second, and the foliage reached out for the precious photosynthetic rays. Across the spongy expanses of the quad, the people lay in their pods, salvaging the net seepage of energy from a receding sun and an expeding intraplanetoid core. Later, the mottled amber sun settled massively onto the tree line as Cal and Eva and Rob sat watching. Fingers of fire lifted from the surface and fell back heavily with hypnotic slowness.

"That was a big one," Rob crowed.

"The moons will be spinning tonight," Eva said. "You can stay up and watch them."

"And they're having cobalt fireworks over Lake Pontchar-train," Cal added. "We can see them easily from here."

"I want to see the bats," Rob said.

"They won't be here until the dark time," Cal said, "but you can see them now if you look carefully at their trees." Cal pointed to the northerly line of acacias and rare ebonies. "Look closely and the trees will seem to come nearer to you." Rob's little eyes elongated to 20X and he steadied his chin against Cal's thigh. "I see them, but not close enough," he said. "They look like big dead leaves, hanging straight down."

"Watch close," Cal said, and vectored a mild hypothalamic beam at the horizon. "Hey, they stirred and rustled," Rob said. "How did you do that?"

"Easy. You'll be able to do it soon."

"Don't use too much energy," Eva said.

They watched the giant sun sink halfway into the horizon, its asymptote still angling down at about twenty degrees. On the opposite horizon, the moons appeared, like scarred metallic globes. Directly overhead, the crown star sparked into luminescence. The family lapsed into silence.

"Today *is* the day, isn't it?" Eva asked Cal, knowing that it was—the day for synod review of productivity-adaptability parameters and the monthly decrement of the population.

"Yes," Cal said vacantly. "Are you worried?"

"No, I don't think so. We're all ranked high enough so that the danger of disconnection has never been a real source of anxiety for me."

"What's disconnection?" Rob asked, sensing that his parents were not quite omnipotent.

"It's like lying in the charger for a long time, when you get old or sick," Cal said.

"Genocide?" Rob's one-word question startled his parents.

"Where did you learn that word, Rob?" Eva asked, her incredulity laced with both quiet pride and fringe sadness.

"From the history tapes."

"Well, I think a two-year-old is just too young to know about such things."

"I'm two chronologically, Eva," Rob said in a quiet tone, "but you know my cognitive parameters are advanced, and expanding daily. I learn fast." Eva gave a little sob and gathered the child in her arms. "Big little boy," she said emotionally. "Young, old, manly baby, let Mama hug you tight." She held Rob a long time.

The huge sun seemed to lumber out of sight, and the three figures went inside the house. They gathered around the trivid deck on valve-stem chaises. Rob toyed with a koala-bear clone and Cal and Eva sipped brandy. The trivid scenes changed as the news program progressed: accidents, personalities, documentary excerpts, humor, sports, business, weather, the usual gamut. Then came births, deaths, and disconnections. The deck fell dark and a single light revealed an announcer programmed for global organismic neutrality in appearance and voice. Three-dimensional histograms budded up from geographical models as the announcer read the data: continent-wide births just over half a million, deaths just slightly higher, and disconnections twenty thousand; southern-quad data congruent with synod-level trend analyses, disconnections four thousand. Rob and Cal and Eva leaned in as the local readouts spun across the background screen in large letters. Cal pressed the regional diverter, then the parish shunting control, and punched in his own code. The readout curled from the trivid console and stopped. He reached for the tape and read:

FAMILIAL ADAPTABILITY CENTILE	92
FAMILIAL PRODUCTIVITY CENTILE	88
AGGREGATE CONTRIBUTORY WEIGHT	90
EMPATHIC BONUS COROLLARY	90
TOTAL CENTILE SCORE	90

you are hereby granted life systems power for the next 30 days . individual readouts available on request. aggregate index shws mild decrement over preceding review period . congratulations on generalized excellence .

Cal hugged Eva and they both hugged Rob. They splurged some of the new energy, levitating a thousand feet up above the house to watch the spinning moons and the cobalt fireworks.

Twenty-nine-year-old MICHAEL BISHOP *is one of science fiction's brightest new stars. Unknown and unpublished until 1971, he startled readers with his ambitious novella "Death and Designation Among the Asadi" (1973), a contender for that year's Hugo and Nebula awards, and with an equally fine long work the same year, "The White Otters of Childhood." A later novella, "On the Street of Serpents," has also attracted wide praise, and Bishop's first novel,* A Funeral for the Eyes of Fire, *is due for publication shortly. Married and the father of two children, Bishop lives in Georgia, where he was until recently an instructor at the University of Georgia; he is now a full-time writer. Academe's loss is our gain, as this sly and high-spirited story demonstrates.*

■

Michael Bishop

■

ROGUE TOMATO

The Metamorphosis of Philip K.

When Philip K. awoke, he found that overnight he had grown from a reasonably well shaped, bilaterally symmetrical human being into . . . a rotund and limbless planetary body circling a gigantic, gauzy red star. In fact, by the simple feel, by the total aura projected into the seeds of his consciousness, Philip K. concluded that he was a tomato. A tomato of approximately the same dimensions and mass as the planet Mars. That was it, certainly: a tomato of the hothouse variety. Turning leisurely on a vertical axis tilted seven or eight degrees out of the perpendicular, Philip K. basked in the angry light of the distant red giant. While basking, he had to admit that he was baffled. This had never happened to him before. He was a sober individual not given to tippling or other forms of riotous behavior, and that he should have been summarily turned into a Mars-sized tomato struck him as a brusque and unfair conversion. Why him? And how? "At least," he reflected, "I still know who I am." Even if in the guise of an immense tomato he now whirled around an unfamiliar sun, his consciousness was that of a human being, and still his own. "I am Philip K. and somehow I'm still breathing and there must be a scientific explanation for this" is a fairly accurate summary of the next several hours (an hour being measured, of course, in terms of one twenty-fourth of Philip K.'s own period of rotation) of his thought processes.

85

As I Live and Breathe

Several Philip K.–days passed. The sufferer of metamorphosis discovered that he had an amenable atmosphere, a topological integument (or *crust,* although for the skin of a void-dwelling variety of *Lycopersicon esculentum* the word crust didn't seem altogether appropriate) at least a mile thick, and weather. Inhaling carbon dioxide and exhaling oxygen, Philip K. photosynthesized. Morning dew ran down his tenderest curvatures, and afternoon dew, too. Some of these drops were ocean-sized. Clouds formed over Philip K.'s equatorial girth and unloaded tons and tons of refreshing rains. Winds generated by these meteorological phenomena and his own axial waltzing blew backward and forward, up and down, over his taut, ripening skin. It was good to be alive, even in this disturbing morphology. Moreover, unlike that of Plato's oysters, his pleasure was not mindless. Philip K. experienced the wind, the rain, the monumental turning of himself, the internal burgeoning of his juices, the sweetness of breathing, and he *meditated* on all these things. It was too bad that he was uninhabited (this was one of his frequent meditations), so much rich oxygen did he give off. Nor was there much hope of immediate colonization. Human beings would not very soon venture to the stars. Only two years before his metamorphosis Philip K. had been an aerospace worker in Houston, Texas, who had been laid off and then unable to find other employment. In fact, during the last four or five weeks Philip K. had kept himself alive on soup made out of hot water and dollops of ketchup. It was—upon reflection— a positive relief to be a tomato. Philip K., inhaling, exhaling, photosynthesizing, had the pleasurable existential notion that he had cut out the middle man.

The Plot Thickens

Several Philip K.–months went by. As he perturbated about the fiery red giant, he began to fear that his orbit was decaying and that he was falling inevitably, inexorably, into the furnace of his primary, there to be untimely stewed. How large his sun had become. At last, toward the end of his first year as a planetary tomato, Philip K. realized that his orbit wasn't decaying. No. Instead, *he* was growing, plumping out, generating the illimitable juiciness of life. However, since his orange-red epidermis contained an utterly continuous layer of optical cells, his "eyes," or The Eye That He Was (depending on how you desire to consider the matter), had deceived him into believing the worst. What bliss to know that he had merely grown to the size of Uranus, thus putting his visual apparatus closer to the sun. Holoscopic vision, despite the manifold advantages it offered (such as the simultaneous apprehension of daylight and dark, 360-degree vigilance, and the comforting illusion of being at the center of the cosmos), could sometimes be a distinct handicap. But though his orbit was not decaying, a danger still existed. How much larger would he grow? Philip K. had no desire to suffer total eclipse in a solar oven.

INTERPERSONAL RELATIONSHIPS

Occasionally Philip K. thought about things other than plunging into his primary or, when this preoccupation faded, the excellence of vegetable life. He thought about The Girl He Had Left Behind (who was approaching menopause and not the sort men appreciatively call a tomato). Actually, The Girl He Had Left Behind had left *him* behind long before he had undergone his own surreal Change of Life. "Ah, Lydia P.," he nevertheless murmured from the innermost fruity core of himself, and then again: "Ah, Lydia P." He forgave The Girl He Had Left Behind her desertion of him, a desertion that had come hard on the heels of the loss of his job. He forgave . . . and indulged in shameless fantasies in which either Lydia P.—in the company of the first interstellar colonists from Earth—landed upon him, or, shrunk to normal size (for a tomato) and levitating above her sleeping face in her cramped Houston apartment, he offered himself to her. *Pomme d'amour.* Philip K. dredged up these words from his mental warehouses of trivia, and was comforted by them. So the French, believing it an aphrodisiac, had called the tomato when it was first imported from South America. *Pomme d'amour.* The apple of love. The fruit of the Tree of Knowledge, perhaps. But what meaningful relationship could exist between a flesh-and-blood woman and a Uranus-sized tomato? More and more often Philip K. hallucinated an experience in which interstellar colonist Lydia P. fell to her knees somewhere south of his leafy stem, sank her tiny teeth into his ripe integument, and then cried out with tiny cries at the sheer magnificent taste of him. This vision so disconcerted and titillated Philip K. that for days and days he whirled with no other thought, no other hope, no other desire.

ONTOLOGICAL CONSIDERATIONS

When not hallucinating eucharistic fantasies in which his beloved ate and drank of him, Philip K. gave serious thought to the question of his being. "Wherefore a tomato?" was the way he phrased this concern. He could as easily have been a ball bearing, an eightball, a metal globe, a balloon, a Japanese lantern, a spherical *piñata*, a diving bell. But none of these things respired, none of them lived. Then why not a grape, a cherry, an orange, a cantaloupe, a coconut, a watermelon? These were all more or less round; all were sun-worshippers, all grew, all contained the vital juices and the succulent sweetmeats of life. But whoever or whatever had caused this conversion—for Philip K. regarded his change as the result of intelligent intervention rather than of accident or some sort of spontaneous chemical readjustment—had made him none of those admirable fruits. They had made him a tomato. "Wherefore a tomato?" *Pomme d'amour.* The apple of love. The fruit of the Tree of Knowledge. Ah ha! Philip K., in a suppuration of insight, understood that his erophagous fantasies involving Lydia P. had some cunning relevance to his present condition. A plan was being revealed to him, and his manipulators had gone to the trouble of making him believe that the operations of his own consciousness were little by little laying bare this plan. O edifying deception! The key was *pomme d'amour.* He was a tomato rather than something else because the tomato *was* the legendary fruit of the Tree of Knowledge. (Never mind that tomatoes do not grow on trees.) After all, while a human being, Philip K. had had discussions with members of a proliferating North American sect that held that the biblical Eden had in fact been located in the New World. Well, the tomato was indigenous to South America (not too far from these sectarians' pinpointing of Eden, which they argued lay somewhere in the Ozarks), and he, Philip K., *was* a new world. Although the matter still remained fuzzy, remote, fragmented, he began to feel that he was closing in on the question of his personal ontology. "Wherefore a tomato?" Soon he would certainly know more, he would certainly have his answer . . .

A Brief Intimation of Mortality

Well into his second year circling the aloof red giant, Philip K. deduced that his growth had ceased; he had achieved a full-bodied, invigorating ripeness which further rain and sunshine could in no way augment. A new worry beset him. What could he now hope for? Would he bruise and begin to rot away? Would he split, develop viscous, scarlike lesions, and die on the invisible vine of his orbit? Surely he had not undergone his metamorphosis for the sake of so ignominious an end. And yet as he whirled on the black velour of outer space, taking in with one circumferential glimpse the entire sky and all it contained (suns, nebulae, galaxies, coal sacks, the inconsequential detritus of the void), Philip K. could think of no other alternative. He was going to rot, that was all there was to it; he was going to rot. Wherefore the fruit of the Tree of Knowledge if only to rot? He considered suicide. He could will the halting of his axial spin; one hemisphere would then blacken and boil, the other would acquire an embroidery of rime and turn to ice all the way to his

core. Or he could hold his breath and cease to photosynthesize.
Both of these prospects had immensely more appeal to Philip K.
than did the prospect of becoming a festering, mephitic mush-
ball. At the height of his natural ripeness, then, he juggled
various methods of killing himself, as large and as luscious as he
was. Thus does our own mortality hasten us to its absolute proof.

THE ADVENT OF THE MYRMIDOPTERANS *(or, The Plot
Thickens Again)*

Amid these morbid speculations, one fine day-and-night, or
night-and-day, the optical cells in Philip K.'s integument
relayed to him ("the seeds of consciousness," you see, was
something more than a metaphor) the information that now
encroaching upon his solar system from every part of the universe was a multitude of metallic-seeming bodies. He saw
these bodies. He saw them glinting in the attenuated light of
Papa (this being the name Philip K. had given the red giant
about which he revolved, since it was both handy and comforting to think in terms of anthropomorphic designations),
but so far away were they that he had no real conception of
their shape or size. Most of these foreign bodies had moved to
well within the distance to Papa's nearest stellar neighbors,
three stars forming an equilateral triangle with Papa roughly
at the center. At first Philip K. assumed these invaders to be
starships, and he burbled "Lydia P., Lydia P." over and over
again—until stricken by the ludicrousness of this behavior. No
expeditionary force from Earth would send out so many vessels. From the depths of ubiquitous night the metallic shapes
floated toward him, closer and closer, and they flashed either
silver or golden in the pale wash of Papa's radiation. When
eight or nine Philip K.–days had passed, he could see the invaders well enough to tell something about them. Each body
had a pair of curved wings that loomed over its underslung
torso/fuselage like sails, sails as big as Earth's biggest skyscrapers. These wings were either silver or gold; they did not

flap but instead canted subtly whenever necessary in order to catch and channel into propulsion the rays of the sun. Watching these bright creatures—for they were not artifacts but living entities—waft in on the thin winds of the cosmos was beautiful. Autumn had come to Philip K.'s solar system. Golden and silver, burnished maple and singing chrome. And from everywhere these great beings came, these god-metal monarchs, their wings filling the globe of the heavens like precious leaves or cascading, beaten coins. "Ah," Philip K. murmured. "Ah . . . Myrmidopterans." This name exploded inside him with the force of resurgent myth: Myrmidon and Lepidoptera combined. And such an unlikely combination did his huge, serene visitors indeed seem to Philip K.

ONSLAUGHT

At last the Myrmidopterans, or the first wave of them, introduced themselves gently into Philip K.'s atmosphere. Now their great silver or gold wings either flapped or, to facilitate soaring, lay outstretched on the updrafts from his unevenly heated surface. Down the Myrmidopterans came. Philip K. felt that metal shavings and gold dust had been rudely flung into The Eye That Was Himself, for these invaders obscured the sky and blotted out even angry, fat Papa—so that it was visible only as a red glow, not as a monumental roundness. Everything was sharp light, reflected splendor, windfall confusion. What was the outcome of this invasion going to be? Philip K. looked up—all around himself—and studied the dropping Myrmidopterans. As the first part of the name he had given them implied, their torso/fuselages resembled the bodies of ants. Fire ants, to be precise. On Earth such ants were capable of inflicting venomous stings, and these alien creatures had mouthparts, vicious mandibles, of gold or silver (always in contrast to the color of their wings). Had they come to devour him? Would he feel pain if they began to eat of him? "No, go away!" he wanted to shout, but could only shudder and unleash a few feeble dermalquakes in his southern hemisphere. They did not heed these quakes. Down the Myrmidopterans came. Darkness covered Philip K. from pole to pole, for so did Myrmidopterans. And for the first time in his life, as either tomato or man, he was utterly blind.

THE TIRESIAS SYNDROME

Once physically sightless, Philip K. came to feel that his metaphysical and spiritual blinders had fallen away. (Actually, this was an illusion fostered by the subconscious image of the Blind Seer; Tiresias, Oedipus, Homer, and, less certainly, John Milton exemplify good analogs of this archetypal figure. But with Philip K. the *illusion* of new insight overwhelmed and sank his sense of perspective.) In world-wide, self-wide dark he realized that it was his ethical duty to preserve his life, to resist being devoured. "After all," he said to himself, "in this new incarnation, or whatever one ought to term the state of being a tomato, I could prevent universal famine for my own species—that is, if I could somehow materialize in my own solar system within reasonable rocket range of Earth." He envisioned shuttle runs from Earth, mining operations on and below his surface, shipments of his nutritious self (in refrigerator modules) back to the home world, and, finally, the glorious distribution of his essence among Earth's malnourished and starving. He would die, of course, from these constant depredations, but he would have the satisfaction of knowing himself the savior of all humanity. Moreover, like Osiris, Christ, the Green Knight, and other representatives of salvation and/or fertility, he *might* undergo resurrection, especially if someone had the foresight to take graftings home along with his flesh and juice. But these were vain speculations. Philip K. was no prophet, blind or otherwise, and the Myrmidopterans, inconsiderately, had begun to eat of him. "Ah, Lydia P.," he burbled at the first simultaneous, regimented bites. "Ah, humanity."

NOT AS AN ADDICT *(or, The Salivas of Ecstasy)*

And so Philip K. was eaten. The Myrmidopterans, their wings overlapping all over his planet-sized body, feasted. Daintily they devoured him. And . . . painlessly. In fact, with growing wonder Philip K. realized that their bites, their gnawings, their mandibles' grim machinations injected into him not venom but a saliva that fed volts and volts of current into his vestigial (from the period of his humanity) pleasure centers. God, it was not to be believed! The pleasure he derived from their steady chowing-down had nothing to do with any pleasure he had experienced on Earth. It partook of neither the animal nor the vegetable, of neither the rational nor the irrational. Take note: Philip K. could think about how good he felt without in any way diminishing the effect of the Myrmidopterans' ecstasy-inducing chomps. Then, too soon, they stopped—after trimming off only a few hundred meters of his orange-red skin (a process requiring an entire Philip K.–month, by the way, though because of his blindness he was unable to determine how long it had taken). But as soon as his eaters had flown back into the emptiness of space, permitting him brief glimpses of Papa, a few stars, and the ant-moths' heftier bodies, another wave of Myrmidopterans moved in from the void, set down on his ravaged surface, and began feeding with even greater relish, greater dispatch. This continued for years and years, the two waves of Myrmidopterans alternating, until Philip K. was once more a tomato little bigger than Mars, albeit a sloppy and moth-eaten tomato. What cared he? Time no longer meant anything to him, no more than did the fear of death. If he were to die, it would be at the will of creatures whose metal wings he worshipped, whose jaws he welcomed, whose very spit he craved—not as an addict craves, but instead as the devout communicant desires the wine and the wafer. Therefore, though decades passed, Philip K. let them go.

Somewhere over the Space/Time Bow

Where did the Myrmidopterans come from? Who were they? These were questions that Philip K. pondered even in the midst of his ineffable bliss. As he was eaten, his consciousness grew sharper, more aware, almost uncanny in its extrapolations. And he found an answer . . . for the first question, at least. The Myrmidopterans came from beyond the figurative horizon of the universe, from *over* the ultimate curvature where space bent back on itself. Philip K. understood that a paradox was involved here, perhaps even an obfuscation which words, numbers, and ideograms could never resolve into an explanation commensurate with the lucid reality. Never mind. The Myrmidopterans had seemed to approach Philip K. from every direction, from every conceivable point in the plenum. This fact was significant. It symbolized the creatures' customary *independence of* the space/time continuum to which our physical universe belongs. "Yes," Philip K. admitted to himself, "they operate in the physical universe, they even have physical demands to meet—as demonstrated by their devouring of me. But they belong to the . . . Outer Demesnes of Creation, a nonplace where they have an ethereal existence that this continuum (into which they must occasionally venture) always debases." How did Philip K. know? He knew. The Myrmidopterans ate; therefore, he knew.

Moving Day

Then they stopped feeding altogether. One wave of the creatures lifted from his torn body, pulled themselves effortlessly out of his gravitational influence, and dispersed to the . . . well, the uttermost bounds of night. Golden and silver, silver and golden—until Philip K. could no longer see them. How quickly they vanished, more quickly than he would have believed possible. There, then gone. Of the second wave of Myrmidopterans, which he then expected to descend, only twelve remained, hovering at various points over him in outer space. He saw them clearly, for his optical cells, he understood, were now continuous with his whole being, not merely with his long-since-devoured original surface—a benefit owing to his guests' miraculous saliva and their concern for his slow initiation into The Mystery. These twelve archangels began canting their wings in such a way that they maneuvered him, Philip K., out of his orbit around the angrily expanding Papa. "Papa's going to collapse," he told himself, "he's going to go through a series of collapses, all of them so sudden as to be almost simultaneous." (Again, Philip K. knew; he simply knew.) As they moved him farther and farther out, by an arcane technology whose secret he had a dim intuition of, the Myrmidopterans used their great wings to reflect the red giant's warming rays on every inch of his surface. They were not going to let him be exploded, neither were they going to let him freeze. In more than one sense of the word, Philip K. was moved. But what would these desperation tactics avail them? If Papa went nova, finally exploded, and threw out the slaglike elements manufactured in its 100-billion-degree furnace, none of them would escape, neither he nor the twelve guardian spirits maneuvering him ever outward. Had he been preserved from rotting and his flesh restored like Osiris' (for Philip K. was whole again, though still approximately Mars-sized) only to be flash-vaporized or, surviving that, blown to purée by Papa's extruded shrapnel? No. The Myrmidopterans would not permit it, assuredly they would not.

THE NOVA EXPRESS

Papa blew. But just before Philip K.'s old and in many ways beloved primary bombarded him and his escorts with either deadly radiation or deadly debris, the Myrmidopterans glided free of him and positioned themselves in a halo-like ring above his northern pole (the one with the stem). Then they canted their wings and with the refracted energy of both the raging solar wind and their own spirits *pushed* Philip K. into an invisible slot in space. Before disappearing into it completely, however, he looked back and saw the twelve archangels spread wide their blinding wings and . . . *wink out* of existence. In our physical universe, at least. Then Philip K. himself was in another continuum, another reality, and could feel himself falling through it like a great Newtonian *pomme d'amour.* Immediately after the winking out of the twelve Myrmidopterans, Papa blew; and Philip K., even in the new reality, was being propelled in part by the colossal concussion resulting from that event. He had hitched, with considerable assistance, a ride on the Nova Express. But where to, he wondered, and why?

SPECIAL EFFECTS ARE DO-IT-YOURSELF UNDERTAKINGS

In transit between the solar system of his defunct red giant and wherever he now happened to be going, Philip K. watched —among other things—the colors stream past. Colors, lights, elongated stars; fiery smells, burning gong-sounds, ripplings of water, sheets of sensuous time. This catalogue makes no sense, or very little sense, expressed in linguistic terms; therefore, imagine any nonverbal experience which involves those senses whereby sense may indeed be made of this catalogue. Light shows, Moog music, and cinematic special effects are good starting places. Do not ask me to be more specific, even though I could; allusion to other works, other media, is at best a risky business, and you will do well to exercise your own imaginative powers in conjuring up a mental picture of the transfinite reality through which Philip K. plunged. Call it the avenue beyond a stargate. Call it the interior of a chrono-synclastic infundibulum. Call it the enigmatic subjective well which one may enter via a black hole. Call it sub-, para-, warp-, anti-, counter-, or even id-space. Many do. The nomenclature, however, will fail to do justice to the transfinite reality itself, the one in which Philip K. discovered that he comprehended The Mystery that the Myrmidopterans had intended him, as a tomato, to comprehend *in toto.* For as he fell, or was propelled, or simply remained stationary while the new continuum roared vehemently by, he bathed in the same ineffable pleasure he had felt during the many dining-ins of the gold and silver ant-moths. At the same time, he came to understand (1) the identity of these beings, (2) his destination, (3) the nature of his mission, and (4) the glorious and terrible meaning of his bizarre metamorphosis. All became truly clear to him, everything. And this time his enlightenment was not an illusion, not a metaphysical red herring like the Tiresias Syndrome. For, you see, Philip K. had evolved beyond self, beyond illusion, beyond the bonds of space/time—beyond everything, in fact, but his roguish giant-tomatohood.

HOW THE MANDALA TURNED *(or, What Philip K. Learned)*

Although one ought to keep in mind that his learning process began with the first feast of the ant-moths, this is what Philip K. discovered in transit between two realities: It was not by eating of the fruit of the Tree of Knowledge that one put on the omniscience and the subtle ecstasy of gods, but instead by *becoming* the fruit itself—in the form of a sentient, evolving world—and then by *being eaten* by the seraphically winged, beautifully silver, messianically golden Myrmidopterans. They, of course, were the incarnate (so to speak) messengers of the universe's supreme godhead. By being consumed, one was saved, apotheosized, and lifted to the omega point of man's evolutionary development. This was the fate of humankind, and he, Philip K., only a short time before—on an absolute, extra-universal scale—an insignificant man of few talents and small means, had been chosen by the Myrmidopterans to reveal to the struggling masses of his own species their ineluctable destiny. Philip K. was again profoundly moved, the heavens sang about him with reverberant hosannas, all of creation seemed to open up for him like a blood-crimson bud. Filled with bright awe, then, and his own stingingly sweet ichor, Philip K.

popped back into our physical universe in the immediate
vicinity of Earth (incidentally capturing the moon away from its
rightful owner). Then he sat in the skies of an astonished North
America just as if he had always been there. Millions died as a
result of the tidal upheavals he unfortunately wrought, but this
was all in the evolutionary Game Plan of the supreme godhead,
and Philip K. felt exultation rather than remorse. (He did wonder briefly if Houston had been swamped and Lydia P.
drowned.) He was a rogue tomato, yes, but no portent of doom.
He was the messenger of the New Annunciation and he had
come to apprise his people of it. Floating 350,000 miles from
Earth, he had no idea how he would deliver this message, the
news that the mandala of ignorance, knowledge, and ultimate
perception was about to complete its first round. No idea at all.
Not any. None.

CODA

But, as the saying goes, he would think of something.

GEORGE ALEC ("PIGLET") EFFINGER *can still be considered a newcomer to science fiction, but he has been around long enough and has been prolific enough so that writers even more recently arrived than he have begun to bombard editors with stories that seem clearly imitative of his. Which is a doubly futile endeavor; for not only is each Effinger story a strikingly individual achievement, unclassifiable and unique, but also we have little need of imitations while the original producer is still keeping his typewriter busy. Still on the trustworthy side of thirty, Effinger has published two novels—*What Entropy Means to Me *(1972) *and *Relatives *(1973)— and a host of short stories.*

■

George Alec Effinger

■

THE MOTHERS' MARCH ON ECSTASY

Hello, my name is Dr. Davis, and I'm here to tell you about the time there was a happiness all around. You couldn't get anywhere; I mean, the dancers in the streets filled the avenues all day, all night. When you tried to push your way through them (there were still a few of us who had to get somewhere) they smiled at you and offered you their flower. You could only smile back, because if you attempted to say anything they would dance away. Dance the night away, under the mad moon of love.

When it all started I was living in Queens. Each morning I would get up and brush my teeth, pick up my notebook and table of logarithms from their place on the television, and take the subway to the laboratory on Manhattan's upper West Side. But as the joy spread, from person to person like an epidemic of the crabs, we scientists found that more and more of those systems that we had come to depend on were going wrong. Why had we never considered and instituted back-up, fail-safe systems? (Wagner, my companion, suggested that we would never admit that the back-up systems might be more reliable than the originals.) In any event, when the conductors and engineers and transit police and repairmen found the subway cars too limiting for the expression of their happiness, the trains ceased to run. Wherever they were abandoned they remained, blocking the dark visceral tubes of the city. The next trains to pass by would have to stop there, of course, and so they collected in huge strings under the boroughs, good only as a breeding ground for the fabled alligators and giant Sumatran rats.

Well, so far, no problem. I walked. I walked through Queens to the Queensboro Bridge, crossed it, went up First Avenue to 72nd Street, turned west there through the park (Central Park was filled with dancing Puerto Rican softball teams) to Central Park West, uptown to 86th Street, west on 86th to Amsterdam, and uptown again to the secret location of the lab.

There was a spareness to the laboratory that I always found offensive. I had rented a storefront on Amsterdam about two months before the onset of the happiness, intending to work on a cure for something. I recall distinctly my elation in finding a place so congenial and so precisely what I had had in mind. I turned to Wagner and handed him the key. "Go," I said, "and find for us those supplies of which we will have need. Do not pay too dearly, neither shall you 'cut corners' so that the difference will fall to your own purse."

"You may trust me, Master," he said. I did, too. We had an understanding.

Well, you can imagine my chagrin when, upon arriving at the lab the following morning, I found the entire wall space within covered with 1 × 8 white pine shelves, and on the shelves hundreds and hundreds of little bottles of chemicals. Calcium carbonate. Manganese dioxide. Copper sulfate. Little bottles with powder-blue labels and white plastic twist-off caps. In one corner was a monstrous pile of microscope slides, cloudy with previous use, unwashed and crusty. In an old liquor carton were thousands of rubber stoppers, some with one hole, some with two holes, and some with no holes at all. Wagner had not bought any glassware to use them in.

"I ran out of funds," he said.

You may picture my pique. I hit him across the face, and he whimpered his apology. I sat down on the stool that he had thoughtfully purchased for me. No worktable. The very first thing that he should have acquired. I couldn't even begin without a slate-topped worktable. No Bunsen burner. No lens paper.

No asbestos pad. No test-tube brush. I was helpless.

"What are we going to do, Master?" asked Wagner.

"Oh, shut up and let me think," I said. I regret those tones that I used on poor, faithful Wagner. But things are different now. He is gone, lost forever, and all that I have left is the knowledge of my responsibility for his lostness. This fearful weight bears me down, forces the very lifebreath of life from me, and I can never ease the pain. Oh, that I could enjoy anew the conscienceless freedom of those long-dead days. But I am sure that it is impossible. I am not a scientist now. (Perhaps you have noticed from the loveliness of the words that I have become a poet. It happened overnight. I had nothing to do with it. Fate, I suppose.) And so an entire lifetime's training and desire are made meaningless. I might as well retire; go learn to play shuffleboard with the others who discovered that they are no longer short-order cooks, bank guards, scissor sharpeners. Ah, the futility of striving. All that we can ask for is to be happy, eh?

And they were, and where did it get them? People just don't know when they're well off. There always has to be something wrong, the serpent in the garden, that sort of thing. At first, when the signs pointed to nothing in particular, I thought it was all very charming. Men and women frolicking in the streets, everybody smiling and emptying wastepaper baskets from their office windows, cars playfully aiming themselves at each other and steering away at the last moment like the Dodgem at Euclid Beach Park when I was a tad. But it couldn't just stay that way, could it? No, not with people the way they are. Larger doses of joy were required. The search for outlets became frantic; people expended enormous amounts of energy, exhausting themselves and their city to show how happy they were. No one (except the scientists, who were immune) slept, or ate, or cried. Early on, singing was the rage. Then skipping down the sidewalk and walking barefoot through the Park Avenue fountains. Then nudity, though never any sort of overt sexual contact. For some unknown reason the abandonment of sorrow brought with it a rebirth of chastity. A sort of forced innocence that turned my stomach. Wagner agreed.

And, finally, dancing. Everybody danced, except us scientists, who continued to work. When things definitely began to look bad we pooled our resources and wrote papers. My friend Larry did a paper on the effect of eight million people dancing on the already overstressed geological formations on which Manhattan rests. He orchestrated a somber score, to coin a phrase: the island sinking beneath the waves, the city sitting like the cracked skin on a chocolate pudding, the people dancing their cares away, the night away, beneath a lunatic moon. It was then that we organized ourselves, made over our already overtaxed fraternity of learning into the ragged irregular army of good-cause mendicants it is today.

Thanks to my years of experience in observation I could tell that the reveling multitudes were not *really* happy. There were moments when an individual had to catch his breath. Then, for just a few seconds, I imagine that he asked himself, "Hey. Precisely *what* are we celebrating?" But then he'd look around and see everyone else dancing away to some hypothetical inner beat, and he'd find it again and smile and begin twisting. I didn't mind the inconvenience they were causing me as much as I was saddened by the overwhelming display of mass delusion. Several times I caught the arm of one of them and said, "You're not truly happy. You millions of people are just fooling yourselves. Come on back to the real thing. Come on back to Life." But I never got anywhere that way. It was as though I had lost touch somehow with my fellow man, as though some impervious wall had been built, shutting me out from the companionship of my race because of an unknown arbitrary standard that I failed in my innocent desire for progress (not necessarily technological, though of course that was the channel through which most of my work had always been done, but social and spiritual as well. Knowledge for its own sake was not, in my youth, the hollow mockery of a goal that it has become today) to recognize, the fools. And now I had no one at all to turn to: about this time

Wagner was due for his two weeks' vacation, which he spent in the Catskills. When he returned he was a changed man.

"Master!" he shouted, slamming the screen door like I've told him a thousand times not to do. "Master, come see! I've taken myself a bride!" It was than that I realized that poor, stupid Wagner never understood exactly what sort of relationship we had. He dragged his new wife into the lab, where I was busily preparing my pencils for the day's work. The girl, to give her her due, was pretty, though not what I would call especially attractive. She smiled shyly; I asked her what her name was, and when she said "Linda" I could see Wagner's surprised reaction. Later I learned that Wagner had met her in a dancing class at the resort where he had spent his vacation. "Linda" loved to dance, as did almost everyone at that time. Wagner, though not a scientist, had been immune to the epidemic through his innate lack of empathy. But evidently "Linda" was a fine teacher, because I saw my former assistant only twice more, the last time frugging his heart out in front of a warehouse on Washington Street. I don't suppose I'll ever forget him. I've kept his room just the way it was, and his dish in the kitchen . . .

After nearly a half-century of scientific endeavor, during which I made it a conscious practice to ignore all "artistic" events, I find it remarkable how quickly I am able to master this business of writing. Who knows where I might have gone had I taken it up instead of the worthwhile pursuits. I admit, Wagner used to come to me in the middle of the afternoon, when our favorite radio programs interrupted the workday, and tell me how much he admired my turns of phrase, my bons mots, the precision of my language. But naturally I discredited all this because he slept curled behind my knees.

It is logical to assume, however, that someone such as I, who was prepared for life in the old days, when, despite a lesser quantity of knowledge being loose in the world, one was expected to have a mastery over a far greater percentage of it, might gain through that mastery an ability to learn new things in alien fields at a faster rate than someone who is expert within only one area, no matter how abstruse that may be. I applaud myself here not out of egoism, as I am sure that it must seem, but rather to indicate to the reader the qualities residing within me from earliest youth which enabled me to meet the crisis about which I am presently writing, and to face the facts of that crisis with the proper mixture of respect and sureness that would best promote those positive results that were, at the time, so desperately awaited by an unknowing world. My sentences lengthen.

I was talking about Wagner, and the change in our relationship that occurred during the crisis. No, actually, before that I was talking about the laboratory itself, and I hadn't really finished describing it. As I said, there were all these shelves of chemicals, most of which I could see would be totally useless for any sort of experiment that I would be interested in. I considered selling them back to the store (Wagner had gotten a good price from Schubert's Bike and Hobby), but the salesman wouldn't hear of it. I phoned in an ad to the *Village Voice*, and only the outbreak of happiness prevented it from being answered. But, at the same time, that inconvenience enabled me to stock the lab by appropriating the necessary equipment from high schools in the neighborhood. Looking back, that time was about the happiest of my life. So early in the episode I had yet no idea of the scope and potential for disruption possessed by an epidemic of joy. I was not concerned and, indeed, at first I gave no thought to looking for a cure. I was still intending to direct my energies into more rewarding areas: dexterity equivalencies, a cure for menstruation, acupuncture research.

We made up long lists, Wagner and I did, lists of materials that we wanted to get. We paged through the Turtox catalogue, our eyes blurry with tears like children looking through the Sears Christmas issue. "Look!" I would say, pointing to a bottle of *Rana pipiens*. I hadn't taken one of those apart since high school. The nostalgia and the abstract drive to *do research* made me giddy. Wagner couldn't appreciate the subtlety of my feelings, but I'm sure that somewhere beneath his hunched back he had something of the same excitement. It was like setting up a new project, a new office, beginning a new job: buying pencils and pads and rulers and gummed reinforcements that you know you'll never use. "Why don't we get a preserved sand shark?" I said, mostly to myself. "I could practice on it, couldn't I?" $300 autoclaves. $300 microtomes. Delicate pH meters that would frustrate me with their fussiness. Racks of test tubes with colored liquids in them. Cages and cages of rabbits and monkeys to poke things into.

I turned the pages of the big red book, and every new thing that I saw I wanted. Wagner sat in a corner with a yellow legal-sized pad. I'd call out to him, "Chart. Male urogenital system." And I'd give him the order number and the price and he'd write it down. He filled up page after page of that pad, and my dreams of the perfectly equipped laboratory became more and more grandiose. After a while I stopped, when I came to the catalogue's index, and I was instantly sad when I realized that I could never have any of it.

Could I have that reaction again? Could I ever feel that way, could I know that longing for *facilities*, now that I am a writer and no more any sort of technologist? I have a copy of an Edmunds Scientific catalogue, and I have not opened it once. It tortures me, where it sits on the bottom of one of my desk drawers; I know it's there, but I rarely acknowledge it. I'm afraid to look, to open the cover and turn the title page and then the contents page and look right at a Van de Graaf generator and feel *nothing*, no stirring in my mental loins. I don't want to find out, but I know that someday I will have to.

If only the infection of joy had been the genuine emotion, my work would have been simpler. Instead of trying to find the antidote I could have gladly worked to understand why certain of us were left unaffected. If that happiness had been the pure and untainted thing that humanity has been awaiting for centuries, I would have jealously wanted to join in the celebration. But it did not take long to see that they were all fools, all deluding themselves with artificial and unclean substitutes.

They were soiling themselves, but from the inside; whether or not the process was voluntary was irrelevant. In fact, knowing that most, if not all, of the victims were unwilling made the situation that much more desperate. Morons and proto-rational types alike were stricken, and it was my sacred trust to release them from the slavery of what they pitifully identified as happiness.

"I do not understand, Master," said Wagner in one of his characteristic attempts to share my success. "Why should you change them? They say that they are happy."

"You fool," I said, looking up from my frog, "haven't you learned that all self-destructive persons claim that they're happy? That's part of it. Don't you remember Rita?"

Wagner seemed to wilt. His face contorted; he frowned and his eyes twitched at the corners when he recalled Rita, his first love who had been sacrificed on the altar of Science. "Master, you are cruel," he said softly, turning away and walking across the laboratory, dragging his dead left leg behind. I went back to my frog, jumping when Wagner slammed the screen door on his way out. I cursed under my breath, but my sense of humor rescued me (and, probably, saved Wagner's life) and I broke into a fit of maniacal laughter.

I needed a subject. My experimentation could go on only so far in theory, as I worked isolated in my Manhattan study. A constant flow of animals passed through my lab, taking up temporary residence in one of the dozen cages that I kept beneath the cot in the back. Mice and gerbils seemed to be the easiest to get, for these small rodents were what Wagner most frequently brought back from his forays to pet shops around town. Once I had a small armadillo, and I was almost sorry to have to use it, it was so cute. I fed it lettuce. I gave it a humorous name, like Eratosthenes or something. It was the only thing that I had ever loved.

The animals lived in the cages until I decided that they were acclimated. I devised an arbitrary scale of noises to indicate what level of at-homeness they had achieved. The less they squeaked, the less alienated I believed them to be. This is why

I never used dogs or cats, although the pet stores must have been crowded with them. They don't squeak the same way. After a few days of good food and companionship the rodents would make little noise. The next stage was comfort, and then actual happiness. The little things would sit in a corner of their cage with a placid smile on their thin lips. Some would whistle, others would push vegetable fragments and newspaper shreds around in a primitive housecleaning activity. I noticed that the happier mice would nod to me when I happened to catch their eye. I have never felt any guilt or sadness about "sacrificing" them at this most contented stage, because I always knew that the future of the human race and my own selfish aggrandizement depended on that step. The frogs were forgotten. I lifted the chosen mouse from his cage and carried him to the drawing board that served me as a worktable. There wasn't a single corner of his mousy self that I didn't explore, and I never learned a thing. But I didn't give up. I did it again and again. Never learned anything, though.

So I needed a live human. Wagner was horrified. I told him that it was for Science, and his pedestrian fears were immediately quelled. "For Science, eh, Master?" he said in his peculiarly thick voice. "Science, eh? For Science, then, all right. If it is for Science you shall have your human subject." He grinned at me strangely and hurried out. He did not return for several hours, and then alone.

"Where is he?" I shouted. "Where is my subject?"

Wagner laughed mirthlessly. "I could not find one," he said.

My anger was uncontrollable. "There are eight million of them out there!" I said. I grabbed his arm and dragged him to the door. I opened the screen and pointed. "Look, you fool! Any one. Any one of them!" He just laughed and I grew more furious. I raised my hand to strike him and he cowered, still laughing. I did not hit him, but instead merely threw the forceps that I was holding. They hit his massive chest and fell to the sawdust-covered floor. "Don't you understand, you monster?" I said. "For the good of humanity!"

Wagner laughed again. "They're happy," he said. I turned away in frustration.

"Get out," I said. "Get out of my clean lab. Go home to that 'wife' of yours." Wagner laughed, and I shuddered to hear it. He did leave, slamming the screen door, and I never saw him again until that time before the warehouse. Perhaps a kind word . . .

But no. It was hopeless. My heart was broken, but involved in my work as I was, I never noticed. Or else it is only now, now that I can no longer hope to regain the scientific objectivity that I prized for so many years, now that I am that which I vilified for most of my life—a poet—that I see things in their broader perspective. I certainly haven't gained anything by this new-found ability.

I didn't know what to do. My friend Larry and my other associates were as puzzled in their labs as I, and could offer little help. I was on my own. Absently I took out one of my last frogs and set it on the drawing board. It was a female, and I really didn't feel like flushing the eggs when I got to that point. I sometimes think about what my life would have been like had that *Rana* been a male. Perhaps my life would have been different. I think about that sometimes, about the different roads I might have taken. Maybe I would have ended up an entirely different person. Who can say? I think about that sometimes.

Suddenly I jumped from my seat, leaving the poor frog where she lay, pinned out against the board like some hapless target in a circus knife-thrower's act. I put on a long gray overcoat and a tan slouch hat, pulled down over my forehead to shroud my eyes in shadow. I looked like *Der Wand'rer* or one of those fellows who exposes himself to little girls in playgrounds. Then I went out in search of my subject.

I was still locking the outside door to the lab when a lovely young lady danced by on the sidewalk. I grabbed her arm and she barely noticed, so happy was she. "Let me take care of that for you," I said, and she smiled without comprehension. I unlocked the door again with one hand, still holding her arm tightly in the other. Then I steered her into the lab.

I removed my coat and hat. "Make yourself at home," I said, trying to appear cheerful. She ignored me, dancing to the buried music in her head. "Tell me, how did it all start?" She said nothing. "How does it actually feel? Do you ever get dizzy, nauseous, thirsty, cold?" Silence.

Perhaps already I was beginning to lose that sense of devotion to method, that necessary coolness of intellect that is essential to valid appraisal. It had to begin somewhere. But why? Fifty years in the field, all to be brought to nothing within a week. To wake up in the morning and suddenly be a whole new person, one who is basically weaker and completely useless (by the old standards), is a terrifying thing. Even worse is this consuming and hopeless yearning for the old self. To be a scientist —and one of the best of the lot—and then to abandon, nay, *misplace* (as the procedure was totally involuntary and darkened with mystery) that carefully cultured turn of mind and find oneself fit only for the stringing together of pretty words, that is a nightmare from which I can never wake.

My subject avoided me. It wasn't a conscious thing, I suppose. She was preoccupied with her happiness, and unaware of her environment. She looked as though she hadn't been eating regularly; she certainly had totally forsaken bathing. I decided that she would have to be treated and acclimated in much the same way as my mice and gerbils. But I didn't understand the danger.

I found myself cutting up frogs or clams and humming to myself. Old half-remembered show tunes would pop up in my mind when I watched the girl (whom I named Mary and clothed in my overcoat so her lovely body wouldn't distract me) move around the lab, curiously picking up knives or mice or bottles of chemicals from the shelves. Sometimes when she was asleep I used to look at her or feel the fine hair along her arms, tickling her, I guess, because she'd smile in her dreams or even wake up and touch me.

After a few days of this seductive madness, I was saved by a visit from my friend Larry. He was accompanied by a tall, slender young woman wearing Larry's overcoat. "This is Janice," said Larry. The young woman smiled. Her eyes were glazed with a kind of joyful fever that had become far too familiar to me. I was beginning to find that same quality attractive in my own specimen, Mary. My friend gave Janice a little shove, sending her off in the general direction of Mary. The two young women bumped about my laboratory for several minutes before their paths intersected. When at last this lucky event occurred, they smiled at each other and wandered off to find the bathroom.

"I see that your research has taken a path similar to my own," I said.

"No doubt," said Larry grimly.

"I have begun training my subject," I said, wishing to impress my friend. Within the scientific community, that is a worthy goal, and one not frequently attained. I was to fail again. "She obeys simple commands," I said, "and is beginning to understand the meanings of 'yes' and 'no.' "

"But not the difference between 'right' and 'wrong,' " said my friend.

"No," I said. "That's scheduled for, let me see, next April." I was naturally somewhat deflated by Larry's lack of enthusiasm, but I attributed his attitude to the probability that Janice had obtained for him already those results. I indicated that Larry should join me for a glass of claret, and he muttered his gratitude. While pouring the wine, I hummed a catchy little tune, remembered from my childhood, from some otherwise insipid musical show. My friend reacted violently. He grabbed my arm, splashing the wine in colorful blotches onto my white lab coat.

"What is that?" he cried, half rising from his seat, further decanting the red fluid into my lap.

"It's cheap wine," I said, annoyed.

"No, not that!"

"The song, you mean? A pleasant number, whose lyrics I have quite forgotten. Would you rather hear something else instead?"

Larry released his grip on my wrist and seated himself once more. He sighed. "Dr. Davis," he said, "I want you to consider your behavior, as objectively as possible. You are humming a tune. Does that indicate anything to your admirably well trained scientific sensibilities?"

"No," I said.

"Had you in the past been in the habit of humming such tunes?"

"No," I said. But I began to get a glimmer of what my friend was trying to say, obviously with difficulty in sparing my feelings. With a sudden rage I turned and looked for Mary, my human subject. She and her new friend, Janice, were emerging from the curtained-off lavatory. They were both smiling and humming to themselves. "And to think," I said in a low voice, "how much pleasure I took, merely from watering the rodents with her at my side. I ought to have been warned."

"Do not blame yourself," said my friend Larry. "It is indeed an insidious menace."

"The Devil himself must lend them aid," I said.

My friend Larry merely stared for a few seconds. He shook his head at last. " 'The Devil'?" he said. "I think maybe you'd better go lie down for a while."

I could feel the blood rushing into my face. I had committed a kind of absurdity before a fellow member of the scientific community. "Forgive me," I said with some embarrassment. "I have noted a certain lack of concretism in my speech and thoughts. But, even you must admit, why, the behavior of the overwhelming masses of people in the world today must fairly reek of the diabolic."

"Of the inane," said my friend. "And in that respect I see little difference with their actions in times past."

At this point I considered that my friend Larry was trying to be a bit *too* technologically cynical. There was every possibility that he was covering up some inner rot of his own. "I have never seen one of those 'happy' people foraging for food. I cannot conceive of how they continue their existence."

"Mostly they eat out, I suppose," said my friend.

I was struck by the patent lunacy of this idea. "Then how," I said slowly, pompously, full of the tingling anticipation of utter triumph, "how do they manage to pay for their meals?"

He only shook his head mournfully. "They're all on welfare, I think," he said.

I was stunned. My victory crumbled, but I scarcely noticed amid the terror of the situation. "But that's . . . that's . . ."

My friend Larry finished the awful sentence for me. "It's a form of creeping socialism," he said.

With what devastating horror I heard those words may well be imagined. My friend Larry concerned himself with the sudden paleness of my complexion and the unshakeable torpor into which I then fell. He carried me over to my cot and covered me with several unpleasant army-surplus blankets, as we had been instructed to do during innumerable poolside courses in first aid. With the passage of time, the shock began to lessen; at last, I was able to move my lips in a crude approximation of speech. I could convey my wishes to my friend, futile as those meager needs were. The same impulse which had sent the world into an interminable plague of joy now plunged me into deepest despair. My talk of devils and deities was, perhaps, well founded, worse luck. And to top it, these eternal powers were enemies of free enterprise.

My friend Larry disagrees, of course. He spends a good deal of time arguing with me, claiming in his snide way that I am mad to insist on supernatural beings. I, though, can see the larger picture; it is a nightmarish landscape indeed, done up in shades of Red. My friend is blind to it entirely; he is merely an unwitting pawn. It seems that I, alone (now that my specimen, Mary, has been transferred to several hundred neatly labeled microscope slides), maintain the battle against the cruelty and injustice of the universe. It is a lonely fight. And I'll need funds to carry on my great work. Those funds will have to come from you. So *give*, and give generously, when I, the Ecstasy Volunteer, knock on your door.

"I was born in 1948," STEVEN UTLEY *reports, "and grew to pulsing young manhood on dinosaurs, super-heroes, and* I Married a Monster From Outer Space. *I'm an ex–Air Force brat and a college drop-out, and I once got arrested for resisting arrest. I've sold, at this writing, fiction and poetry to the likes of* Vertex, If, Alternities, Emphasis, Universe, *and* Stellar." *One of the pieces Utley has sold is an ingenious novelet, written in collaboration with Howard Waldrop, about General Custer's air force; originally it was to have appeared in this issue of* New Dimensions, *but for complex and uninteresting reasons is being published in a rival anthology. The poem here is partial atonement for that.*

■

THE LOCAL ALLOSAURUS

The local allosaurus
doesn't get around much these days:
he's gotten a bit long in the tooth
and contents himself with his hard bed,
and with constant bitching about how badly
the whole place has run down
since *he* was running the show.
He claims to remember better times,
one hundred or so million years ago,
when the air had a different taste to it,
and he was the lord of the world.
I can get away with a faint smirk
(his eyes aren't what they used to be),
but I know better than to remind him
that he was only a steam-roller of a lizard
with far more muscle than brain
or that he was surely capable of no desires
other than eating and mating
and was, just as surely, incapable
of distinguishing between the two.
He still has a temper
and still has a most impressively
wicked-looking head.
So I let him wallow in his nostalgia,
and he uncomprehendingly lets me call him
Yorick.

When DAVID WISE *was six years old, all the way back in 1961, he took up filmmaking in a serious way, producing an animated short that won several awards and was widely shown. Other films followed, and between the ages of seven and thirteen the precocious moviemaker lectured at universities, schools, and film societies, was the subject of interviews in* The New Yorker, Time, *and* Life, *and enjoyed the other benefits of being the nation's leading pre-adolescent cinematographer. Now, in his maturity, Wise seemingly has abandoned film for prose fiction; he has sold stories to* Clarion III, The Last Dangerous Visions, *and other anthologies, and is working on "a novel or two." He lives in Los Angeles' wild, untamed Laurel Canyon district.*

■

ACHIEVEMENTS

We don't know one millionth of one percent of anything.
—EINSTEIN

The following is a story about achievements. Every minute someone is inventing Poly-grip. Every other minute someone is inventing thumbscrews. And a few seconds after that, someone is inventing a peaceful use for the postage scale. WARNING: The Surgeon General has determined that being run over by a Mack truck may be hazardous to his health. So have we all been warned. Now, read on . . .

◆

My goal in life was to have my own split-level house in New Rochelle. When I finally achieved this goal, my house was in Pasadena, California, but even so, it was mine. There were, of course, complications. We must all make sacrifices. Some people struggle all their lives without attaining their goals. I guess I was lucky, that's all.

◆

Watson and Crick discovered the true nature of the DNA molecule. They did it just in time for Christmas and the Nobel prizes.

Linus Pauling choked on some culture he was sucking into a pipette at the time when he was told the news. "Aw, nuts!" he said.

◆

Nikola Tesla, a lab scientist (they were called "inventors" then) who occasionally worked with Thomas Edison, invented and perfected a means of drawing electrical power from the natural electromagnetic waves which are carried constantly throughout the earth. His device required no power stations, no maintenance, no gargantuan monopolistic business guidance: simply a pole which could extract hundreds of thousands of kilowatts of electricity from the atmosphere.

All of Tesla's theories and plans for his direct-current high-potential power system, as well as his papers on the "stationary waves" in the earth, mysteriously disappeared when the FBI ransacked his apartment directly after his death in 1943, in the hopes that his polyphase system of literally *free* worldwise power would remain a secret. A working model of the Tesla Coil remains, however—on display at Griffith Observatory.

◆

I told my mother I was building a house for myself. I was in Burbank at the time. She was in the Bronx. She told me that she opposed the idea. "I oppose the idea," she said.

I asked her why. "A single man has no right building a house for himself. A house will do you no good without a wife to take care of you in it, livening it up; adding, so to speak, a 'woman's touch'—a quaint expression, don't you think? How dare you go through such an audacious scheme without consulting me first? And you, a Fifth Amendment communist at that. No son of mine."

And so on.

The invisibility formula was invented in 1946 by J. Allan Phelps. No one remembers the formula because little was seen of its inventor afterward. Sources indicate that Phelps was an out-of-work paint technician who had been laid off shortly after the surrender of Germany, allowing him time to work out a method of altering molecules to cancel out their ability to reflect light. His first test subject was, naturally, himself. Unfortunately the formula worked. Phelps had not realized that if the whole of his body were invisible, his retinas would be unable to catch light. Thus he was not only invisible, but blind as well. This made the rendering of an antidote—another detail he had neglected to attend to—somewhat impossible. He spent his last days bumping into things and mumbling, "Where's a men's room?" He finally drowned when he accidentally walked off the side of the 16th Street Pier in Manhattan, taking his formula with him. His memory lives on today, a typographical error in a footnote in the pages of history.

◆

Construction of management networks in the Southeastern agribusiness sectors: Crosscut mid-economic factors w/ managerial clusters for optimum control efficiency. Achievement of top-grade quality of market production combines w/ sound corporate structure for complete stockmarketability. Trustees in agribusiness community receive equal net shares, according to on-the-floor trading and off-the-shelf income, determined by consumer attraction, necessitating mass-marketing. Agency-oriented campaign sweeps nation, bringing in new funds, new shareholders. Profits climb. Managerial networks spread from Southeastern sectors to Northeastern. Pattern repeats. Etc.

◆

"Tell me all about your race," the eight-tentacled creature said, "and I shall grant you anything you may so desire. Wealth, fame, estate, those kinds of things you Earthlings are so fond of. Oh yes, we know much about you. We have studied you for a great deal of time. We are far more advanced than you puny creatures. But there is still much we have to learn. And *you* can help us. You will be greatly rewarded, but first you must let me . . ." The orange tentacles snaked through the air, reaching out. ". . . *drain your mind!*"

And so, Serial Number 78104 became the first fire hydrant to make contact with a creature from another planet.

◆

THE ACHIEVEMENTS OF NATURE
     The Grand Canyon
     Snow
     Random mutation
     Cripples
     Grass
     Sound waves
     Mathematical laws of the universe
     Vegetables
     Riverbeds
     Epilepsy

◆

Professor Barrington paced around his office furiously. "Take my word, Hoskins," he said. "Destroy your notes and never tell a soul what you've discovered!"

"But why, Professor? Why?"

"You're just a lab assistant, boy. You're too eager. Besides— don't you realize, son," said the elderly man, leaning over Hoskins' shoulder and whispering into his ear, "what would happen if this discovery fell into the wrong hands?"

◆

THE ACHIEVEMENTS OF MAN
     Laurel Canyon
     Soap flakes
     Fallout
     Thalidomide
     AstroTurf
     Memorex recording tape
     Scientology
     Natural foods

The Panama Canal
Jitterbugging

◆

The Bremer Construction Co. man had piercing eyes and a voice so hard you could split logs on it. "So you want to build a house, eh?" he said in an attempt to impress me with his attentiveness.

"That's right," said I. "You hit the nail right on the head."

"We don't use nails here no more," he said. "We're strictly a white glue and staples firm."

"Oh," I said. (I was later to regret having said this.) "Well, then. How much will it cost to have the job done?"

Past the window behind the man's head the sun set, turning his face into a silhouette, gentle and menacing. In the darkness the keen light in his eyes burned, pinprick-sharp. I could barely see him lift his head. He shifted cryptically in his chair. "Mister," he said in a low whisper, "it'll cost ya plenty."

◆

Robert Ira was sitting in his apartment one evening watching *Dragnet* when a man appeared next to him. The man was wearing blue overalls. "Wow!" he said. "1781! I'm actually here!"

Robert crunched on a Dorito chip thoughtfully. "Who the bloody fuck are *you?*" he said after a moment.

"I'm from the future!" the man said. "My time machine actually works! I'm in the year 1781! Where's George Washington?"

"I think he's dead," Robert said, glancing at the TV. Harry Morgan and Jack Webb were running out of a police car.

"Dead? But he isn't supposed to die until 1799! Golly! I must have set the controls too high!" The man began walking around the apartment. "Fascinating! The colonial design is remarkably similar to our own!"

"It isn't colonial," Robert said, still watching the TV. "It's Early Goodwill."

"Gosh!" the man said. "I didn't know Early Americans had television! What a discovery!" The man stood by the set. "Do you have a horse-drawn carriage? Or a blunderbuss?"

"I'm afraid not. Would you like to see my electric toaster?" He put another chip in his mouth. "What year are you from, anyway?"

"I'm from 1971," he said, puzzled. "What year is *this?*"

"Congratulations," Robert said. "You've made it all the way back to 1968."

The man blanched, pulled a control unit out of his pocket, fumbled with it embarrassedly, and disappeared into the year 1692. A bunch of people spotted him and began shouting "Witch!" He was promptly burned at the stake.

◆

Dr. Anto Leikola sat down one day with his scribe and a flap of metal and wrote a memo to himself at a density of 85 letters per square millimeter, a record for miniaturization in handwriting.

"2 lbs. butter," he began. "4 loaves sourdough bread . . ."

◆

Sri Krishna is said to have achieved a state of constant enlightenment, commonly known as static *nirvana*, although he still pays high taxes.

◆

Millions.

◆

"How much longer is it going to be?" I asked the Bremer Construction Co. man.

"Don't rush us!" he said. "If you rush us we work sloppily and get white glue and staples all over everything!"

"But it's been *five years*," I said. "If it weren't for those damned lunch breaks . . ."

"Union says my men gotta have a four-hour lunch break. I make them work through their lunch break, I get the union on my back. I get the union on my back, I get a backache. My workers all quit. I don't get no profits to get Ben-Gay for my backache."

"Well, that certainly seems to make sense," I said.

◆

"And, son, that little boy grew up to be . . . Abe Lincoln!"

◆

One cloudy afternoon on February 6, 1970, Roger Martinez walked into the lounge of his dorm at St. Mary's University, followed by ten other students, each carrying a tank of goldfish. Martinez then sat down and proceeded to unceremoniously eat all 225 of the goldfish in the ten tanks, breaking the previous record. His only comment as they carried him out was, "Needed more salt."

◆

Eulby VanDerNeerg flung wide the glass doors of the accordion shop. "Liberate those accordions, brothers!" he said. "Accordions for all the people!" One of us dropped an accordion, a big Wurlitzer. Its keys, like a perfect shattered crocodile's smile, skittered and clattered against the display window. We stood around the dead accordion, weeping chrome-like tears.

"It died in the act of freeing the inner Lawrence Welk of the spirit."

"Gee, Dad! It was a Wurlitzer."

"For every martyr to the cause, a thousand new accordion revolutionaries will rise and take arms."

Eulby took control. "There will be an eight-bar rest to mourn the passing of our comrade," he said. The next day Eulby cancelled what was to be his greatest achievement, the Great Accordion Revolution. Little was heard from him until, almost a decade later, he was arrested in Barstow, California, for selling second-hand nuns. A nanny goat was also arrested in connection with the incident but was not charged.

◆

Jonas Salk discovered the polio vaccine.

◆

Flannery O'Connor's posthumous "Complete Stories" won the 1972 National Book Award.

◆

I walked away from the site in Pasadena where the Bremer Construction Co. was slowly building my house, and hopped on my rhinoceros, which was double-parked out in the street.

"Giddyap."

◆

Neil Armstrong was the first Earthian to set the soles of his spaceboots on the moon.

"This is one small step for man," he said, "and one giant leak for mankind."

"What's the matter, Neil?" Houston Control asked. "Can't you hold out till the Jack-in-the-Box on the way back?"

◆

Fenster Stowe broke up one of his late mother's best crystal wineglasses into little bits, then ground the little bits into dust with a rolling pin and put the glassdust in his father's evening Scotch-and-soda. Later, he watched as his father writhed in agony for several hours. When he finally flopped to the floor, dead, Fenster dragged his corpse to the bedroom and there performed anal intercourse on his late father.

Fenster Stowe's great achievement in life was getting his name in all the papers when he was apprehended after going on a binge of cutting up chairside dental nurses with a power saw. "The part I liked best," he told a reporter from *Newsweek,* "was sawing off an arm and then slicing the flesh off it and hitting them in the face with it." A famous novelist later wrote a famous novel about what Fenster had done, although it did not win the National Book Award.

◆

Bill Jones was the 139th man to set the soles of his spaceboots on the moon. "This is one small step for me," he said, "and one big bore for mankind."

◆

LITTLE ROCK, ARK.

◆

God created the universe in seven days, receiving no substantial overtime.

◆

Ronald MacDonald sat down to dinner with Col. Sanders, his old drinking partner. "Say, Colonel," Ronald said as the Château Rothschild '59 was served, "that sure is swell chicken you make."

"Whah thank yo'," the Colonel said. "Those burguhs you serve at yo' place are stu-pendous, and the fries can't be beat."

"And the coq au vin is excellent this evening, don't you agree?" Ronald said, adjusting his red wig. "What say you to a dark burgundy *après dîner?*"

"Mah mah!" said the Colonel.

"Now, Colonel, the way I see it," Ronald said, "with Chile in our pocket, it should be easy to knock off the rest of South America. Once we get funding for more revolutions in underdeveloped communist countries and get more juntas in our side of the court, it should be easy to set up an auxiliary government here at home. Then we can . . ."

◆

THE ACHIEVEMENTS OF NATURE (continued)
>   Starry nights
>   Monsoons
>   Extinction
>   Genius
>   Tobacco
>   Elephants
>   The Great Lakes

◆

I walked into my newly finished house. There were staples and patches of white glue everywhere. My rhinoceros had already made mincemeat of the garage. All the upstairs windows were broken. The pump didn't work. The fourth tier of the chandelier was missing. I felt ripped off. I pondered my next move.

◆

THE ACHIEVEMENTS OF MAN (continued)
>   The Hayden Planetarium
>   Rain machines
>   Genocide
>   *Mensa*
>   Cigarette-smoking machines
>   Smokey Robinson and the Miracles
>   Fires on the Cuyahoga River

◆

Rufus Kane Winterbottom built himself a time machine in 1995 and proceeded to put it to use for the good of mankind. He set the controls at three o'clock, and turned on the machine at three o'clock exactly, thus successfully making an exact reproduction of himself outside the laws of temporal cross-paradoxes. Taking a tip from Fenster Stowe, he proceeded to murder his original and perform a sodomistic act on his corpse, thus inventing the art of autonecrophilia.

◆

Carter Steele was the first Earthian to set the soles of his spaceboots on Ceti VII. "This is one giant step for mankind," Carter said.

"You forgot to say 'Mother, may I?'" Poughkeepsie Control said.

"Oh, did I?" Carter said. "I'm sorry, it's just that I've never been on television before."

"Quite all right. Just take two steps back."

◆

Augustus Q. Moultifent invented the antimatter suppository in 2006. "Whudduh rush!" he commented to newsmen as his innards tied themselves into a knot and slowly disappeared.

◆

"I'm sorry, it's just that I've never been on television before," the voice of the man in the television said. Watching it at the time, I admitted that the Ceti VII mission was most interesting, if somewhat lacking in charm. I was 97 at the time. The Bremer Construction Co. was due to fix the garage any day now, even though my rhino had been dead for some time. "Excuse me. Is this the oxygen regulator?" the man asked. "I think I'm suffocating."

◆

America fell out of bed and woke up. It had all been a dream!

◆

The last great discovery made by an Earthian for nearly five hundred years was made in 2021, when Julius Cholmondley, an American astronomer at the Mount Wilson Observatory, pinpointed what he claimed was an unknown group of objects headed for Earth at faster-than-light speeds.

"Ridiculous!" his peers said.

"Ridiculous!" the *New York Times* said.

"Ridiculous!" the President said.
"Ridiculous!" the public said.

◆

The Earth was invaded in 2022 by large green men with huge eyes who said they came from the Crab Nebula. "Say," the leader of the aliens said, "you humans sure do make good-looking suits and swell transistor radios and televisions and are terrific basketball players and sing and dance and play fantastic guitar and make wonderful little cars and lightbulbs and pencils and teabags and knives and shoes and we think we'll enslave you." Then the leader of the aliens turned to his second-in-command and told him, "Cart off everyone who's capable of doing heavy labor. Take the rest off somewhere and eat them."

◆

Humanity was released from bondage in the year 2023. "Say," the leader of the aliens said, "this suit's too small and I can't get anything worth listening to on the transistor radio and the shows are all reruns on the television and your basketball game's gone completely to pot and your voices have changed and you're getting too old to dance and your guitar's out of tune and my wonderful little car's out of gas and the lightbulb burned out and the pencil's dull and the teabag is steeped out and the knife's blunt and the heels just came off my shoes and we think we'll free you now," whereupon they all disappeared in a puff of smoke, leaving behind only some empty bottles which, unfortunately, were not returnable for deposit.

◆

Human civilization was destroyed in 2024 when, in a heated argument over who should rule Earth now that the aliens had gone, several nations pressed the same buttons at the same time, unleashing a series of plagues that wiped out 99 percent of the human population of the planet, sparing only areas of Nairobi and northern New Jersey.

◆

Fire was discovered in 2531 by Glimp Ook (2488–2531), who, in a fit of pique, attacked an abandoned gas pump with a flint spear and was blown 450 feet straight up.

The blaze attracted many of his tribe, who stared in wonder at the roaring flames. This in turn soon revived the age-old arts of burning-at-the-stake and weenie roasts.

◆

The art of painting was invented by Plag Glik, who ripped off one of his friend's arms in a casual fight and beat a cave wall with it. The designs created by this struck him as profound, and he subsequently went around ripping off his friends' arms and beating walls with them until his friends, tiring of his behavior, dropped a water heater on his head.

◆

The wheel was invented by Mwale P'toto, a Nairobi jungle-dweller. The rest of the tribe, upon seeing his achievement, informed him that, as people who lived in an area where mechanized travel was unfeasible, they had no use for a wheel. Then they shoved a palm tree through his chest and burned his wheel.

◆

The gun was invented by Lorraney Mustumper, who needed something to shoot himself in the head with.

◆

The stained-glass window was invented . . .

◆

The invention of the digital wristwatch:

◆

Penicillin . . .

◆

. . . the typewriter:

◆

. . . who realized that the speed and velocity of any given object could be ascertained by squaring the . . .

◆

. . . "Say! $n^2(rs \cdot e^4) = Gr^7 + 46° - 2(dR^2)!!$" he said, throwing himself from the third-story window . . .

◆

. . . was discovered by Jom Simth, who tied wings to his back and jumped out of a . . .

◆

. . . who discovered the polio *shmensh* . . .

◆

. . . Earth was invaded . . .

◆

. . . DNA . . .

◆

THE ACHIEVEMENTS OF MAN

JACK DANN's *stories have been appearing in science-fiction magazines and anthologies since the early 1970s; one of the best known is the 1973 novella "Junction," deemed worthy of a Hugo or Nebula trophy by many readers. He edited an anthology of science fiction on Jewish themes,* Wandering Stars, *and, with George Zebrowski, has co-edited the collection* Faster Than Light. *Dann is currently at work on an elaborate cycle of novels spanning a vast segment of the future. His work is marked by vivid narrative energy and—often—a concern for traditional Judaism and its metamorphoses in times to come.*

■

Jack Dann

■

THE DYBBUK DOLLS

Chaim Lewis had opened the store early. He did not especially mind Undercity, even though Levi Lewis, his half-brother, told him he would become sterile from radiation (which was nonsense) and lose his eyesight. So after two children, why did he need to be potent, and what eyesight? If he went blind—which couldn't happen; Dr. Synder-Langer, his eye doctor, was a state affiliate and went to seminars—what did he care? He could get a cheap unit in Friedman City (Slung City they called it)—or if he had saved enough, he could plug a room into the self-contained grid built into Manhattan City. A bright façade of metal would be much better than the Castigon Complex. Shtetlfive, located in the qualified section of the complex, was a very nice upside ghetto, very rich, semi psycho-segregated, and sensor-protected. But Chaim would only move into a shtetlsection; he needed the protection of familiar thoughts and culture. That wouldn't be so bad. He could still visit Shtetlfive—it would not move for a while, maybe never. Business, unfortunately, was too good.

Above Shtetlfive was the tiny Chardin Ghetto, poor in material wealth but high in spirit. They gave all their money (which was considerable) to their colony on Omega–Ariadne. Koper Chardin ran one of the best pleasure houses in Undercity with impunity. He even advertised organ gambling, "for those who want to experience the ultimate gamblers' thrill." In fact, it was located on Chelm Street—which was rented by the

Shtetl–Castigon Corporation at an exorbitant exchange—and
had been built on mutual contract to better serve all business
interests. Its overflow (and the poor that could not afford it)
provided a moderate part of Chaim Levi's business. But most
of his money was made on collectors.

"Collectors they call themselves," Chaim said to no one in
particular as he studied the afternoon trade sheet on the fax
hidden behind his waist-high counter. The small room was
dusty and badly lit, but it was expensively soundproofed so that
only a low level of thoughtnoise could penetrate and influence
his customers.

A young woman, dressed in a balloon suit, turned from a
display of magazines on the wall and said, "Those 'Stud' magazines. The price?"

She's got to be upside, very much upside, he thought as he
closed his eyes in mock contemplation. And she's older than she
looks. That's a falseface, he told himself.

"Well?" Her balloon suit changed color to fit the surroundings. This front room, the showroom, was dingy for effect. A
dingy shop was a lure for the passing bargain hunter. Magazines
protected by shock fields lined the soiled white walls, and plastiglass cabinets displayed small telefac units, pornographic
tapes, and assorted self-stimulation devices: second-hand handy-
randies—robots designed and programmed to caress—and vi-
brators complete with controlled frequency and amplitude of
vibration, variable size and surface texture, and temperature
control. And a small sign above Chaim's counter read non-
telepathically: DOLLS IN STOCK.

"Those magazines are very rare." Give her time, Chaim told
himself.

"Price now, no bartering," she said, walking over to Chaim's
counter. Her face was red and smooth—taut synthetic skin over
a wire frame.

"Well," Chaim said, "twentieth-century porno, why the paper is itself worth—" He paused the proper amount of time. She
did not respond properly. Instead of demanding price-by-law,

producing a recorder, and then haggling within the well-known parameters determined by her own collectors' guild council, she pursed her lips and scanned the wall above Chaim's head.

Perhaps this is a new touch, Chaim thought, but his concentration was broken by the shouts and jeers of new customers. A boy of about nineteen, naked to the waist and obviously proud of the male and female sex organs implanted on his chest and arms, led a dozen people into the store. He wore his long blond hair in braids and his face was rouged and lined. He sported one large breast to prove he was a male. That was the latest fashion. The other six boys also flaunted sex organs on their arms and chests, but the women were modestly clothed, so Chaim could only guess at what was concealed.

"Where's your hook-ins?" asked the blond boy in undercity gutter tongue.

"In the next room," Chaim said. "But mind yourselves. There are plenty of sensors in there." Another thrill family, Chaim thought. Kinkies. He guessed from their accents that they were from one of the nearby manufacturing undercities, although one of them—a spindly girl with a large mouth and flushed face —spoke with an affected upside accent. All the undercities were identical spheres, one mile in diameter, buried one thousand feet below topground. But Undercity was the first; the others were named after such families and personages as Ryan, Gulf, Rand, Lifegarten, and other lesser luminaries. Lifegarten was the most powerful. It connected twelve spheres and had to be governed as a state with its own undergovernor.

The girl with the upside accent nervously shook her head— another upside affectation, Chaim thought—and flirted with the blond boy. She wore her long blond hair in greased ringlets that left tiny stains on her dress. "Dolls," she said. "This is the place that sells dolls. Herbesh was talking about—"

"Shut up," said another girl, her accent thick with factory twang. "When you're slumming with us, shut up."

"That's all right," said the blond boy, laughing. "She's not even a collector, much less a creep."

The woman in the balloon suit stiffened, but ignored the kinkies. They left to try the feelies, and the room was quiet once again.

So she is a collector, Chaim thought. But she doesn't want porn, she wants a doll. For the grace of God and less comments by that unsympathetic holy man, the *Baal Shem,* he would have to try to dissuade her. Chaim would have to hurry, though, for Levi would be here soon, and he did not believe in divine religion—he was trained by atheists in the army. Now he's a spy, Chaim thought. And my own bloodspirit.

"You do, I believe, sell dolls," said the woman in the balloon suit. "I wish to purchase one, and I'm willing to stand here and bicker for as long as you like. I know price-by-law doesn't apply to alien goods."

"You seem to know what you want. But why want this—"

"Make it fast, but I've made up my mind."

"Then you know about dolls?" Chaim asked, his thoughts drifting. Something about the kinkies bothered him, but he couldn't decide what it was. Perhaps it was something they said. "It's a perversion," Chaim said. "You cannot satisfy yourself with dolls."

"That's the idea, isn't it?" she asked.

"But sex is not supposed—"

"Sex doesn't concern me." She rested her hands on Chaim's counter. Her suit was changing color, affected by the shifting colors that streamed in through the small high windows shaped like pentagrams. "I'm a neuter—by choice, of course. You should be familiar with that. Doesn't your church advocate neutering your young until they are ready for marriage to keep them pure?"

Chaim finished the sentence in his mind. *In the eyes of God.* He studied her face. It was too perfect a job, he thought. There were no character lines, no deviations, no pocks or scars, and her pug nose (that was the style) did not cover enough of her face and her mouth was too thin. But that's the way it's supposed to be, he thought. He could find no sensuality there, only bland purpose.

"So then why do you want a doll?" he asked. "It is for sex where the thrill lies. What more?"

"That's the point; I want to experience it without my groin. I want it in my head."

"But dolls are for frustration, to build up pleasure and then trap it inside you until it becomes pain. Unbearable pain. Nothing can get out."

"Must we continue this? I have enough credit. You've done your duty. What more do you want? You Jews want to make money."

"We just want to live," Chaim said, thinking about the kinkies again. Something they said. He had been through this conversation too many times.

"Doing this?"

"This is all we're permitted. It's a long story, and like everything else, all politics."

"But your sect has money, in fact it's very rich."

Chaim sighed and ran his thumb around the reinforced edge of his pocket. *Live in Gehenna or be separated. The Diaspora of the rich.* But almost everyone is rich, Chaim thought. *To overthrow Satan you must know him. Know him, yet not be corrupted.*

"Money is only good for certain things," Chaim said. "That is part of Paskudnak's plan. You have heard of that?" It was working. She might not buy a doll yet.

She laughed, her mouth twitching at the corners for effect. "That's a myth, a fairy tale. There's no test. No one is trying to corrupt you. No game. That's made up to scare your children."

She's intent on having that dybbuk, Chaim thought.

"Well," she said. "The doll. Price."

"If you even look at a new doll, it will take something away. Something good that lives inside you."

"Yes, I know." She grinned. "Price."

A fool, he thought. "It will actually take the shape of your frustrations."

"Price."

"It is not even known if the doll is some sort of mechanical toy, or if it is alive. No one knows."

"Price. Pricepriceprice."

So you win, he said to no one in the room. *Herbesh.* That was
the word that upside girl used. Where had he heard it before?
Herbesh. Something about . . .

"Your time is up," said Levi Lewis, stepping in from the
street. For an instant the small showroom was bathed in a lurid
yellow light. Old magazines turned yellow, silver handy-randies
glittered, and Levi's face—framed between a red-and-silver
beard, curled earlocks, and a black hat with a fur brim—looked
withered and pocked. Then the door closed and the room became dim again. Levi was dressed exactly like Chaim. He wore
a black caftan that reached to his knees. His pants were red,
pleated and cuffed. A glitter belt separated mind and heart
from his most corrupted parts.

"You've worked your requirement," Levi said. "That's the
law." He winked at the woman in the balloon suit. Another
yellow glare as a couple entered the store and browsed in the
corner. Both wore sequined cloth dresses, lightbeads, and metal
dangles in the form of stars and grotesque faces. "See," he said.
"More customers to be titillated. My turn, Chaim. Go away.

"It's another *nechtiger tog* outside again," Levi said. "Day is
night, morning is noon. Feh. They're using beadlights and that
lousy hoof-foof thoughtnoise to make more business. And everything is yellow. I hate yellow. It hurts my eyes. May I help you?"
he asked the couple in the corner, who were examining the
poor selection of pornographic telefactapes. They ignored him.

"So the street will earn its name," Chaim said after a pause.
"Chelm, Chelm, a foolish place."

"Go get her doll," Levi said, suddenly serious. "You will not
talk her out of it."

He's right, Chaim told himself. What matter; she's only a
balloon. Although the room had returned to its former dusky
state—the small pentagram windows could not offer much light
and the lamps were turned low—her balloon suit was radiant.
It seemed to bulge. Chaim could not look at her face. More

tsores for me, he thought. Every day brought its share of troubles. Sticks to make a holy fire.

Chaim tried to shut out the thoughtnoise that was blaring in his head. The thoughtnoise had to be coming from somewhere inside the store, he thought, because it was too strong to be just echoes from outside. It was giving him a headache.

"Well," the woman said. "I'm waiting."

So wait, Chaim thought. The fax screen was blinking. No one could see it but Chaim. It was set into a dead spot in the glasstex counter.

:Attention. Intruder FaChrm #4. Police notified/Sil. Pro.:

The kinkies set up a mindblock, Chaim thought. That's why I couldn't hear the alarm. Chaim was mindlinked with the store's alarm system. They must be rich, Chaim thought. Rich enough to disrupt with their own equipment the most expensive alarm and control system he could afford. He daydreamed for a few seconds. *Herbesh.* That same word swam in his mind. He remembered: Herbesh was a powerful member of a Chartist Clan. The shtetl had many political enemies, and the Chartists were the most rabid. Many money feuds had been lost because of anti-Semitism. But the Chartists were more than just political enemies; they derived their strength and community from hatred and thus gained Machiavellian access into high-level politics.

Herbesh, Chaim thought. A Paskudnak. They're one and the same. Paskudnak was a Jewish myth, an ongoing legend born and maintained out of paranoia. He was considered to be the focus of evil, "the mount of darkness." Some said he was deformed and called him Shimen Hunchback; others said he was ugly as sin, but seduced all the beautiful women that came his way. Fruma, Chaim's wife, thought he must be beautiful, a misled innocent. A *nefish.* He was the imagined superman-conspirator who took on different faces at different times to frustrate the Jewish alliance. Chaim half believed in Paskudnak. After all, he would tell himself, there obviously is a conspiracy against the shtetl.

One of the kinkies said something about Herbesh, Chaim thought. So they must be related to him. They have the money to steal, and buy mindblock equipment. They must want the dolls. *Gottenyu*. The kinkies would stuff themselves with the dolls and begin another scandal, another feud. But why steal the dolls? If they could afford mindblock equipment, they could simply buy the dolls outright.

Then it must be a setup. What else? Chaim thought. And a setup could only mean scandal. Herbesh's kinkie clansmen would be psychologically deformed for life—that's what the fax would read. He could already see tomorrow's scandalfax. Herbesh's *Reyakh*, who knows only one tune, will make up a new song. And Paskudnak, who forces our lives, will win. That would be too much for the shtetl's weakened morale. They certainly had *chutzpa*, Chaim thought.

"Red light," Chaim said to his brother. Levi shrugged. There could be no blame on him: he wasn't officially working. Attempted robberies were common, and Chaim had made it a rule not to upset the customers. It was all routine. The sensors would mindscan every customer, deactivate any heat weapon, throw up a shock field if necessary, and notify the police. Since concealed projectile weapons were by law denoted "Civilian Punishable," it was the proprietor's choice. Chaim could not remember whether he had programmed paralysis (temporary) or mindshut. It didn't matter now, he thought.

"I'm going to see what's going on," Chaim said to Levi. The police were probably around the corner. It was probably too late to get out with the dolls.

"For what? It will be finished in a few minutes."

That's what I'm afraid of, he thought, as he walked across the room.

"But you place yourself in danger . . ."

He should care, Chaim thought. He would lie with Fruma. He should be glad I'm not telling him. What could he do, anyway, but ruin everything? Mumbling a prayer, Chaim stepped into the feelie room. Both telefac units were being used, as were the less exotic cerebral hook-ins. A boy and girl, both naked, were strapped into the telefac stirrups, their backs resting against the supporting pads that stimulated their spinal nerves and activated the pornotapes. A network of microminiaturized air-jet transducers provided them with tactile information, and they also received audio, visual, and motion feedback. The girl's knees were buckling. The spinal pad quickened her heartbeat with a rerun of "Bestial Love." Her friend in the other telefac was in the throes of orgasm. The ultimate vicarious thrill.

Chaim looked away from them. The others, plugged into the small hook-in consoles, were dazed. But the blond boy and the upside girl were standing beside the back door. The door was open, revealing part of the sensor-protected storeroom. The dolls were hidden in a lockup at the far end of the storeroom wall. He hoped they had not been able to open the lockup and find the dolls.

"The police will be here soon," Chaim said. He tried to stop his shaking.

"We'll wait," said the blond boy. He reached for the upside girl's hand.

"So it is a setup," Chaim said.

"No," said the girl. "It's for fun. We're just doing this to pull on your parts and have a good time. As children we're entitled to a little fun."

"Are you part of Herbesh's clan?"

"He's my uncle," the boy said. "Aren't you afraid of Paskudnak's wrath?" The girl giggled. "If he found out you were selling dolls to children, swamping their innocent souls with alien filth, it would make scandal. And then where would you work?"

"Hungry Jews," said the girl.

"You may be from Herbesh's clan," said Chaim, "but you're not children." Chaim knew they had him. Herbesh would call for a literal interpretation of the black-letter law, fold the courts, and denounce the shtetl on every fax channel for peddling filth to innocents. But if there were no dolls, there could be no proof.

"Police will be here soon," the boy said. "It's all set. You just might"—he slipped into guttertongue—"have enough time. Just a game."

"You know the commercial," the girl said. "Today's newsfax is tomorrow's scandalfax."

"Are the dolls opened?" Chaim asked. The boy and girl laughed at him.

"That's for us to know and you to find out."

"Azzes ponim," Chaim mumbled in a last effort at pride. They laughed as he walked past them into the storeroom. The storeroom had been ransacked: ancient magazines had been torn apart and left on the floor with streamers of telefac tape and broken plug-ins. A kinkie girl (Chaim wasn't sure, since he or she was undressed) huddled against the wall, hiding whatever organ was between spindly legs. Chaim hoped she was not cradling a doll against the wall.

The lockup was closed. But Chaim had no time. His ears burned. Like an animal, he thought, I'm running from these children—they should be running from me: they've broken the law. What's the difference? he asked himself. Eat dirt now, turn to dust later.

He had to get the dolls out of the store. A chill went through him—could they have done something with the dolls? What if they've tampered with the lockup? he asked himself. What could he do but close his eyes and pray. The police should be here by now, he thought. No time. So let it be finished. Could they have fixed that too? Sure, with the *Shtot Balebos.* What does he care.

Chaim slipped his fingers into a coded depression in the lockup cabinet. A soft burst of light and the door opened, revealing glasstex trays of neatly placed dolls. And each doll had taken the shape of a distorted human face. Chaim's face.

They've unpacked the dolls, Chaim thought. Plasticine packages were neatly piled on the top shelf.

Little tongues wrapped around little teeth, squinting porcelain eyes, wrinkles, and bald heads.

THE DYBBUK DOLLS145

Petrified screamers.

All looking at Chaim from their glasstex trays.

Chaim screamed, pressing his palms against his eyes so the dolls couldn't reach into his head. But it was already done. Even with his eyes closed, he had "imprinted" each and every one of them. Within a fraction of a second he was transferring his every impulse and emotion to the dolls, namely fear. They drank it up, transmogrified themselves into a pattern best fitted to frustrate and titillate him.

"Dybbuks have entered me," he shouted, trying to exorcise the spirits. He could feel each one burrowing into his mind, confusing his thoughts, tasting his most sinful desires. Chaim could hear the kinkies laughing. Like tinkling bells, he thought. Let them laugh; it should be on me if it's God's choice.

"Scandalfax," the girl said. "You'd better gather up your dolls and take them with you. No time"—a slip into guttertongue, an upside affectation. "The police will be here soon, and the kids are hanging from the telefacs with red faces and erections and sitting on the floor with hook-ins plugged into their pink heads. Looks very bad."

"Very good," the blond boy said, pinching her cheek.

It was probably a ruse, Chaim thought. There would be no police. But he couldn't take the chance. Herbesh would not stand for opened dolls anywhere near his kin. The hook-ins and telefacs would only incur small punishment. Let Levi worry— that *loksh* spy.

"And we say you imprinted us with those dolls," said the boy, "while we scream and make obscene gestures and laugh and hold our heads. Alien thoughtscum, you know."

They must have used a mindblock to unpack the dolls, Chaim thought. He fantasized that the blond boy and upside girl were naked. They stood in the dark, heavy cloth stretched tightly over their puckish faces, and meticulously opened each package. *Gottenyu*, he thought. The dybbuks are changing me already, soiling my thoughts. He gathered up the dolls—they were the size of his large hands—and dropped them into a carrybox. They'll melt together, he thought. So let them. They'll suck out my soul. What black soul could you have? The girl is pretty, not fat and earthy like Fruma, but delicate and shriveled like Raizel the wet nurse.

"Take them home with you, sleep with them," the girl said, twisting a greased curl around her forefinger.

What small breasts she must have, Chaim thought. He felt strong unnatural urges welling up inside him, filling him up, beating against the inside of his skin to be free. His body was no longer a holy vessel, and he felt dispassionately removed from it. He drove it like a car toward the back door. His glands secreted the wrong juices, anesthetized him, fooled him with oceans of sexual sensation—all directed toward the kinkie girl, always ebbing instead of reaching new heights. Frustrating him. But there was sickly-sweet beauty in that frustration.

He could not, would not, have her. So the dybbuks pushed against him, sandpapered his delicate conscience against his flesh to produce guilt. That heightened the sensations, strengthened the brew. Chaim turned for a last look at the girl as he pressed against the door, and then stopped himself. No, he thought. God shouldn't see me brimming with filthlife. The dolls were not mechanical; they were alive.

The door opened and Chaim was in the street, squinting his eyes in the strong yellow light. "Not even a look behind," he said to the dolls in his hand and the dybbuks in his head. Chelm Street was to his right, bustling with people, a river of rollers and slidewalks rushing in-town and back on the other side. Like boats on the water, platforms and movetels drifted slowly down the middle of the street. Beyond Chelm Street, and to his left, drawing an arc around him, the skyscrapers rose out of the yellow thoughtfog, sparkling like glass stalagmites in a crystal cave. Tiers upon tiers of fenestrated glasstex, studded with sunlights, reaching like inverted roots toward the bright surface of the dome above. Set into this glass landscape was a circular park, barely visible in the settling fog. Its boundaries were only a few yards from where Chaim was standing. A few feet from

him was a transpod rut that extended as far as he could see to
his left and descended into the ground a few yards to his right.

Chaim felt giddy. The fog was a lure. Its fumes and the hoof-
foof thoughtnoise excited him, made him feel glamorous, a part
of the partycrowd. A small transpod stopped in front of him.
The silver egg was computer controlled and driven by a propulsion system built into the narrow rut. Chaim climbed into the
transpod with some trouble, intoning the eternal *oy-oy-oy*. He
punched out the coordinates to go home, called the shtetl to tell
them of his dilemma, and by the time he settled into a comfortable position he was almost topside.

He tried to compose himself. Just as I thought, there were no
police, he told himself. Looking at the carrybox on his lap, he
thought: I should throw this filth into the disposer. But who
knew what would destroy it? By throwing it away, he might be
putting the dybbuks out of his reach forever, and their spirits
would remain inside him, corrupting him, until he was only a
hollow shell filled with dybbukfilth. He needed the dybbuks'
flesh to exorcise them.

Chaim's heart was pounding. The car seemed to be getting
smaller. (You're making this up, Chaim told himself. Stopit.) He
was afraid of closed spaces again, like when he was a child
locked in Makher's closet with Dvora Shiddukah.

"So this is the way it is to be," he said, trying to ignore his
fantasies. He braced himself, arms outstretched, fingers touching the silver side panels, and murmured the *Shema Yisrael*.
The air was suddenly filled with noxious smells. (Stopitstopit,
Chaim told himself. This is a dream. Don't set the stage.) He
tried to pray. It was difficult to breathe. Too hot. Chaim was
sweating. (You are dry as a mat.) His *talis koton*, a fringed cloth
undergarment, was soaked through, defiled, he thought, by his
dreams. He found himself with an erection.

He dreamed about Dvora, sweet skinny Dvora with her
bumps for breasts and squeaky voice. The closet was dark and
Dvora was naked and making mouse noises. Air, Chaim said to
himself, gagging. Too small. Can't breathe. (Liar. Dybbuk-

dreamer. You're smiling and breathing clean recycled air.) Chaim reached forward to dissolve the gray walls, but couldn't touch the switch. (Stop acting and press the button.)

And then he was pushing the switch and screaming. He was an actor without an audience. But there was no release. His throat hurt and his head ached. Now there was too much air and space. The city was all around him, and he was being swept through a glass tunnel, one of the billions of transparent cables that linked up the city, toward a canyon formed out of glass and steel and light. Above him was a rush of perspective lines drawing together in the distance. A roof covered this part of the city, melded all the buildings into a ceiling. Below him were slidewalks and runshops and millions of people dashing about, spoiling the clean geometrical lines of the city ways. But Chaim was too high to see them.

He hoped for a rush of relief. He was close to home now. But the exhilaration was too much for him. It became bone-crushing pain. And then just fear. He had only been afraid of heights once in his life, when he climbed onto a parapet on a dare. He slipped and almost fell. That's how he felt now. He was falling again, grasping for a transparent edge.

Before him was a glass wall. Then he was inside it. The transpod followed its course to a lift-rut where it rose like an elevator toward the upper levels of the largest living units in New York. Castigon Complex consisted of two risers, each a thousand stories high and linked together by hookwalls and emergency passtubes. The uppermost stories looked down upon the smooth snow-covered surface of the city's roof and swayed very slightly. But from Chaim's position, the building was too large to be seen as anything other than interlocking linelevels and arbitrary shapes. It was as if these were risers that had been set into a glass template, which was itself another building.

As the pod slowed to a halt, Chaim's head cleared and he sighed and closed his eyes. "Thank you, *Kvater* of both demons and angels." The door opened onto a platform strewn with plastipaper, but Chaim made no move to get out of the pod. A few people rushed by. He prayed. Thank you, Chaim said to himself. Let me rest a moment. A familiar face leaped out of his mind and dissolved before his mind's eye. It was Dvora. Her deep-set eyes were tiny blue stones set into the caverns of her bony face. He dreamed that she was lying on the glass parapet. She was waiting for him, breathing in short gasps, exposing her worm-white body to the chill wind. There would be no respite.

"But it's all illusion," Chaim shouted at the air. This is false as a telefac or hook-in, he thought. I'm drawing on my filthpile of carnal thoughts and experiences. But they're not real. (Yes they are.) I'm suffering for forgiveness. (God will punish. Liar.)

A group of children, dressed in knee-length caftans, heads shaved but earlocks untouched, all wearing *yarmelkehs* or black hats with imitation fur tails, were on their way home from *Kheyder*, where they had spent the morning studying Torah. They hooted and sang. High-pitched voices echoed. Translucent walls became mirrors of sound.

"Stop that," Chaim said. "It's a sin." Their echoes would dissipate their fragile souls.

"Bim, bim, bam," they sang. "Sleep soundly at night—

"And learn Torah by day. And you'll be a rabbi—

"When I have grown gray."

They walked backward past Chaim. For each step they took, so the legends told, their guardians or watchers would burn a year in Hell. Technically, at that moment, Chaim was a watcher. So he closed his eyes, but the children had taken at least five steps. They should play with shadows. *Sheyneh* loafers. (Stopit. Dybbukfilth.)

A buzzer sounded, reminding Chaim that he was taking up space. He tried to ignore it. Soon the pod would direct enough thoughtnoise at Chaim to make him leave. Think. Something about those children on the platform, he told himself. They were dressed like *Sheyneh*, the rich, but they had the red faces of the *Prosteh*, the poor. He felt a coldness in his groin. Think-think. Something familiar. (Another lie.) Something beautiful. (Dybbuktalk. Close your ears.)

Chaim squeezed the carrybox on his lap, felt a thrill radiate down his legs. A flame was coloring everything he thought and saw, dulling the ever-present frustration that glowed like coals on his lap. There was no rush, he told himself. He had to remember something. That's it, he thought. Those children all look like me. (Dreamer. Liar. Make-up-man.) Like my children. (Dybbukspawn.) Again, the coldness. His lap was wet. He shook off the dark things crawling in his mind and found himself kneading soft flesh, holding it between his large palms. His hands were inside the carrybox.

"Gottenyu," he cried, pulling his hands out of the box and closing the lid. "Now they have my flesh, too." He watched the people rushing past the pod. Although there were a few women hurrying about in old dresses and work aprons, the men—dressed in knee-length caftans and sporting full, untrimmed beards and carefully curled earlocks—were clearly in the majority. There were several other pods backed up behind Chaim. It was still early, workers hadn't returned home yet, and housewives were in their rooms, frantically preparing for *Erev Shabbes,* the Sabbath eve. It was called "Short Friday," because after sundown no work could be performed. Any woman found in the building's ways on Short Friday became known as a *yideneh* and was shunned by the other women of her shtetl level, unless she had a good excuse. *Shabbes* was a time for the family, a time for prayer and study.

Chaim found that he could block out most of the thought-noise easily. He was having fantasies that Raizel the wet nurse looked just like him. Fearing for his life with every movement, he was making love to her on a parapet. He was a glutton, pulling the life juices out of her frail, skinny body.

"So what are you waiting for?" asked Feigle Kaporeh, an old woman wearing a rumpled ankle-length dress, a kerchief around her thick neck, and a wig over her cropped hair—she was known to be senile and still considered herself beautiful enough to attract sinful glances. "How much noise does the pod have to make before you get out?"

Still thinking about Raizel, Chaim swung one of his legs out of the pod. Feigle Kaporeh can't look like me, he told himself, as he pulled the carrybox along behind him. (Onanist.)

"*Oy,*" she said. "It's you. Get away from me. *Tatenyu.*"

"*Yideneh,*" Chaim mumbled and rushed across the platform, pushing through the few people that were in his way. He could smell the sweet fragrance of *challah,* the Sabbath bread, mingling with the stale air of the transpod tunnel. Chaim felt himself being pulled into a knot that would explode, flinging the trapped juices out of his corrupted body. I have to be alone with the dolls, he thought. Just for a few minutes. (Fight them.)

An arch decorated with golden lions and tablets of the Ten Commandments led into Shtetlfive's ways, a maze of hallways running parallel and perpendicular to a defunct rollway. The low-ceilinged rollway was the size of a small street or alley, and had become the neighborhood meeting place. It was poorly lit and poorly ventilated, but in an area where space was at a premium, this free tunnel was a luxury. It was hoped that the authorities would not be quick to turn the rollway into transients' space. Located nearby were the auditoriums and meeting rooms that functioned as synagogue, *besmedresh*—a study and prayer center, wailing room, Bundcongress, and local schools such as the *Talmud Toyreh* and *Gemoreh Kheyder.*

But there were few people about, only visitors, early workers, tardy gossipers, and children returning from trades and rich *Kheyders.* The "Queen-Bride" of the Sabbath had to be escorted in; there was no time for dallying. The *shammes,* a synagogue functionary, was going about his duties early. He walked along the rollway calling, "Jews to the bathhouse," for the ceremonial *mikva* of purification.

"Hey, Chaim," he shouted. "We have news of what happened. Go quickly. Rabbe Ansky has found more than enough men to make a quorum. And, he-should-be-blessed, the *Baal Shem* from Menachem Ghetto will preside."

Chaim ignored him and stepped into a small corridor that would lead to his rooms. I must be alone, he thought. Just for

a minute, just to see . . . He would have to look into the box;
there would lie his catharsis. But the quorum will save me. Why
do I need Raizel, anyway? he asked himself. I only need myself.
(Dybbuktalk.) But Raizel is a lustbowl. No matter. I have it all
inside me.

He could hear the buzz of garbled conversation before he
reached his rooms. I have to get past their quorum, he thought.
The doorslide was open. He walked into his front room and
found it filled with people, more than enough for a holy quorum
to exorcise the dybbuks. Chaim paused before his wife, Fruma,
who took a step backward. She was wearing a black dress, a lace
scarf over her matron's wig, and all her jewelry, which consisted
of three gold pins, two necklaces with Mogen David dangles,
and several silver bandbracelets. "I'm sorry," she said. "The
year in Hell should be sent to me. It's the dybbuks—"

She, too, looks like me, he thought. The same strong face.
(Stopit. Here is safety.)

"We heard from Levi," Fruma said. "This must be one of
Paskudnak's tricks. But we are strong. Look, the *Baal Shem*,
he-should-be-blessed, and Rabbe Ansky will preside over the
quorum. And, just in case, Mordcha Lublin has brought us the
shofar from Newtemple."

Everyone but Rabbe Ansky stood behind the *Baal Shem*, a
holy man of about eighty with a full white beard and greased
earlocks. He wore a black caftan of the finest satin and a skullcap with a tassel. Fruma was about to speak again when the
Baal Shem spread his arms for proper effect and said, "It is time.
Let us begin. Chaim Lewis, give me that box of filth."

"You may prepare the other room now," the *Baal Shem* said
to Fruma. "Then leave us. Your *zogerkeh*, or whichever woman
you choose, will lead your prayers for Chaim in this room. But
remember, do not listen to our holy words."

A few of the other men—prayer shawls draped over their
shoulders, holy phylacteries strapped to their foreheads and
bare arms—were already rocking back and forth, mumbling
prayers. Chaim looked around the room. He knew most of the
men: Yitzchak Meyvn, Solomon the cantor, Avrum Shmuel,

Yudel, who cheats on his wife with his neighbor, and Moishe Makher, Yussel, Itzik, Yankel, and others whose names he couldn't remember.

"The box now, Chaim," the *Baal Shem* said. "We must hurry. *Shabbes* will not wait for us."

"No," Chaim said. "I must have myself alone." (Give them the box.) It's almost done, he thought. (The dybbuks are sucking you in.) Just for a moment. (You can't have yourself that way. *Treyftreyf.* Impure.)

"What kind of talk is that?" asked Rabbe Ansky, a dark man with a shaved head, frizzy earlocks, and a coarse black beard. He took a step toward Chaim. "Now come on, give me that box."

Chaim tasted worms in his mouth. He ran toward the bedroom, knocking down Rabbe Ansky's wife, a small wrinkled woman who was screaming for help. Fat Yitzchak tried to cut him off, but Chaim had already passed Fruma. He pushed her out of the doorway and locked the slideshut. I'm safe from them for a few minutes, he thought. It would take some time to have the power shut off. Until then, they couldn't get in.

He pulled a chair into the middle of the room, sat down, placed the carrybox on the floor, and then greedily opened it. All the men in the other room look alike, Chaim thought. But they're only poor impressions of me. (Open the door.)

Chaim peered into the box. Hurry, dybbuks, he thought. Get it over with. His parts were clawing at each other. Spirit-pus. I'm filled up with it. I'll burst. Release me. (Open the door.)

The dolls had melted together into a gray lump of clay. Its shape changed as Chaim stared at it. It became a human head. (Stop it now.) It's only a mask, Chaim thought. Wait. The mouth was open, lips pulled over blue gums. (Stopit.)

Chaim saw what he wanted: his face without blood, without life. Give it back, he thought. But there could be no release. His soul was passing into the open mouth of dybbukflesh. He could not get back into himself. He would be stuck in the dybbuks' mouth.

Shaking and crying, he tried to fight the dark things that were

sucking at his thoughts and memories. But he had lost too much
of himself. I can't stay outside. (Then open the door.)

I can't.

The lights went out. Chaim paid no attention: he was drown-
ing in his own thoughts. (Listen. The door.)

"Quickly, before he soils himself," said the *Baal Shem*,
"remove him from that *thing.*" The doorslide was stuck at an
odd angle, and the men had to pull in their stomachs to squeeze
through. Fruma and the other woman watched from the other
room. The men lifted Chaim out of his chair and braced him in
a standing position.

"Can you hear me, Chaim?" asked the *Baal Shem.*

"Yes," Chaim said. His heart was beating faster. A spot of
goodness grew larger, then was swallowed by alien thoughts.
He dreamed of Fruma, how she smelled and the noises she
made. FrumaDvora. Panting together. Like me. They smell like
me. Taste like me. He reached for Fruma, but could only find
himself.

The *Baal Shem* began to pray. He rocked back and forth on
his heels, sang, and raised his eyes toward the ceiling. "We must
draw the dybbuks out of him," he said to the other men, who
were praying with their hands over their faces. "You must not
be afraid. Look at it. Destroy it. We will take it into ourselves,
but with God's help we are strong."

As the men looked into the carrybox, the *Baal Shem* read the
Ninety-first Psalm aloud. At first his words were strong and
clear, but as he went on he began to falter. He gripped his
prayer shawl until his knuckles turned red. "Look at it," he
whispered to the others as he bent over to stare into the box.
"Draw it out. God will protect."

Chaim could feel everyone's presence. He tried to pray, but
his jaw was locked and the words were jumbled in his mind. The
lump of dybbukflesh was changing. Sometimes it looked like the
face of the *Baal Shem*, only wicked and full of lust, and at other
times it looked like Rabbe Ansky, afraid and trying to become
a woman. Chaim could see the faces of all the others in the clay

lump. He knew their fears and thoughts. Yudel was spitting up blood and Yussel was trying to run away from a man that he hated. The others choked quietly on everyone's memories.

> " *'He will cover you with his pinions,*
> *and you shall find safety beneath his wings.'* "

"Help me, Mayer Ansky," said the *Baal Shem,* as he dropped the holy book. But the Rabbe, like the rest of the men, could only stare catatonically into the carrybox.

" *'I will satisfy him with long life,'* " said Chaim. He had to fight for every word.

" '. . . *To enjoy the fullness of my salvation,'* " intoned the *Baal Shem.*

"Dybbuks," the *Baal Shem* shouted, "vacate the body of Chaim Lewis and the other members of this holy quorum. In the name of the most holy, go off to eternal rest."

The lump of clay was changing color. It would soon turn into dust. Chaim felt the darkness leave his mind, but the sour memories remained strong. The others had destroyed the dybbuks by making Chaim's sins their own. Now they were all stained. They would share each other's sins. They would always be bound together. The *Baal Shem* would never become a martyr. Chaim could almost hear everyone's thoughts.

"*Mazltov,*" said the *Baal Shem.* "*Shabbes* has come."

But Chaim and the others had fallen asleep. The *Baal Shem,* finally giving in to weakness, fainted. The "Queen-Bride" of the Sabbath would be escorted into Shtetlfive by sleepers to the trumpets of snorers.

GIL LAMONT *lives in Los Angeles and has written a number of novels for California-based publishers. He was one of the earliest contributors to the short-lived and lamented Essex House line of experimental novels, with* Roach *(1969). This is his first short science-fiction piece.*

■

Gil Lamont

■

THE MIRROR AT SUNSET

In the dream I am running, I don't know from what or which, but it is of the utmost necessity that I run and keep running. I suck in great mouthfuls of sweet air, feel my lungs expand. I breathe hard, harder, and drops of sweat begin to bead on my brow. My legs are pumping, pumping. My arms are swinging, swinging. My feet fly over the cinders, toe heel sole, pushing, thrusting, and I am driving myself to the limits of exhaustion. My throat burns as I gasp. Salt sweat attracts a thin layer of dust and dirt, on my face, on my neck, under my arms. My shirt is plastered to my back. I am running and sweating and dying with the agonies of being alive, and it is glorious.

In the dream my heart thumps in my chest cavity as I run, thumps a little louder as I add a burst of speed, and then its beat is ragged, it tears, it breaks, it bursts, and this time I am really dying. You must stop this running, I tell myself. You'll kill yourself like this. And then I begin to fall forward on my face.

At which point I always wake up. This time consciousness snaps to with a jolt, there is no easy segue from dream to waking, and before I remember that it cannot be, there is for the briefest of moments a tingling lingering ache in my calves and thighs. Then I fix time and space. All the external pangs are gone. I am standing, so: arm upraised in greeting, torso half-twisted toward my invisible friend, the other arm dangling stiffly at my side. I am dressed in clothes that do not quite fit, though they are at least pinned in the back. I have, after this

157

uncertain passage of time, become used to them. In fact I ignore them most of the time. They are not part of me, they have nothing to do with me, their style is not my style, and personally if I had the choice of what I would wear I would wear nothing. If I had the choice I would not be where and who I am, and I think it would be wonderful to feel all the elements raging against my naked skin: fire and ice and pain and love and beauty. I get none of these from the clothes I wear—correction, the clothes I have been dressed in. This time, however, I have reason for discomfort, as whoever dressed me has somehow twisted my feet until the toes point at a common locus. I am pigeon-toed.

We all have our crosses to bear, I once heard a fat woman from Midwich say. She'd come in to buy something for her husband, an anniversary present, and she spent a great deal of time looking through the entire stock of sport jackets before she found one her husband wouldn't like. It was a loud item in checks and stripes, garish colors (the details escape me now, of course), pockets everywhere and not enough buttons. Seeing her buy that monstrosity restored my faith, allowed me to accept the singular advantages of my position. In addition, that coat was the last the store had in stock, and I was not the only one happy to see it blare its way out of our lives.

I am not alone here, of course. The hired help is here from gray dawn to orange twilight, hustling amid the bustling, sneaking coffee breaks and bitching about the boss. A quick life, flickering with delight. A life full of friends, acquaintances, enemies. The clash of personalities. Jealousies and hatreds. Fear and understanding. I understand the last of these. I understand understanding, as I must, because I have nothing else to do all day long, and I have in my brief existence formulated several thousand utterly remarkable interpretations of the underlying philosophy of life. I understand the importance of light to the motility of man. When it is light they come. When it is dark they go.

Now it is growing dark, orange floods knee-deep, lights are

flicked on here, off there. The cleaning staff is coming through, picking up the spoor of the last customers, and the store is closing. A lady whose face I have never seen adjusts the collar of my shirt; then, dissatisfied with the cast of my countenance, shifts the angle of my chin a few degrees. Then she is gone and I am staring across the aisle at a mirror.

Understand that I cannot see myself in the mirror. Understand that the mirror was not there yesterday, that if it had things might be a lot different. Now the mirror is something new, something I have seen before but never studied. Before, I have only glanced into the mirror as it, or I, was carried past. Now I can look into that reflected world until I have had my fill.

I stare for a long time before I begin to sort out which is what. It takes me a while to understand that all is backward—I knew that but did not realize it—and once I have that straight I can pick out the gondola of overstock blouses with the hosiery display at the near end, behind that the racks of dresses in every conceivable size, beyond that the changing rooms of orange board and frosted glass. I stare at the shadows on the glass and think about my dream and the end of my dream, especially the end. The running and the dying. The dying. A chill rivets my attention back to the shadows on the glass, at which point the door opens and a woman steps out of the dressing room. She is wearing such-and-such and so-and-so, walking with undulating grace easily and fluidly toward me. She is more motion at once than I have ever seen before.

I think she is quite beautiful, filling amply all the current criteria. I am eager for her to get close enough to see that I am pigeon-toed and correct it. Yet even as she steps nearer someone is entering my field of vision. He cuts across the aisle, slows down (and she is slowing down) and blocks the mirror.

I can still see her, but she is blocked by him and will advance no farther. He moves and she apes him, scratching her shoulder as he scratches his. Neither says a word. I stare and I do not understand. And then I do.

She is the reflection of him.

I do not understand how it can be so, nor why it is so, but I cannot doubt what I see, that isn't my style, and so I must accept that she is his reflection, and possibly he hers, and that is the way it is. So I study him before I go back to studying her. He's of fair height, as tall as she anyway, and he has a fine healthy head of hair, good posture, nothing in his back pockets, boots with moderate heels. I do not like him. Her I could love, that compassion in her eyes, the perfection of her face and body according to the current criteria. But she is looking at him, and smiling.

Smiling in that vaguely predatory affectionate manner. Smiling and smiling, as I suppose on our side of the glass he is smiling and smiling, lips puckering up into cheeks with the joy and glory of it all.

I can read the signs. Love has reared its head.

He looks at her and she looks at him for long dull seconds. I think about the world back of my left shoulder: a gondola of overstock shirts, socks at this end of it, behind racks of suits and the changing cubicles. And I think about the mirror, and I think of the world behind the glass . . .

They are still looking at each other, but now her mouth moves in silence. I cannot make out the words but it is long enough to say "I love you" and no more. Then her hand moves to the front of her dress. From the flapping of his elbows I detect that he is opening his shirt, but quickly I am more interested in her. This will be my first opportunity to personally appraise taboo areas of the body. I am curious about her breasts.

She drops her dress to the floor and is standing there naked with a knowing smile, and yes the current criteria! praise be the current criteria! I am fascinated and repelled, awed and uplifted.

He, the idiot, is still struggling with his pants, but he gets them down in time to win her approval. They nod at each other, lean forward, lips touching the glass. There is a quick private communication, I am sure of it, for suddenly there is an aura about them that I cannot completely place. I will in time, but now is not the time. They are pulling their clothes back on and his head turns to the right and he nods back at me and says something. She laughs, showing a fine throat, looks back over her shoulder, says something to him with a significant glance at me. He peers into the glass at something I cannot see, confers with her earnestly. She has not all this time taken her eyes off me, and when she replies the lines of her mouth are for a moment hard. Then suddenly they both burst out laughing.

But I understand. It is not unkind. They are not laughing at me, only at my predicament, so I ignore the twinges inside and laugh with them.

With a shrug he turns back to me, gives me a thumbs-up, puts his hand to the mirror, fingers splayed on the surface. Her palm has risen to meet it, her fingers flatten themselves against the glass between them. Again there is that secret communication, and now there is no glass between them. Their hands touch, palm to palm, an eddy of distortion around his fingers. He pushes his arm forward and his hand disappears to the wrist and I jerk in alarm. He withdraws his hand and it is still there, looks real, probably is real. And she has done the very same thing, now putting her hand back up to meet his, now pushing forward until their wrists are meeting and their hands are nowhere to be seen.

I think I begin to understand, a shift of mental attitude which somehow communicates itself to him, for he turns back to me and smiles, smiles, turns back to the mirror and puts both hands through it and sticks out his foot, leans forward, begins the very process of walking. His leg disappears into her leg as hers disappears into his. Then one arm is gone to the shoulder, his head goes, half his torso is left, now only one leg, now the heel of a boot, now nothing, not even a flaw left in the glass by their passage.

Some time has passed since he came and they went, and I have stood here with my pigeon toes, thinking and thinking. I am trying to understand, more so now because since that time the boss has shifted my chin back to where it had pointed before. I have accepted the circumstances of their escape because I have no choice, but I am plagued by questions about them. He and she. The Couple, as I think of them now. What was that conferred business about? What were they saying about me? Was that significant glance one of recognition? of pity?

Did she, just for a moment, think of turning the glass? Who did she want me to see? Who did she want to see me?

And I wonder why he stopped her, and I have come to understand. In understanding their motives I have come to understand my predicament and my immobility and myself, and I would gladly embrace all of these and accept them were it not for my need to know the shape and form and current criteria of that which I have lost.

Now most of my time is spent in dreaming, and when I run I pay attention less to the breathing and the pounding and the churning, and more to the breaking and the bursting and the dying.

BARRY MALZBERG's *stories—this is the sixth to appear in New Dimensions—have many virtues, but lightheartedness is not generally considered one of them. I think this is a lighthearted Malzberg story, though, as Malzberg stories go: an account of human/alien relations which, though superficially somber, is informed by an underlying playfulness that is always present on the deepest levels of his fiction.*

■

Barry N. Malzberg

■

REPORT TO HEADQUARTERS

Gentlemen: With considerable difficulty I have managed to compile the following primitive glossary of the X'Thi. Working under great pressure and in difficult circumstances as I have been, this was not an easy job and may be riddled with inaccuracy. Nevertheless, considering that I was able to assemble it within two cycles and *under exceedingly embarrassing personal situations* I think that it is a job of some quality.

Conditions here remain as stated in previous reports, and I hope that the rescue party is continuing with all due haste. I do not know how much longer I can hold out in these circumstances irretrievably alien, although they are, of course, trying to do everything to make me comfortable. Mooning season is approaching, however, I am warned by the X'Thi, and with it their apparent "decampment" (I think that this is the equivalent I am seeking) and they cannot take me with them. What am I supposed to do then, gentlemen? Stay here with diminishing supplies and die? You can understand my problem. You must render me help.

AZAPLI: The act of triring or having just trired, the retraction of tentacles; the tendency of tentacles to constrict the blood vessels when extended, leading to vascular suffering and, in extreme cases, sudden death. For this reason the X'Thi trire as little as possible, although triring is inevitable during Hok, a metaphysical situation. They are trying to reduce Hok, however.

BLOLOMITE: The principal substance of reduction, that substance which appears to be a metaphor for the Cosmic Jolt which, the X'Thi believe, resulted in the creation of the universe and their own central, crucial role in it. Blolomite can neither be seen, touched, tasted, heard nor felt but it is the major source of all energy. During Hok, Blolomite may be seen for brief flashes in the light of the paralleled moons.

COSMIC JOLT: That central, lurching force with which the X'Thi believe that the universe began; alternatively, that C.L.F. (I am using abbreviations in order to save transmission time and costs and hope that you appreciate this gesture) with which the universe will end; their conception of the known universe, and all of time for that matter, as being a loop or thread suspended between the poles of Cosmic Jolts. The interval between the first Cosmic Jolt and the second appears to be calculated, as neatly as I can manage this, as being in reductions of sixty to seventy trires.

A panic appears to have been created by the landing of the vehicle upon Coul's Planet; the impact sprang up little filaments of Blolomite and many of the X'Thi took this to be the second and the more jarring of the Cosmic Jolts. It may have been for this reason, the impact and the panic, the assault of the X'Thi upon the vehicle, which caused me to use the reactor. I regret this very much. I have communicated this regret to the X'Thi. They have accepted my apology. I do not believe that they will seek retaliatory action since they are a gentle and spiritual people, but cannot guarantee this.

COUL'S PLANET: I do not believe that there is any megalomania in my referring to this rather bucolic if gaseous world as the above. As *Coul's Planet.* The naming of territory after its discoverer has an old and honorable tradition dating back to the maritime industry and also from the early days of interplanetary survey. Coul's Planet, along with the remainder of the universe, was, as stated by the X'Thi, formed from the Cosmic Jolt an unimaginable interval ago and will similarly terminate in another. In another Cosmic Jolt. In the meantime it is composed of a series of noxious gases suspended by light gravity above a liquefied core: methane, hydrogen and nitrous oxide in equal parts circulate rather energetically around the unseen core. Here at the heart of Coul's Planet I reside, surrounded by the friendly steel and metal alloy bulkheads of this ship which protect me from the environment and which also through an intricate series of viewscope devices permit me to remain in contact with the X'Thi, the lords of this planet. I am located, to the best of my knowledge, some twenty-five hundred miles north of the equator, rather near to one of the snow-capped poles. The X'Thi have no name for their own planet. The stupid creatures! They say that its name is ineffable, known only to the Creator of the universe. Therefore I have given it its proper name.

DECAMPMENT: Shift of Coul's Planet in the cosmos which, according to the X'Thi, results in a necessary redistribution of gaseous materials which would otherwise become stagnant. Forming waste. Reconstitution of Blolomite during the decampment renders the planet safe until the next period, but grave shocks to the environment force the X'Thi into their annual rite of displacement which takes them to the northern pole through this period of readjustment. They cannot take me with them and that is why recovery efforts must be accelerated and why you must do everything within your power to save me from the horrors of unreconstituted Blolomite, slowly encircling this little craft in their dread dread tentacles which *I cannot retract.*

DISPLACEMENT, RITE OF: See DECAMPMENT.

E: That cosmic sound (emanating of course from the Cosmic Jolt) with which all creation began. According to myth of the

X'Thi, "E:" was the shout of the Creator as, in his anguish, he caused Coul's Planet to be.

HOK: Apparently a religious festival preceding decamp-ment. (See DECAMPMENT, DISPLACEMENT.) Alterations in the eco/geological balance signaling the advent of decamp-ment cause physical changes in the environment. Blolomite appears in dull flashes of energy, suddenly revealed to the naked eye. One can, during Hok, reach out and physically touch the Blolomite or endure the illusion that it can be touched as seen in the vibrating, varying light swinging from the equator to the poles, revealing the substance in all its dull luster, recapitulating as it were the appearance of the planet as it might have been during the Cosmic Jolt. During Hok the nor-mally tight sociopolitical patterns of the X'Thi are deliberately altered; there is a relaxation of stricture, prurience occurs, ran-dom contacts between individuals, a shattering of the socioeco-nomic sector so that all elements of the culture interweave and intermix during this celebration. During Hok even the lowest and humblest of the filthy creatures may cohabit with the rul-ers; even the rulers are allowed to throw off the necessary dignity of their office to fornicate with the populace: all of them fornicate and cohabit together; it is this which brings Hok to its climax and in the general exhaustion, guilt, debilitation which follow, the decampment and its consequent displacement then occur; but through all of this and after I will be confined to this vessel, the simulated bulkheads, the thick metal shielding, un-able to participate because exposure to the deadly gases of Coul's Planet would instantly kill me; all I would be able to do would be to rotate slowly in the contrived weightlessness of the ship, penitent, suffering, awaiting rescue and then, *after* Hok, in the darkness after decampment when all of them have gone to the poles and it is as if I will be the only individual left on the surface of the world . . . well, you should surely see why I await the rescue party with such unusual eagerness and anticipation and why it is all I can do to keep myself from tearing at the very bulkheads with frustration and rage; I can hardly bear the emotional exhaustion of Hok which, the X'Thi assure me, is almost upon us. *How much more of this can I stand to take?*

COUL, LEONARD (see also COUL'S PLANET): The discoverer of Coul's Planet. The intrepid and solitary voyager out of the Service who has dedicated his life to adventure, to the search for and achievement of new terrain, who has cheerfully, steadfastly, unblinkingly accepted the loneliness and danger of his trade, who has asked (until the moment of this disastrous event) absolutely no assistance from the Service but has merely accepted his duty as a given condition, now thirty-seven years old and fallen upon difficult times but still, still, gentlemen, of good courage and spirit, continuing his negotiations with the X'Thi, working upon this glossary which is a keyhole into their consciousness, performing his tasks within the difficult confinement of the ship uncomplainingly . . . all the time putting to one side any consideration of his wizened genitals, his tormented psyche, his diminished and abused consciousness which has put up with more, more, I must tell you, than any of you could conceive. Who, nevertheless, is Coul to complain? Hok comes upon him; Cosmic Jolts lay both before and ahead of him, somewhere in the middle of that great Loop of possibility he hangs doing his tasks, keeping up his optimism, knowing that in his hour or hours of need ye will not abandon him but will save him from all of this.

PARALLELED MOONS: Two moons track Coul's Planet, revolving around it in tandem much as Coul's possibilities may be said to darkly devolve around his core. The moons are linked yet separate, they are in similar orbits following duplicate trajectory separated only by a small wisp of space; for this reason they are referred to as "paralleled," although certain of the X'Thi disagree with this, saying that "simultaneous" would be a better mode of reference. The Cosmic Jolt has both an origin and a conclusion, the X'Thi (they are in their way a rather mystical people although they have no organized religion) state, all of the universe may be perceived as a duality, within each of us are not only (in many cases) paired organs but opposed motives, and these paralleled moons are projections of that duality, circling, circling Coul's Planet in the perpetual night of its sky. During Hok, Blolomite is revealed in flashes in the light of the paralleled moons (see BLOLOMITE). The paralleled moons, however, are composed of the same gaseous substance as is Coul's Planet; that is to say that it would be very difficult to get hold of them, even if they were not so impossibly distant, so impossibly huge.

TRIRE: See AZAPLI.

X'THI: The cheerful residents of Coul's Planet. The *natives* of Coul's Planet I should say rather; indigenous to its ecology and terrain, that essentially ebullient population whose rather arcane linguistics are at least mapped in this glossary, that essentially ebullient population with whom I have been in almost constant contact since my crash-landing and subsequent unsuccessful escape attempts from Coul's Planet some time ago.

The X'Thi are mystical without being religious, efficient without being organized, proprietary without being domineering; it can be said that they combine both the best and worst traits of their ecology in so being, although again this may merely be a projection of my own admittedly limited view of them and they may be both more or less than can be readily ascertained. What is there to be said of the X'Thi? Their physical appearance is amorphous; dimly glimpsed through the viewports of this sinking vessel they take on different colors and aspects with the changes of the day; part of this having to do with their own rather chameleonlike ability to partake of features of the terrain, part of it having to do with my own rather dazzled perceptions which due to hunger and increasing fright cannot be trusted as to consistency. The X'Thi themselves testify that their changing aspect may be due not to difficulties in sight or terrain but to the presence of Blolomite itself throughout the atmosphere: Blolomite has the sinister ability to distort reality into changing shapes and aspects; coming from the Cosmic Jolt and being put in place by the squawking "E:" of the Creator (whose identity, gentlemen, is unknown at the present time, the Creator being ineffable), it partakes of many qualities which may be beyond our ken and it can be said that to live on Coul's Planet as I have been forced to for this period of time may simply mean to be *immersed in Blolomite* as strange as this thought may be, immersed in Blolomite and circling forever dimly under the light of the parallel moons, the parallel moons streaking the heavens in their very duality. The X'Thi say that they cannot sustain me much longer in this environment, that as the time of decampment approaches they must more and more attend to their own difficult and necessary tasks preceding said decampment, that they will have to abandon me to my own devices in order that they may protect themselves. There is, they assure me, nothing at all personal about this abandonment, they are rather fond of me, they are fond of Leonard Coul, abandoned voyager in their midst, but their own survival is paramount and they must go about it in their own way. After all, Coul's Planet, the Cosmic Jolt, Hok and the decampment were around long before I was (to say nothing of Blolomite) and will similarly survive me by a good long period; they must pay proper obeisance to their traditions because without their traditions, where are they? An unanswerable question, gentlemen. Hok will begin, in glimmers of Blolomite as seen in the light of the parallel moons the Cosmic Jolt may be apperceived but the X'Thi will be gone, they will all be gone and I will be here alone, always alone, *unless efforts are made to speed up the rescue party at all costs,* to accelerate, that is to say, its efforts. In the meantime there is nothing to be done but to continue on my routine and essentially timekilling tasks, maintenance of the environment, eating, sleeping, the preparation of this glossary and so on. What will I do when Hok comes? The answer to that is unspeakable and I will cheerfully leave that question to you, gentlemen, being unable, quite, to deal with it myself.

Y: That cosmic sound (emanating, it is said, from the second Cosmic Jolt) with which creation will end. (See E.) According to the myths of the X'Thi, the Creator will cry "Y:" as Coul's Planet comes to an end, imploding toward ash in the sickly light of the wasted moons, small scraps of Blolomite dancing in the gases as in that explosive "Y:Y:Y:" all that the X'Thi will ever know shall end.

This haunting, dreamlike vision of the remote future is DREW MENDELSON's *first published story. He is a native of Kansas City, not quite thirty years old, and has lived in the San Francisco area since his college days. After studying astrophysics and communications at the University of California, he dropped out of college in 1967 to enlist in the army, serving as an officer in Vietnam. He returned in 1970 and is currently a free-lance writer and journalist.*

■

Drew Mendelson

∎

MUSEUM PIECE

If it is a Starry Night with Cypresses, this future twice a million years from now, it will be a scene that painters paint with palettes no more rich than Vincent's. With stars he bends the fabric sky to velvet maelstroms, pinwheel lights; they buffet flames of cypresses; they whorl the crystal night.

We are entering a colonnaded hall, the Lady and I. We are entering a hall with a floor of marble and tall stone pillars and a lofty ceiling arched high to climb above balconies. We are entering the gallery, the museum of the year 2,000,000 A.D. It is a breathtaking sight to stop and take in at once. Footsteps reverberating, whispers echoing, diminishing, heartbeats thundering, our breath hisses through teeth in a gale of possibility. All futures are here.

The Van Gogh hung at the gallery entrance is a painting as engulfing as any of those portraying the far future, and as evocative; for we find that the future is never the same place. No physicist discovers the same structure, no chemist the same composition, no biologist the same organisms, no anthropologist the same cultures, no archeologist the same history as any other visitor on any other visit.

"It was their choice to send a sculptor first to the future," says my Lady. "It is said that the future is for scientists, for those who can interpret it with a micrometer exactitude." But she notes, staring up at this finely proportioned mass of bronze we are seeing: "I am glad that they first sent an artist."

175

Here is a creature of the underground, huge eyed, slack lipped, who surfaced in the blackest night. It is locked in frozen battle with the highly evolved grandchild of man. The human descendant has a heavy skull buttressed with flying archways of bone appearing to contain the multifarious convolutions of an advanced brain. But, spindly frame buckling and straining, this intellectual giant out of the distant future of man is losing his battle with the fiendish creature out of the Earth's depths.

A whirl of potential is playing itself out in my head. Is the subterranean also a descendant of man? The statue haunts me. It is the ultimate combat.

A carillon rings us away while other couples gawk. The scale is an impossible construction of eleven tones. It is absolutely confusing unless you follow the skein unraveling with deliberation until it circles back. The elusive notes seem to climb continuously, teasing the ear with illusion as men climb a staircase in a closed upward spiral only to end at the first step.

Musicians explore our alternate space/time futures and return with melodic structures. Painters are found here also, their art reproducing the views they have captured. About this great hall the people of our time are circulating through paintings hung with glimpses of variant tomorrows.

A short chubby man stands before one painting where lead-soldier troops of a toyland army are marching. Their land is a place of puffball trees and sawdust-stuffed horses and gilded cannon and matchstick caissons. At the fore of the procession a tubby trumpeter with a furry high-peaked powder-blue hat raises his horn. Beside him is a nearly as short and fat drummer boy. Does the little man viewing this painting hear the note of the trumpet? Does the drum rattle his bones? Whose buffoon army is this, pennants unfurled and no foot out of step?

The Lady whispers to me as we pass him by, "Do you suppose he finds himself there in that marching column? Do you think he wishes he were there?" I smile as we step to the next.

Maple trees are rooted in an infinite lawn. The colors of the maple leaves are brilliant. The lawn recedes to an indefinite

horizon splashed with the vermilion excesses of the fallen
leaves. Where leaves do not stain the grass, the growth luxuri-
ates in a wash of sunlight touching it, pure, green. Seen from
a rocky knoll, randomly furred with moss, the landscape is perfect: Autumn.

"Who would have thought such a place as this could be
found?" Dancing voices in front of the hanging canvas chime
in agreement, with appreciation of color and brushwork and
inner light surpassing reality.

Spires rise to pierce the mist. A long-limbed man stares at this
canvas. His face mirrors the radiance of a hotter sun spreading
itself across a higher, whiter sky. Parapets stretch to become
lace walkways spanning the distance between towers. The most
lofty of the towers are so far away that the people placed by the
painter on ledges and bridges and filagreed escarpments are
only tiny bits of humanity. Perhaps the tall viewer finds here a
more perfect world than ours. The Lady again notes that the
viewer might almost be at home in the scene.

Touring the hall we find painters who see Earths as the obvious extrapolations of Now, and the strange expressions of Earths
alternatively to the one we know. The grotesque mixes with the
exquisite; the future extends itself with as many variations as
the past.

Nature fills her ecological ledges and crevasses. Nature fills
them as the nooks and crannies in an old roll-top desk, each with
her creations, each creature to its own niche, small or large,
short-lived or eternal. A variegated past stretches behind us. It
is inhabited by nightmare monsters that lived and died in the
Jurassic, filled with volcanic eruptions and solar flarings, earth-
quakes, tsunami, and storms. Can we expect the future to be
less?

The ultimate painting is purposefully hung to be the final
touch of art. For here, every bit as cruel and affecting and
eternal as the crucifixion of Christ, a painting of religious mar-
tyrdom hangs.

The eyes of this man are ethereal in their total unconcern for the anguish painted on other faces. One arm, an extra jolting joint long, extends toward his six fingers, delicate, spidery; gripping a binding rope, not in agony but in transfixion. It is as if this soul feels nothing of pain, carnal or spiritual.

Mixed despair and delight washes the faces of his tormentors, faces long with high cheekbones and deep-set eyes and pale feathery hair seeming to float away from the heads. It is night; the figures at the edges of the canvas fade into indistinct darkness, but the faces, hands and bodies of those close to the center are lighted in a burning incandescent glow by the climbing tongues of flame eating the pyre beneath the martyr's feet and licking upward along his robe.

Though there is no further evidence of religious union beyond this painting, no bible, no legend discovered, the alien-human caricature clothed in flames has inspired the birth of religion. It is crowded here. Before the turning in the corridor, the converts stare at the face: passage is impossible.

The whispered chants of a billion sects, prayer wheels flapping, follow us. Is the soft insistent clack just our footsteps touching on the hard marble floor, or is it the percussive lyric of the beadsman's litany clicking bead by bead through a morning's prayer?

The bright clear sun in an open court dissolves into the sound of the cloistered hall; the notes resolve into the crystal tinkle of a gemstone rose. We stop, touch.

The rose is a ruby flower twining its thorny vine about the double tier of a small fountain. It is singular. Where do crystal roses grow? Are there also brittle china birds in this world? Are there tourmaline dogs and cut-glass cows whose milk is onyx and porcelain froth? Who are the people? Does such a flower light the eyes of children, attracting bits and pieces of their hard polished world?

But though the rose glows, its thorns sting my fingers with a nettle's hotness, shattering the mood and sending us away.

Hardly released from the courtyard's dazzle, we are ensnared by the complex mysteries of the force engine. It is a delicate construction, giving us our first view of future science. The Earth of this engine is a port planet, the center of intragalactic enterprise. Vast starclippers, sprinting many times the speed of light, ply the deep space vacuums between the many suns. The secret of faster-than-light flight is tantalizingly simple. The schematic of this engine is an easily duplicated structure involving bronze and zinc and gossamer fine-drawn steel wire, inexpensively made. But some twist or mutation in the fabrics of our twin universes keeps the force engine from operating in our own space-time. Here, the space-sundering energies cannot find the perfect balances they require.

A physicist is standing here in wistful contemplation. It is possible that his fingers were the ones that formed the malleable metals. His thoughts follow the calculations which break the barrier of the speed of light, again and again affirming the same painful conclusion. The engine becomes nothing more than an enigmatic sculpture like the bronze combatants in the central hall.

."Come," bids my Lady, impatient to be off, "there is so much to see!" Spinning out and away from this central spot, the gallery is a helix and each display a vortex in its rising curve.

What we first encounter is the dreamland of entomologists and herpetologists. Here, we discover an ecological matrix entirely uninhabited by mammals. Creatures of every size and status peer out from photographs; smiling with mandibles, or sniffing with antennae, they fight gravity, wind, and sun with chitin in the place of skin and bone. In furious competition for these same life-sustaining ecological plateaus are the reptiles. Captions beneath the frames explain:

"Lizard efficiency at overcoming the natural forces of day-to-day life is pushing the reptiles to the fore. Here, reptilian life is replacing insect life in much the same manner as the dinosaurs were replaced by the mammals."

But does the slowness of the reptile brain preclude thought? Does the relative chemical simplicity of the insect biology prohibit intelligence? Is the cockeyed man-sized beetle really smiling with hidden glee at our smug analysis of its shortcomings? The mirage caused by the camera angle shows the alligator-snouted creature examining the pictured scientists with equal sly attention as they examine it.

The Lady is already past the exhibit and tugging me along by the hand. "See here," she cries. "What is this? A stone spear?" And she follows the striated rock from end to end along its stone pedestal.

It is, says the note, a core sample pierced into Earth by an unmanned expedition. We read its findings by means of a graph specially ruled to correspond to the age layers of the stone. Its story is that the Earth 2 Million is composed of rock of igneous birth. In the layers and compactions of tremendous depth nothing grows, nothing penetrates indicative of any life. What forces squeezed this Earth at an early age to diamond hardness? The scientists are baffled, and they refuse to offer conjecture. The stone is solid through all its length. Following the time line back to the point which atomic dating finds to be two million years old, no trace of our existence, no indication of our presence can be discovered in the preserved strata.

The Lady sniffs in disbelief. "One investigator," I offer to her in explanation, "claims that this phenomenon results from the myriad of potential futures to be examined. Proving, at least to his own satisfaction, that in some alternate time streams man never exists at all."

But we turn from one small discomfort to a larger one. If it is deflating to our egos to find the planet can get along just as well without the complication of humanity, it is doubly disconcerting to examine a solar system where the Earth itself never came to be. I am not alone in seeing the humor in this. My Lady is asking a man why he is laughing.

"You know what we have here?" the great pudgy gentleman inquires as his belly jiggles in an earthquake motion. His words dart out where and when they can between huge guffaws. "A joke, the funniest thing in the whole universe. It's funnier than clowns or comedians. It's funnier than a whole barrel full of monkeys!"

It is contagious mirth. Grinning ear to ear and rumbling again with his laughter he listens as the Lady asks, "Tell us, please!" and her mouth begins to grow into a delighted grin. The infectious laughter shakes all three of us, and the man tries to explain the joke.

"It is . . ." and he laughs, "that . . ." and he laughs. But he cannot continue and ends up by pointing at the huge photograph hung on the wall.

The joke, on us, is of cosmic proportions: While instrument readings prove that this is the exact point in space and the precise point in time where the Earth should be, an empty space hangs. No atmosphere intrudes to cloud the perfect observations of the telescopes. No planet revolves about the sun, or rotates through the diurnal cycle of day and night. No Earth disturbs the orbit of the moon. Only empty space is decorated with distant jewels of stars and the span of the Milky Way.

The moon, bloated by some of the matter which in other sequences makes up the bulk of the Earth, becomes alien with a thin atmosphere, fuzzy representations of clouds and pale blotches of green surrounding glints which may be water. How extraordinary for those who think the Earth to be the center of creation to find this scene. Will they laugh too?

"Here," she says. "Let's enter here." And she reads aloud the sign above an entryway: "This is perhaps the most alien space of all, the least understandable, the most unfathomable. Inside here you will encounter a substance which is only color. Two hundred thousand separate shades, hues and tones can be distinguished by the human eye. They are all here and more!"

What we see is: aquamarine to turquoise hues, blue as a baby's eyes, and beryl blue and cobalt blue . . . jade green and peacock green . . . verdigris so tinctured it seems to be the microscopic surface of some bronze statue turning to a sudden Nile green almost before you are aware of the change. Amethyst becomes lavender becomes plum bringing an instant of ripe fruit to the tongue before it is dashed in a carmine bath of excellent red which is now blood red then ruby red, scarlet and wine. These are the colors with names, the colors which can be picked out, defined, and remembered. They are familiar islands of stain across a vast spectrum; the mind cannot begin to recall all the infinite nuances.

Is this the palette of an artist working on a universal scale, the rainbow skin of another Earth whose constituent fabric has not the familiar palpability of matter but rather the guise of frequencies exposed to us one thread at a time?

At the exit an attendant leads away the color-dazed viewers. We stand blinking as he tells us: "It is many days before someone steeped in this varicolored wash can shed the memory and again see the world for what it is and not simply a pale tint of itself. You are lucky. See there!" and he points to the visitors whose rescue he has effected from the hypnosis of the display.

Earth, though, is the habitat of humanity. The ghost folk, the goblin creatures of impossible tomorrows, are below us now, stalking the lower corridors, the possible halls. But we have arrived at the highest balcony now to see others, like us, to see the diverse futures that were devised.

An elderly gentleman on whose arm an equally elderly and quite elegant lady is leaning turns the pages of an anthropological expedition.

They see a tribal warrior with a horrifying living mask tattooed on his face. He is wielding a vicious-looking spear and is apparently menacing the cameraman. The background is a jungle of riotous color and profuse life. The text explains:

"The dominant tribe is the Obofu, numbering about eight hundred. They inhabit the lowlands of a northwestern river valley, engaging in a rudimentary economy of slash-and-burn agriculture. They are seemingly very warlike, a highly protective people, but their actual sophistication in weaponry and battle tactics is slight. They attempt to avoid actual combat by fierce displays designed to frighten away their enemies.

"The Obofu are the most advanced race on the planet and have an involved and complex social structure . . ."

The elderly man and woman are following this breathtaking narrative of a primitive planet with its highest inhabitants barely out of the stone age, while behind them on the gallery wall is a towering photograph taken on another Earth. It depicts a monument to the preeminence of technology.

But not all means of warfare are so simple. Rounding a corner we are shocked by a grim chamber filled with military artifacts. She and I stand close.

A series of photographs of a space war fought in the absolute-zero vacuum shows an engagement with Laser heat weapons. Diaphanous clouds screen the ships from Laser energy. Now ships maneuver and penetrate the screens. Plates boil away from starship hulls. The traces of almost intelligent missiles weave through the battle, tracking, following, engaging, destroying the ships of the opposing fleet.

"I wish there were a way to know who won." But the outcome extrapolated from the evidence is a foregone conclusion. What I mean: Was it we or they?

Set in the center of this war room is a combat robot evolved nearly to the limit of destructive potential. Even frozen in eternal stasis it is still so menacing that few of the visitors will approach or examine it. This is the sole remaining relic of one future. It was found frozen amidst the ruin of a nearly perfect civilization. The Lady's eyes peer into mine. Have we taken a Tiger by the tail? There is nowhere to hide.

Battle maps hang from the walls. Lines of demarcation and axes of advance and fire concentrations and unit assaults speak in a language of military tactics and techniques. What does he think, the resplendently dressed general of our own army, standing before these maps?

What does he think especially (the Lady whispers to me) of the horrifying delineation of the conquest of the world of Now, this year, complete with casualty lists and martial-law decrees and refugee tallies? In one of our many possible futures will we experience the terrible degradation of a conqueror from the stars?

Though neither of us wishes to examine it, one record in this display indicates the method of disposition, whether by firing squad or slave camp, for every human now alive.

To complete this chamber are cases and cases of weapons, from stone-chipped flint to neutron blasters; the ultimate weapons of every age of man.

A low musical tone, very clear, very perfect, with delicately matched harmonics, peals out, abates and peals again. It becomes a background rhythm for a cascade of liquid notes. The music recedes as we move on through the balconies.

At the touch of a button a film plays out. People in strange dress of bright colors, mostly green and gold and scarlet red, with feathered caps, soft boots, and billowing pantaloons, are passing across the camera's eye, and the camera tracks to follow them. They are dancing, pirouetting, skipping along the way. As they pass, one of the people turns to stare with wide-open eyes at the camera. With vacant eyes he looks, an undecipherable smile playing on his face. Now, revolving away, he exits to join the throng skipping down the path. The eerie notes of a medieval piper trill among the moving humans. The tune is a spell to mesmerize and bind the listeners. At the front of the procession the tall, spare form of the piper twirls, leaping, dipping in time to the tune. This is the scene of Hamlin Town replayed; these are people who have tried to cheat the Pied Piper of some promised reward: they tread the same sad road.

The music awakens a longing in the listener: even separated by years and film and sound recording there is a compulsion. A cage of velvet ropes has been twined about this alcove where the images dance to protect the observers from blindly walking into the screen.

The enchanted characters of the time dance away along the path and the film ends abruptly. Was the photographer mesmerized by the song, so he, dancing, abandoning the camera, entered the ecstasy of the piper? The last few seconds of the film are undirected and whirr at an indefinite horizon.

"The camera?" I ask. The Lady's hand which I know holds mine is a ghostly sensation. Words are whispers through air gone thick as glue.

"I wonder," answers my Lady, "if this is what the crippled child felt when the mountain closed before him." And before the button can be pushed, enmeshing us, we pull ourselves out from this alcove where velvet ropes are scant guardians.

Suddenly haunted by this gallery we are now only skimming by the artifacts. An age-muted tapestry displays a sorcerer in the act of conjuring some terrible demon. The silly thought that this is merely imagined magic of a simple time flies before the fact that the tapestry is floating unsuspended by wire or wind or magnetic pulse.

A minute and beautiful china doll perches in a nook. But is it china? For the doll changes position with every blink of my eyes; first smiling, then serious, before she bursts into tears.

We stop to taste the wine. What is the vineyard? a master vintner asks. Through the ritual test of Bouquet, Body, Clarity and Taste, we see the tears welling in his eyes. He has encountered vintage Perfection before and will again. But not this. This wine was returned from the finest vintage year ever to grace the Earth. This, an unmatched excellence, trickles down my throat, trickles only, for the decanted drop is a precious rarity which cannot be replaced.

As the vintner leaves, the attendant explains, watching our faces as we sip, and gloating a bit with proprietary enjoyment: "That vintner will never practice his craft again; he knows he can never achieve this."

There is nowhere, yet, a finished chronicle. As we search out the museum's displays we find ourselves in a small auditorium. Two civilizations unfold themselves here, contrasted across the depths of social possibility.

One portrays a life of absolute freedom with but one law: No hurt shall be done to anyone. It is the nature of the viewer watching the projection of slide after slide and listening to this recounting of the good and wise and loving culture to be almost fearful of anything such as this ever coming to pass.

"How?" is questioned, echoed back and forth across the chamber through an audience digesting this information. The anthropologists who studied there came back to explain: These folk have no word for kill and none for pain and none for steal or hunger or death.

"Empty lives!" mutters a skeptic at the end of the showing.

"All enjoyment has been taken from them," complains a second.

"Balance," another agrees. "Without evil there can be no good, and thus there is no balance!"

"It must be boring."

But boredom is hurt, and humbleness taken to its extreme becomes haughtiness, and without expectation there can be no surprise. So the authors of this most perfect utopia planned for all objections. What is most apparent is that the scientists returning here found they could not understand this way of life.

"There is a magic formula here," admits one of the anthropologists, "and we didn't find it. We were told we could return to our own time with no more than the image of their civilization. They said that as long as we feel the need for such contrasts we will be fated to search in vain for their secret." Peering out over the audience he concludes in a wistful voice, "It is as if one had found the key to unimaginable wealth; the secret being to stir a kettle full of boiling lead until it turns to gold. But never never through all the process to think of a green rhinoceros."

Beyond his whisper a structure of evil is appearing. It is one so ugly that the observer is infected with a nameless horror and a terrible chill. The hideous days of the Nazi Reich are multiplied and imposed once more upon the planet and echoed, reinforced, magnified in intensity. Again the marchers gather in blackest night, raising torches to scrawl across an achingly familiar landscape the twisted fire cross. Again the banshee wails of chained voices rise, flailing at the night and the flaming torches, thundering loyalty to a manic master. Boxcars are filled with persons as no more than human refuse until they are led away to be denied life. Ovens gape, and mounds of starved corpses hardly human for lack of anything but skin stretched over fragile bone gaze blankly at us.

"Unspeakable!" cries the audience.

"Hideous!"

"How could they show this here? Nightmares will destroy my sleep. Why did they have to present me with these deathmongers?"

But the question not asked is even more horrendous: How could such an evil come to be? The precedent is far too familiar to be misunderstood. The audience escapes.

Down the splintered mirrored Earths we are pursued by the images of possible existences. Bursting through planets of ape-men and across the courtyard of the gemstone rose, through the shifting spectrum of marble halls we stand gasping at last at the door to reality. The crowd is dispersing one by one into the fractured tomorrows.

Is it imagination? Does the man exiting from the gallery before us seem to be growing taller, more angular of limb? He is stepping out on a diamond path rising above the flagstone walkway. His eyes glitter now with icy brilliance; his gaze sights on an ephemeral landscape composed of onion domes and high minarets.

The elderly couple strolling arm in arm find it strange that their footsteps are falling on the delicate skin of fragile tundra above an Earth of permafrost. The physicist stepping out from the portal begins to traverse a foothill slope. He continues on toward highlands peaked in snow cascading crag upon crag down to where the gnarled pines exist upon the snowline.

The chubby cherubic gentleman is hardly surprised that his feet are marching in step to martial music of drum and high clear trumpet call while his frame grows still more squat and his clothing becomes a baggy uniform.

Can the tall general in his own resplendent uniform be altering into a stooped, fur-clad cave creature? Do his fingers become short and stubby, itch to take up brush and paint to smear cave paintings in earth colors of stick-figure men and larger-than-life beasts; pictures portraying heroic conquests spanning only acres of the whole wide world?

Is it imagination? The jungles become meadowlands, become pampas, become veldt. The high specks in the bright sky alter from eagle soaring, to impossible roc flailing the almost too thin atmosphere, to helicopter flaring, to rocket, to kite triangular tugging at the end of a mile-high string, and for an instant to batwinged furry human who plummets down along a swift parabola skimming the night side of Earth.

Is it our imagination? The Lady and I begin to walk into our own version of the future. Is it not chimera, this ridge, this slope, this incline, grade? Behind, the gallery disgorges visitors. But the Lady and I climb up the steep hill and find unveiled beyond: a pale green sky, a yellow-lime sun. Can the shape below the mandala sun ever be Vincent's Sower again? Stretching across iced clouds, thick with blunt knife strokes, is the stark black stump of a truncated branch in its reach to heaven. Is it not illusion? If not, whose Earth is this?

Alabama-born GREGORY BENFORD *is a theoretical physicist who took his doctorate at the University of California at San Diego; for the past few years he has been Associate Professor of Physics at that university's Irvine campus, where he does research in controlled thermonuclear fusion. His science-fiction stories have been appearing professionally since 1965; they include two novels,* Deeper Than the Darkness *(1970) and* The Jupiter Project *(1972), the novella "Threads of Time" (1974), and several dozen shorter works. Though his fiction has always been marked by strong emphasis on scientific extrapolation, he has in recent years also become concerned with contemporary modes of literary expression.*

■

Gregory Benford

∎

WHITE CREATURES

> And after let me lie
> On the breast of the darkening sky.
> —JOAN ABBE

The aliens strap him in. He cannot feel the bindings but he knows they must be there; he cannot move. Or perhaps it is the drug. They must have given him something because his world is blurred, spongy. The white creatures are flowing shapes in watery light. He feels numb. The white creatures are moving about him, making high chittering noises. He tries to fix on them but they are vague formless shapes moving in and out of focus. They are cloudy, moving too fast to see, but he knows they are working on him. Something nudges his leg. For a moment something clicks at his side. Two white creatures make a dull drone and fade into the distance. All sensations are formless and cloudy; the air puckers with moisture. He tries to move but his body is lethargic, painless, suspended. There is gravity; above, a pale glow illuminates the room. Yes, he is in a room. They have not brought him to their ship; they are using human buildings. He cannot remember being captured. How many people do they have? When he tries to focus on the memory it dissolves and slips away. He knows they are experimenting on him, probing for something. He tries to recall what happened but there are only scraps of memory and unconnected bunches of facts. He closes his eyes. Shutting out the murky light seems

191

to clear his mind. Whatever they have given him still affects his body, but with concentration the vagueness slips away. He is elated. Clarity returns; thoughts slide effortlessly into place. The textures of his inner mind are deep and strong.

Muddy sounds recede. If he can ignore the white creatures things become sharp again. He knows he must get free of the white creatures and he can only do that if he can understand what is happening. He is absolutely alone and he must fight them. He must remember. He tries. The memories resolve slowly with a weight of their own. He tries.

◆

He cut across the body of the wave, awash in churning foam. The clear Atlantic was startlingly cold. The waves were too small for boards but Merrick was able to body-surf on them easily. The momentum carried him almost to shore. He waded through the rippling currents and began jogging down the beach. After a moment his wind came to him and he ran faster. His long stride devoured the yards. He churned doggedly past forests of firm bodies; the beach was littered with Puerto Ricans. The tropical sun shimmered through a thin haze of sweat that trickled into his eyes. As his arms and legs grew leaden he diverted himself with glimpses of the figures and faces sliding by, moving stride by stride into his past. His mind wandered. Small families, leathery men, dogs and children—he made them all act out plays in his head, made them populate his preconceived universe. That was where he saw Erika Bascomb for the second time. He had met her at a reception some months before, known her only as the a distant smiling wife of the Cyclops director. She sat on the sand, arms braced behind, and followed his progress. Her deliciously red lips parted in a smile more than mere welcoming and he slowed, stopped. His thickening waistline showed his age, thirty-eight, but his legs were as good as ever; strong, tanned, no stringy muscles or fine webbed nets of blue veins. Erika was a few years younger, heavily tanned from too much leisure time. So he stopped. He

remembered that day better than any of the others. She was the
first fresh element in his life for years, an antidote to the tedious
hours of listening that filled his nights with Cyclops. He remembered her brown nipples pouting and the image dissolved into
the green and brown swath of jungle that ringed the Cyclops
project. The directional radio telescopes were each enormous,
but ranked together in rigid lanes they added up to something
somehow less massive. Each individual dish tipped soundlessly
to cup an ear at the sky. The universe whispered, exciting a
tremor of electrons in the metal lattice. He spent his days and
nights trying to decipher those murmurs from eternity. Pens
traced out the signals on graph paper and it was his lot to scan
them for signs of order and intelligence. Bascomb was a pudgy
radio astronomer intent on his work who tried to analyze each
night's returns. Erika worked there as a linguist, a decoder for
a message which never came. Merrick was merely a technician,
a tracer of circuits. Project Cyclops had begun in earnest only
the year before and he had landed a job with it after a decade
of routine at NASA. When he came they were just beginning to
search within a two-degree cone about the galactic center, looking for permanent beacons. If the galactic superculture was
based in the hub, this was the most probable search technique.
That was the Lederberg hypothesis, and as director Bascomb
adopted it, supported it; and when it failed his stock in the
project dropped somewhat. One saw him in the corridors late
at night, gray slacks hanging from a protruding belly, the perpetual white shirt with its crescent of sweat at the armpits.
Bascomb worked late, neglected his wife, and Erika drifted into
Merrick's orbit. He remembered one night when they met at
the very edge of the bowl valley and coupled smoothly beneath
the giant webbing of the phased array. Bascomb was altering
the bandwidth of the array, toying with the frequencies between the hydroxyl line and the 21-centimeter hydrogen resonance. Merrick lay in the lush tropical grass with Erika and
imagined he could hear the faint buzzing of hydrogen noise as
it trickled from the sky into the Cyclops net, bearing random

messages of the inert universe. Bascomb and his bandwidth, blind to the chemical surges of the body. Bascomb resisting the urgings of Drake, Bascomb checking only the conventional targets of Tau Ceti, Epsilon Eridani, the F and G and K stars within thirty light-years. Politics, a wilderness of competition and ideals and guesses. He tried to tell Erika of this but she knew it already, knew the facts anyway, and had tired of them. A linguist with nothing to translate. She waited for a mutter from the sky, but waiting dulled the mind and sharpened the senses. She shook her head when he spoke of it, fingers pale and white where she gripped the grass with compressed energy, head lowered as he took her from behind. Blond strands hung free in the damp jungle twilight. Her eyelids flickered as his rhythm swelled up in her; she groaned with each stroke. The galaxy turned, a white swarm of bees.

◆

The aliens seize him. He struggles against the padded ghost-like webbing. He moves his head a millimeter to see them but he cannot focus, cannot bring things to a point. The white creatures are patches of light. They make chittering shrieks to each other and move about him. Their images ripple and splinter; light cannot converge. They are performing experiments on humans. He tilts his head and sees a plastic tube snaking in from infinity. There is a fetid smell. The tube enters his nostril and penetrates his sinuses. Something flows into him or out of him—there seems little difference—and his perceptions shift and alter again. The white creatures make a nugget of pain within him. He tries to twist away but his body is full of strange weaknesses, limbs slack. His face crinkles with pain. He feels delicate tremors, minute examinations at points along his legs and belly. He is an animal on the dissecting table and the white creatures are high above him, taller than men. Their rapid, insect-like gestures melt into the murky liquid light. They are cutting him open; he feels the sharp slitting in his calf. He opens his mouth to scream but nothing comes out. They will break

him into parts; they will turn him inside out and spill his brains
into a cup. His fluids will trickle onto cracked linoleum, be
absorbed into the parched eternal earth. Do they know that he
is male? Is this what they want to find out? Siphon away hor-
mones, measure blood count, trace the twisted DNA helix, find
the sense of rotation in body sugar? What are they after? What
could they use? He shuts them out, disconnects from the dense
flooded universe outside his eyelids. He thinks.

◆

Erika continued to meet him. There were sly deceptions,
shopping expeditions in the town, Erika in a Peter Pan collar
and cable-stitch cardigan; tan, arranged, intent, as much a
monument to an America now vanished as a statue of Lincoln.
Neat, making casual purchases, then into the back hotel room
and coiled about him in sweaty ecstasy. She whispered things
to him. That Bascomb was pale and soft underneath his clothes,
a belly of suet, mind preoccupied with problems of planning,
signal-to-noise ratios, search strategies. Listening to her secrets,
Merrick thought uneasily that he was not that different from
Bascomb, he believed the same things, but his body was hard
and younger than the other man's. Erika had gradually drifted
into the public relations office of Cyclops; as a linguist she had
nothing to do. She escorted the oil-rich Arabs around the bowl-
shaped valley, flattered the philanthropists who supported the
project, wrote the press releases. She was good, she was clever,
she made connections. And one day when Bascomb appeared
suddenly in the hotel room, entering into the holy place of sighs
and groans unannounced, she was ready. Merrick did not know
what to do, saw himself in a comic role of fleeing adulterer, out
the window with half his clothes and into the streets, running.
But there was none of that. They were all very civilized. Erika
said little, simply put on her clothes and left with Bascomb. The
silence was unnerving. Merrick did not see her for two weeks
and Bascomb never came into Merrick's part of the technical
shop. A while later the rumor spread that Erika had left Bas-

comb, and before he could check it she was gone. She went to South America, they said, and he wondered why. But he knew quite well why he got the less desirable shifts now, why he was passed over for promotion, why he was transferred to the least likable foreman in the project. He knew.

◆

The white creatures are gone for a while. Perhaps it is night. He lies with prickly points radiating in his body where they had cut him. He feels pierced and immobile, a butterfly pinned to a board. Blurred globs of cloudy sensation wash over him. Occasionally an alien passes through the murky light in the distance. The pale glow from the ceiling seems yellow. He wonders if he can deduce anything from this. He must try to gather scraps of information. Only through knowledge can he discover their weaknesses. Yellow light. A G-type star? The sun is a G-type and appears white in space. What would it look like beneath an atmosphere somewhat different from Earth's? It is impossible to say; there are so many kinds of stars: O and B and A and F and G and K and M. The O's are fierce and young, the M's red, aged, wise. O Be A Fine Girl, Kiss Me. He remembers Drake arguing that the search strategy should not include M types because the volume around them supporting a terrestrial-type planet would be so small. They would be locked by tides to their primary, said Dole. Merrick cannot follow the argument.

◆

He left Puerto Rico after two years of gradual pressure from Bascomb. Erika severed her n-year marriage contract with Bascomb from Chile. Merrick was in Washington, D.C., doing routine work for NASA again, when he received her first letter. She had become a guide for the wealthy rising capitalists of Brazil, Chile, Argentina. She showed them the North American continent, carefully shepherding them around the polluted areas and the sprawling urban tangle. There was a market for that sort of talent; the insulation between social classes was breaking down in America. Erika could shuttle her group of rising capitalists from hotel to sea resort to imitation ranch, all the while preserving their serenity by taking care of all dealings with the natives. Her customers invariably spoke no English. She passed through Washington every few months and they began their affair again. He had other women, of course, but with Erika new doors of perception opened. Her steamy twists and slides never failed to wrap him in a timeless cloak. The dendrites demanded, the synapses chorused, ganglia murmured and the ligaments summoned; they danced the great dance. She forced him to cling to his youth. Between their rendings in the bedroom she would pace the floor energetically, generating piles of cigarette butts and speaking of everything, anything, nothing. He did not know if he ever really learned anything from her but that furious drive onward. She was no longer a girl: the slight slackening of age, the first bluntings of a world once sharp-edged, had begun. She could not deal with it. He saw the same beginnings in himself but ignored them, passed them over. Erika could not accept. The thought of juices souring within her made her pace furiously, smoke more, eat with a fierce energy. She knew what was coming. She saw. She had forgotten Alpha Centauri, Tau Ceti, the aching drifting silences.

◆

The white creatures move in the watery light. He wonders suddenly if they swim in a liquid. He is in a bubble, moored to the bottom of a pool of ammonia, a plastic interface through which they study him. It explains much. But no, one brushes against his bed in passing and Merrick feels the reassuring vibration. They can breathe our atmosphere. They come from some place quite similar, perhaps guided by our UHF or VHF transmissions. He thinks this through. The North Canadian Defense Network is gone, victim of international treaties. There is cable television, satellite relay. Earth no longer emits great bursts of power in those frequency bands. It has ceased to be a noisy signal in the universe. How did the white creatures find

Earth? Why did Cyclops find nothing? We are not alone, the white creatures found us, but are all the other civilizations simply listening, can no one afford beacons? The white creatures do not say. Except for them is it a dead wheeling galaxy of blind matter? He cannot believe that.

◆

He transferred to California in his late forties. There were still Mariners and Vikings, gravity-assisted flights to the outer planets, Mars burrowers and balloons for the clouds of Venus, sun skimmers and Earth measurers. He wanted that sort of work. It seemed to him as the years went on that it was the only thing worth doing. Cyclops was sputtering along, torn by factionalism and the eternal silence at twenty-one centimeters. He went to Los Angeles to do the work even though he hated the city; it was full of happy homogeneous people without structure or direction. While on the bus to work, it seemed to him Los Angeles went on long after it had already made its point. There were women there and people worth talking to, but nothing that drew him out of himself. Instead he concentrated on circuits and design work. Mazes of cold electrical logic had to be planted in delicate substrates. There were details of organization, of scheduling procedures, of signal strength and redundancy probability. To Erika all this was the same; she had lost interest in these matters when she left Bascomb. Her business was thriving, however, and she had picked up a good series of contacts with China's subtle protectors of the people. These gentlemen were the new international rich who vacationed in the New World because the currency differential was favorable and, of course, increasing such contacts was good for the advancement of the ideas of Marx and Lenin and Mao. They came to see Disneyland, the beaches, the few tattered remnants of California history. But they remained in their hotels at night (even Los Angeles had muggers by then) and Erika could come to him whenever she chose. She was drinking more then and smoking one pack of cigarettes after another, choking the ash-

Table 2. Comparison of Forecasts, 1964 and 1977 Developments

1964 statement	1977 statement	1964 median	1977 median	correlation
Availability of a machine which comprehends standard IQ tests and scores above 150	Same; comprehend is understood as ability to respond to questions in English, accompanied by diagrams	1990	1992	About the same; larger deviation from median in 1977
Permanent base established on the moon (ten men, indefinite stay)	Same	1982	1992	Later, a less optimistic forecast
Economic feasibility of commercial manufacture of many chemical elements from subatomic building blocks	Same	2100	2012	Earlier, a more optimistic forecast
Two-way communication with extraterrestrials	Discovery of information that proves the existence of intelligent beings beyond Earth (note change of wording; bias for earlier forecast)	2075	2025	Earlier, as expected
Commercial global ballistic transport (including boost-glide techniques)	Same	2000	2030	Later, though less deviation from median in 1977

tray. The lines were lengthening around her eyes and on her forehead. Despite tanning and exercise and careful diet, age was catching her and in her business that was nearly fatal. She depended on her charm, gaiety, lightness; the South Americans and Chinese liked young Americans, blond Americans. Erika was still witty and shrewd, sometimes warm, but her long legs, thin wrists, tight and sleek tanned skin were losing their allure.

So she came to him frequently for solace and did not notice that he aged as well. She came to him again and again, whenever possible. He opened her. She stretched thin in the quilted shadows of his apartment, a layer one molecule thick that wrapped him in a river of musk. They made a thick animal pant fill the room until the sound became larger than they could control; they left it and went back to speaking with smoke fingers. He knew what to say. Erika moved under him. Above him. Through him. Some natural balance was lost in her, some sureness. He saw for a moment what it was and then she groaned and no longer did he know what he was about. O Be A Fine Girl, Open To Me.

♦

They come to him in watery silence and slice him again. The smokelike strands keep him from struggling and needlepoints sting, cut, penetrate to marrow. These are no coded cries across hydrogen. These are real. The white creatures dart in and out of the mosaic around him. He looks beyond them and suddenly sees a cart go by with a body upon it. A human is trussed and bound, dead. The white creatures ignore the sight. They work upon him.

♦

She began to lose patronage. The telephone rang less often and she made fewer trips to California. She began smoking more and picked at her food, afraid to ingest too many carbohydrates or fats that lengthen the lines and make the tissues sag. You have always lived in the future, she said. You love it, don't you. That's why you were at Cyclops and that's why you are with NASA. Yes, he said. Then what do you think of it now, she said. What do you think of your future? He shrugged. What do you think of mine, then? he said. A long slide down the back slope of the hill. It's harder for a woman, you know. I haven't got anyone. Bascomb is dead, you know. She snuffed out a cigarette. The failure of the project killed him, Merrick said.

Erika studied the back of her hand. Her lips moved and she traced the fine webbing of lines with a fingernail. It's all down-hill, she said absently. And then, abruptly: But not me. I'm not going to let it happen to me. He gave her a wry smile and lifted an eyebrow. She had drunk a lot of red wine and he attributed everything she said to that. No, I really mean it. She looked at him earnestly. I have some money now. I can do it now. What? he asked. The long sleep. He was shocked. He fumbled with his apartment keys and they made a hollow clanking sound in the sudden silence. You won't do that, he said. Of course I will. Her eyes blazed and she was suddenly filled with fire. Things will be different in the future, she said. We can't even get organ re-placements without special approval now. I'm sure that will be different in a few decades and I know there will be some way to retard aging by that time. He frowned doubtfully. No, she went on, I'm sure of it. I'm going to have myself frozen. I would rather take the chance on that than live out my life the way it must be from now on. Merrick did not know how to deal with her. He took her home and saw her again the next day but she was an Erika changed now. In the long dry California night she sat astride him and rocked and wriggled her way to her own destination. Her breasts loomed over him like gravestones. Even when he was within the sacred pocket of her she was an island bound for the frozen wastes. He did not let her see him cry.

◆

Stephen Dole. Parameters for quasi-terrestrial planets.
—surface gravity between 0.68 G and 1.5 G.
—mean annual temperature of 10% of planetary surface be-tween 0 and 30 degrees C. Seasonal variance not to exceed $\pm$ 10 degrees C.
—atmospheric pressure between 0.15 and 3.4 Earth sea level. Partial pressure of oxygen between 107 and 400 Torr.
—surface between 20% and 90% covered with water.
—rainfall between 10 and 80 inches annually.

—dust levels not to exceed 50 million particles per cubic foot. Winds and storms infrequent. Low seismic activity.

—ionizing radiation must not exceed 0.02 Rem per week.

—meteor infall rate comparable to Earth normal.

—oxygen-producing life forms or suitable ammonia or methane-based biochemistry.

—star on main sequence between types F2 and K1.

—no nearby gas giant planets. Planet must not be tidelocked to primary star.

—stable orbits within the ecosphere.

—for habitation by men, eccentricity of planetary orbit must not exceed 0.2. Period of rotation between 2 and 96 hours. Axial tilt must be less than 80%.

◆

Throughout the next year he tried to reason with her. There was so little hope of being revived. True, they were successfully bringing back people from nitrogen temperatures, 77 degrees Kelvin, but the cost was enormous. Even if she put her name on the public waiting list it could be decades before she was called, if ever. So she carefully took out the papers and documents and showed him the bank accounts in Mexico City, Panama, Melbourne, San Francisco. She had concealed it from him all the years, her steadily amassing assets that never showed in her style of living or her choice of friends. He began to realize that she was a marvelously controlled woman. She had leeched an Argentine businessman of hundreds of thousands while she was his mistress. She had made sound speculations in the land markets of rural Brazil. She withdrew from the stock market just before the catastrophe of '93. It seemed incredible but there it was. She had the money to insure that she would be revived when something fundamental had been achieved in retarding aging. He realized he did not truly know her, yet he wanted to. There was a long silence between them and then she said, you know this feeling? She threw her head back. Her blond hair swirled like a warm, dry fluid in the air.

Yes, sure, Merrick said. She looked at him intensely. I've just begun to realize that isn't what you're about, she said. You're married to something else. But that instant of feeling and being alive is worth all your ideals and philosophies.

He mixed himself a drink. He saw he did not know her.

◆

The white creatures come again. He is so small, compared to his scream.

◆

He went with her to the Center. There were formalities and forms to be signed, but they evaporated too soon and the attendant led her away. He waited in a small cold room until she reappeared wearing a paper smock. Erika smiled uncertainly. Without makeup she was somehow younger but he knew it would be useless to say so. The attendants left them alone and they talked for a while about inconsequential things, recalling Puerto Rico and Washington and California. He realized they were talking about his life instead of hers. Hers would go on. She had some other port of call beyond his horizon and she was already mentally going there, had already left him behind. After an hour their conversation dribbled away. She gave him a curiously virginal kiss and the attendants returned when she signaled. She passed through the beaded curtain. He heard their footsteps fade away. He tried to imagine where she was going, the infinite cold nitrogen bath in which she would swim. She drifted lazily, her hair swirling. He saw only her gravestone breasts.

◆

Merrick worked into the small hours of the morning at the Image Processing Laboratory. The video monitor was returning data from the Viking craft which had landed on the surface of Titan the day before. Atmospheric pressure was 0.43 Earth sea level. The chemical processors reported methane, hydrogen,

some traces of ammonia vapor. The astrophysicists were watching the telemetered returns from the onboard chemical laboratory and Merrick was alone as he watched the computer con-
trast-enhancement techniques fill in line by line the first
photographic returns. Through his headphones he heard the
bulletins about the chemical returns. There was some evidence
of amino acids and long-chain polymers. The chemists thought
there were signs of lipids and the few reporters present scurried
over to that department to discuss the news. So it was that
Merrick became the first man to see the face of Titan. The hills
were rocky, with dark grainy dust embedded in ammonia ice.
A low methane cloud clung to the narrow valley. Pools of methane lay scattered among boulders; the testing tendrils of the
Viking were laced through several of the ponds. There was life.
Scattered, rudimentary, but life. With aching slowness, some
simple process of reproduction went on in the shallow pools at
167 degrees Kelvin. Merrick watched the screen for a long time
before he went on with the technician's dry duties. It was the
high point of his life. He had seen the face of the totally alien.

◆

Some years later, seeking something, he visited the Krishna
temple. There was a large room packed with saffron-robed
figures being lectured on doctrine. Merrick could not quite tell
them what he wanted. They nodded reassuringly and tried to
draw him out but the words would not come. Finally they led
him through a beaded curtain to the outside. They entered a
small garden through a bamboo gate, noisily slipping the
wooden latch. A small man sat in lotus position on a broad swath
of green. As Merrick stood before him, the walnut-brown man
studied him with quick, assessing yellow eyes. He gestured for
Merrick to sit. They exchanged pleasantries. Merrick explained
his feelings, his rational skepticism about religion in any form.
He was a scientist. But perhaps there was more to these matters
than met the eye, he said hopefully. The teacher picked up a
leaf, smiling, and asked why anyone should spend his life study-

ing the makeup of this leaf. What could be gained from it? Any form of knowledge has a chance of resonating with other kinds, Merrick replied. So? the man countered. Suppose the universe is a parable, Merrick said haltingly. By studying part of it, or finding other intelligences in it and discovering their viewpoints, perhaps we could learn something of the design that was intended. Surely the laws of science, the origin of life, were no accident. The teacher pondered for a moment. No, he said, they are not accidents. There may be other creatures in this universe, too. But these laws, these beings, they are not important. The physical laws are the bars of a cage. The central point is not to study the bars, but to get out of the cage. Merrick could not follow this. It seemed to him that the act of discovering things, of reaching out, was everything. There was something immortal about it. The small man blinked and said, it is nothing. This world is an insane asylum for souls. Only the flawed remain here. Merrick began to talk about his work with NASA and Erika. The small man waved away these points and shook his head. No, he said. It is nothing.

◆

On the way to the hospital he met a woman in the street. He glanced at her vaguely and then a chill shock ran through him, banishing all thoughts of the cancer within. She was Erika. No, she only looked like Erika. She could not be Erika, that was impossible. She was bundled up in a blue coat and she hurried through the crisp San Francisco afternoon. A half block away he could see she did not have the same facial lines, the same walk, the bearing of Erika. He felt an excitement nonetheless. The turbulence was totally intellectual, he realized. The familiar vague tension in him was gone, had faded without his noticing the loss. He felt no welling pressure. As she approached he thought perhaps she would look at him speculatively but her glance passed through him without seeing. He knew that it had been some time now since the random skitting images of women had crossed his mind involuntarily. No fleshy feast of thighs, hips, curving waists, no electric flicker of eyelashes that ignited broiling warmth in his loins. He had not had a woman in years.

The hospital was only two blocks farther but he could not wait. Merrick found a public restroom and went in. He stood at the urinal feeling the faint tickling release and noticed that the word BOOK was gouged in square capitals in the wall before him. He leaned over and studied it. After a moment he noticed that this word had been laid over another. The F had been extended and closed to make a B, the U and C closed to O's, the K left as it was. He absorbed the fact, totally new to him, that every FUCK could be made into a BOOK. Who had done the carving? Was the whole transition a metaphysical joust? The entire episode, now fossilized, seemed fraught with interpretation. Distracted, he felt a warm trickle of urine running down his fingers. He fumbled at his pants and shuffled over to the wash basin. There was no soap but he ran water over his wrinkled fingers and shook them dry in the chill air. There was a faint sour tang of urine trapped in the room, mingling with the ammonia odor of disinfectant. Ammonia. Methane. Titan. His attention drifted away for a moment and suddenly he remembered Erika. That was her in the street, he was sure of it. He looked around, found the exit and slowly made his way up the steps to the sidewalk. He looked down the street but there was no sign of her. A car passed; she was not in it. He turned one way, then the other. He could not make up his mind. He had been going that way, toward the hospital. Carrying the dark heavy thing inside him, going to the hospital. That way. But this —he looked in the other direction. Erika had walked this way and was moving rather quickly. She could easily be out of sight by now. He turned again and his foot caught on something. He felt himself falling. There was a slow gliding feel to it as though the falling took forever and he gave himself over to the sensation without thought of correcting it. He was falling. It felt so good.

◆

The aliens are upon him. They crowd around, gibbering. Blurred gestures in the liquid light. They crowd closer; he raises his arm to ward them off and in the act his vision clears. The damp air parts and he sees. His arm is a spindly thread of bone, the forearm showing strings of muscle under the skin. He does not understand. He moves his head. The upper arm is a sagging bag of fat, and white. The sliding marbled slabs of flesh tremble as he strains to hold up his arm. Small black hairs sprout from the gray skin. He tries to scream. Cords stand out on his neck but he can make no sound. The white creatures are drifting ghosts of white in the distance. Something has happened to him. He blinks and watches an alien seize his arm. The image ripples and he sees it is a woman, a nurse. He moves his arm weakly. O Be A Fine Girl, Help Me. The blur falls away and he sees the white creatures are men. They are men. Words slide by him; he cannot understand. His tongue is thick and heavy and damp. He twists his head. A latticework of glass tubes stands next to his bed. He sees his reflection in a stainless-steel instrument case: hollow pits of his eyes, slack jaw, wrinkled skin shiny with sweat. They speak to him. They want him to do something. They are running clean and cool. They want him to do something, to write something, to sign a form. He opens his mouth to ask why and his tongue runs over the smooth blunted edge of his gums. They have taken away his teeth, his bridge. He listens to their slurred words. Sign something. A release form, he was found in the street on his way to check in. The operation is tomorrow—a search, merely a search, exploratory . . . he wrenches away from them. He does not believe them. They are white creatures. Aliens from the great drifting silences between the stars. Cyclops. Titan. He has spent his life on the aliens and they are not here. They have come to nothing. They are speaking again but he does not want to listen. If it were possible to close his ears—

But why do they say I am old? I am still here. I am thinking, feeling. It cannot be like this. I am, I am . . . Why do they say I am old?

One of the least enthralling chores of editorship is to write the introductory copy—"blurbs"—that occupies the space in front of stories. Here is MICHAEL BISHOP *again, with what I hope is a set of blurbs to end all blurbs.*

■

Michael Bishop

■

THE CONTRIBUTORS TO
PLENUM FOUR

PLENUM *is a continuing anthology-package of the best original holovistic universes now being conceived in our galaxy.*
PLENUM FOUR *is the latest distinguished entry in this series.*
PLENUM'*s editor, Ethelstan Bem, has culled these totally com-
pelling and utterly involving universes from literally millions
of submissions. In the three years its selections have been eligi-
ble, universes from* PLENUM *have won five of the Apotheo
Awards given by HVMW (Holo Visionaries of the Milky Way),
not to mention two of the Yahweh Awards bestowed by hv
fandom at its annual Galactic Cons.*

THE CONTRIBUTORS:

Daphne Deirdre Dubose ("Quasars and Cumquats") has
gained an enviable reputation in the last eight years for her
inimitable "mood" programs in this and other anthology-pack-
ages. "My intent," Daphne lasers from her home in the Austra
Outback, "is to develop a schema of interlocking universes that
overwhelm the experiencer by their cumulative evocativeness
and make the chauvinist son of a bitch cough up his delusions
about how reality operates." With her lifeperson Bruce and her
two littl'uns, Daphne lives in a magnificent crater hole, one of
the many topological changes in Earth's terrain precipitated by
last century's Cobalt Galas. In this secluded Eden nearly four
thousand kilometers from the nearest cit-site, she brings her

209

holovistic universes to slow fruition and incidentally teaches a special course called "John Milton and Introductory World-Shaping" via satellite to thousands of subscribing students all around the globe. Many of Creative-Person Dubose's previous full-length cosmoses appeared in inexpensive two-paks from AC/DC Distributors. Since the success of her Yahweh-winning program *Rib of Chaos,* however, several of these cosmoses have been reissued in platinum-paks (@ 10^{18} inflated georges, Daphne bids me to remind you).

◆

S. K. Sullnan ("Black Hole Blues") is one of a tidal influx of sardonic young holo-visionaries who are attempting to extend the range and techniques of holovistic programming. Sullnan's universes are darkly engrossing experiences. He neither gives nor asks quarter. The maelstromic fragmentation of his method, initially confusing, ultimately holds a glass up to the experiencer in which he recognizes himself and feels a cathartic revulsion. With such universes as "Up Yours, Life" and "The Incredible Shrinking Élan" Sullnan has enraged long-time hv addicts and traditional world-shapers alike by attacking many of the field's sacred cows. In "Black Hole Blues," for instance, he once again questions the necessity of existence.

◆

"Faster Than the Speed of Love" marks the fourth appearance of Benjamin Bacaruda's work in the *PLENUM* anthology-package. Bacaruda is one of the few active holo-visionaries whose career spans the contemporary history of our field. His first holovistic universes were associated with the "Golden Age" of *HYPNOTIC,* back in those glorious but vaguely reprehensible days when we bought our hv paks from pedwalk Vend-O Dispensers and slunk guiltily home to experience them in the shameful privacy of our delta-coves. (Who in those days had either the wherewithal or the spunk to buy a fully equipped plenarium?) Even then, though, Bacaruda was raising the standards of the field. His universette "More Than Megacosmic" is still frequently anthologized; its introduction of sensual and deific motifs was an ether-breaking step in the development of modern hv. In the last decade Bacaruda has been exploring the manifold possibilities of relativistic meiosis. He is a past secretary-treasurer of HVMW and in this capacity urges me to report to the membership that ballots for last year's Apotheo Awards are on the way.

◆

Harmony Shadrack ("Hallucinogengineers") is, along with Benjamin Bacaruda, the only world-shaper whose work has appeared in each number of the *PLENUM* series. She is the only contributor to place more than one universe in a single package (*PLENUM THREE*, which contains "Time's Lapse Gap" and the universella "The Philosopher's Stone Considered as a Hemorrhoid"). Viewed by the hv community as a member of the new generation, Shadrack has startled her experiencers by creating gut-and-cut programs which are painfully absorbing on several levels. Her contribution to this package signals the beginning of a series dealing with the cosmological effects of universe-expanding stimulants. Her next full-dimension cosmos will be entitled *The Eye-Scream Clone;* it is scheduled for immediate distribution. In standard time Harmony Shadrack is the lifeperson of editor Ethelstan Bem.

◆

Pfara ' 'A'ra' 'pf ' s "The Other Worldly, the Other Wise" marks the first appearance in the *PLENUM* series of the work of an alien. Pifi, as he/she/it is known by its/his/her friends, is a master of thirty-three different sensory complexes. Entity ' 'A'ra' 'pf has translated the beautiful and moving "The Other Worldly, the Other Wise" from the Vegan sensory complex into our own auditory-gustatory-olfactory-tactile-visual system. Experiencers of this wonderfully strange universe will no doubt admit that it is unique among all their many hours of hv-ing. We look for more good work from Pifi and wish her/it/him a successful alternate-cycle estivation this summer on Vega II.

◆

R. Ron Golightly ("Fifth Moon in the Corner Pocketa") is the unpigeonholable loony in the pantheon of holovistic programmers. He has been known to create universes from back to front and from the middle to both sides out, breaking rules lesser talents don't even know exist. "Microminiaturizing Andromache" in *PLENUM ONE*, for instance, was a hilarious restructuring of the Welsh *Mabinogion* into a cowboy love song about unrequited entropy. A recent wrinkle in his work has been the introduction of robot solar systems which wind up, and down, and round about, in accordance with the rules of tri-dimensional, mechanistic snooker. Golightly tells us that for a lark he is now retranslating "The Other Worldly, the Other Wise" back into Vegan. "Where it always belonged to begin with," he adds facetiously.

◆

Asa C. Mach, whose universella "Doomdrop" is the featured program in *PLENUM FOUR*, has long been known for the impeccable scientific grounding of his work. Like Bacaruda, Mach had his start in such Vend-O paks as *HYPNOTIC*, *HEAD-FUL*, and *VERTIGO*.

"I got 1½ semi-inflated georges per amp back then and, upon occasion, used to pump up the voltage to no real purpose just to be able to keep body and soul together. My idols were the Big Bang Phenomenon and wind erosion (yes, I know, this last smacks of faddishness), and I tried my damnedest to create programs combining the dynamism of the one with the delicate aestheticism of the other. Even so, many of my early universes were the products of a technology-struck hacker, altogether devoid of style but long on spectacular effects. Hopefully, I've learned a few things over the years."

Mr. Mach's contribution "Doomdrop" attests to the fact that

he has. Its sensitive delving of the simultaneous occurrence of binary supernovas is a *tour de force* of holovistic programming, one which I'm sure few of our experiencers will be able to forget.

"Actually," the estimable Asa C. Mach lasers us, "I got in over my head with this program. Its seeming realism derives from the fact that I induced an ultra-delayed neutron chain-reaction in the atoms at ole Sol's core, did a little undercrust holography by means of three ESPer-eye, plasma-glide waldos, withdrew with a complete spectrum of sensory-complex images, recombined the lot with a bi-scopic mixer, and—*voila!* Unfortunately, the core explosions will probably surface within the next two years in the guise of an annoying pseudo-nova. Except that the effects of the nova will hardly be *pseudo*, the term refers only to the manner of its initiation. But you know how this business is, Stan; a real world-shaper will sacrifice anything for a synapse-boggling holovision."

Experiencers of the *PLENUM* series will no doubt agree that "Doomdrop" was worth it.

◆

For reasons stemming from Asa C. Mach's creation of "Doom-drop," PLENUM FIVE—to appear early next year—will probably be the final anthology-package in this distinguished series. We hope that it gives you as much pleasure as PLENUM FOUR is sure to.

RICHARD LUPOFF's *"After the Dreamtime," in* New Dimensions 4, *was a sensitive and moving account of life aboard the bizarre sail-powered open-decked starships of the far future, crewed by the descendants of Australian aborigines. That story ended in violence and mutiny; now Lupoff carries his narrative onward, in a sequel that stands up as an independent story for those who may not have read its predecessor.*

■

Richard A. Lupoff

■

SAIL THE TIDE OF MOURNING

Nurundere, captain, ordered his lighter to be hauled from the storage deck of *Djanggawul* and fitted for use of Jiritzu. Sky heroes bent their efforts, sweat glistening on black skin, dirt of labor staining white duck trousers and grip-soled shoes.

Much thought was given to their work and the reasons for it although little was said of the matter. The people of Yurakosi were not given greatly to speech: a taciturnity, self-containment was part of the heritage of their race, from the days of their desert isolation in the heartland of Australia, O'Earth.

They alone of the scattered children of Sol carried the gene that let them sail the membrane ships. They alone carried in their skin the pigment that filtered out the deadly radiation of the tracks between the stars, that permitted them to clamber up masts and through rigging as had their ancestors on the pacific waters of O'Earth centuries before, while spacemen of other breeds clumbered and heaved about in their massive vacuum armor.

The brilliant light of the multiple star Yirrkalla wheeled overhead; *Djanggawul* had completed her great tack and pointed her figureheaded prow toward home, toward Yurakosi, bearing the melancholy tale of her voyage to N'Jaja and N'Ala and the death of a passenger, Ham Tamdje of N'Jaja, at the hands of the sky hero Jiritzu.

Djanggawul bore yet the scars of the attempt by surner meat to seize control of the membrane ship and force from her crew the secret of their ability to live unsuited in space. At N'Ala she had shuttled the surviving surners to the orbiting Port Corley, along with the bodies of those killed in the mutiny.

And now, passing the great tack at Yirrkalla, *Djanggawul* heeled beneath the titanic solar wind that would fill all sails that bellied out from the rows of masts on her three flat decks. With each moment the ship gained momentum. Under the careful piloting of her first officer Uraroju she would sail to Yurakosi on this momentum and on the force of the interstellar winds she encountered on her great arcing course. There would be no need to start her auxiliary engines, to annihilate any of the precious rod of collapsed matter that hung suspended through the long axis of *Djanggawul*, where it provided the artificial gravity for the ship.

Sky heroes swarmed the storage deck of the ship, readying Nurundere's lighter for Jiritzu. They fitted the tiny ship with food concentrate, tested her recyclers, tried her hinged mast fittings, and clamped the masts to the hull of the lighter in anticipation of her catapulting from the deck of *Djanggawul*.

When the lighter was fully prepared, the sky hero Baime went to *Djanggawul*'s bridge to inform Nurundere and Uraroju. Others in the work party hauled the lighter from its place in the storage deck, refixed the now vacant moorings that had held the lighter, and worked the tiny ship through a great cargo hatch onto the main deck of *Djanggawul*.

High above the deck Jiritzu stood balanced lightly on a spar near the top of a mainmast. He was dressed like any sky hero of the crew of *Djanggawul*, in white trousers and canvas shoes, black knitted cap and turtleneck sweater, the costume declared by Yurakosi tradition to have been the costume of the sky heroes' ancestors on O'Earth.

A tiny radio had been implanted behind one ear, and strapped to his thigh was a close-air generator. The oxygen-rich mixture that it slowly emitted clung to Jiritzu, providing him with the air he needed for breath, insulating him from the extreme temperatures of space, providing an invisible pressure suit that protected him from the vacuum all around.

He watched the cargo hatch roll slowly back onto the deck beneath him, the one of *Djanggawul*'s three identical outer decks most easily accessible from the lighter's storage place, and watched his fellow sky heroes haul the lighter onto the deck. He kept his radio turned off, and by tacit agreement no man or woman of *Djanggawul*'s crew, not even Jiritzu's kunapi half Dua, approached the mast he had climbed or made any sign of knowing of his presence.

Nurundere himself strode from the bridge of his ship to inspect the lighter, now standing empty on the deck. Jiritzu could tell him easily, not merely by his distinctive cap of white with its wide black band, but by his pale skin, the protective pigmentation of the Yurakosi almost totally faded now, whited out by the passing years and long exposure to the radiation of the naked stars.

Soon Nurundere would have to return to Yurakosi himself, give himself over to the life of a ground squirmer, crawl with the small children and the old men and women of Yurakosi, the only inhabitants of the planet whose able sons and daughters were desperately needed to sail the membrane ships between the stars.

Not so Jiritzu.

Again and again his mind flashed to the terrible scene inside the passenger tank of *Djanggawul,* the moments when the surner meat, the passengers whose payments financed the flights of the membrane ships and filled the coffers of the sky heroes' home planet, had shown firearms—an act unknown on the peaceful, neutral ships—and had briefly imprisoned much of the crew.

Again Jiritzu relived the horror of finding his betrothed, Miralaidj, daughter of Wuluwaid and Bunbulama, dead at the hand of Ham Tamdje.

Again Jiritzu relived the pleasure, the terrible pleasure of killing Ham Tamdje himself, with his bare hands. At the thought he felt sweat burst from his face and hands. His leg, where a bullet fired by Ham Tamdje had torn the flesh, throbbed with pain.

He closed his eyes tightly, turned his face from the deck below him to the blackness above, reopened his eyes.

Above him gleamed the constellation Yirrkalla, beneath which *Djanggawul* had made her great tack. The colored stars formed the facial features of the Rainbow Serpent: the pale, yellow-green eyes, the angry white nostrils, the blood-red venomous fangs. And beyond Yirrkalla, fading, fading across the immensity of the heavens, the body of the Rainbow Serpent himself, writhing and curving across the void that separated galaxies.

A drop of sweat fell from Jiritzu's forehead, rolled to the edge of one eye where it stung like a tiny insect, then rolled on, enlarged by a tear.

He looked downward, saw that the work on the deck was completed, the lighter ready for his use. With heavy heart he lowered himself slowly to the deck of *Djanggawul*, avoiding the acrobatic tumbles that had been his great joy since his earliest days on the membrane ships.

He walked slowly across the deck of the great ship, halted before the captain's lighter. A party of sky heroes had assembled at the lighter. Jiritzu examined their faces, found in them a mixture of sadness at the loss of a friend and fellow and resignation at what they knew would follow.

Nurundere was there himself. The captain of *Djanggawul* opened his arms, facing directly toward Jiritzu. He moved his lips in speech but Jiritzu left his implanted radio turned off. The meaning of Nurundere was clear without words.

Jiritzu came to his captain. They embraced. Jiritzu felt the strong arms of the older man clasp about his shoulders. Then he was released, stepped back.

Beside Nurundere stood Uraroju, first officer of *Djanggawul*. Some junior officer, then, had been left upon the bridge. Uraroju was a younger person than Nurundere, her protective pigmentation still strong, barely beginning to white out; she would have many years before her as a sky hero, would surely become captain of *Djanggawul* with Nurundere's retirement to Yurakosi.

They embraced, Jiritzu for a moment closing his eyes, permitting himself to pretend that Uraroju was his own mother, that he was visiting his old people in their town of Kaitjouga on Yurakosi. The warmth of Uraroju, the feel of her womanhood, comforted Jiritzu. Then they released each other, and he turned to other men and women he would never again see, men and women who must return to Yurakosi with the tale of the tragic things that had transpired between Port Upatoi and Yirrkalla on the outward leg of their sail, and with the tale of the end of Jiritzu.

Watilun he embraced, Watilun the machinist and hero of the battle against the mutineers.

Baime he embraced, a common sailor, Jiritzu's messmate.

Kutjara he embraced, Kutjara with whom he had often swarmed the lines of *Djanggawul*.

Only Dua, kunapi half to Jiritzu of the aranda, spoke in their parting embrace. Radios mute, Dua spoke in the moments when his close-air envelope and that of Jiritzu were merged, when common speech could be carried without electronic aid.

"Bidjiwara is not here," Dua said. None but Jiritzu could hear this. "The loss of her aranda half Miralaidj is too great for little Bidjiwara to bear. The loss of yourself, Jiritzu, is too great for Bidjiwara. She remains below, weeping alone.

"I too have wept for you, my aranda half, but I could not remain below. I could not forego our parting time."

He kissed Jiritzu on the cheek, his lips brushing the *maraiin*, the swirling scarifications born by all kunapi and aranda, whose meaning he, Dua alone of all Jiritzu's shipmates, understood.

Jiritzu clasped both Dua's hands in his own, saying nothing. Then he turned away and went to inspect the lighter given him by Nurundere. He found all in order, climbed upon the deck of the tiny membrane craft, signaled to the sky heroes on *Djanggawul*'s deck.

Watilun himself operated the catapult.

Jiritzu found himself cast from *Djanggawul*, forward and upward from her deck, the distance between the great membrane ship and tiny lighter growing with each moment. He sighed only once, then turned to the task of sailing his new ship.

Above him lay the writhing length of the Rainbow Serpent. By conference with Nurundere and Uraroju over many days it had been settled that Jiritzu would not return with *Djanggawul* to Yurakosi. His act in killing Ham Tamdje was understood. There was no question of trial, no accusation or even suggestion of crime.

But the tradition of the sky-hero peoples held sacred any passenger on the membrane ships.

Death of meat, membrane-ship passengers, ground squirmers traveling between the stars in the tanks of sky-hero craft instead of sealed in the bellies of massive conventional spacecraft, was almost unknown. There was the half-legendary story of Elyun El-Kumarbis, traveler from the pan-semite empire of O'Earth sailing aboard *Makarata* to Al-ghoul Phi, who had passed as a sky hero and died of space radiation, his body later launched into deep space at his dying request.

And there was the new tragedy of Ham Tamdje and his killer Jiritzu who could never again be permitted to ride the membrane ships as a sky hero.

Beneath Jiritzu and the lighter, *Djanggawul* dwindled, her great membrane sails bellied out with starwinds, her golden skin reflecting the multicolored lights of the Yirrkalla constellation.

And above Jiritzu, Yirrkalla itself, the serpent face, leering and glowing its brightness.

He erected the masts of the lighter, fixed their bases on the three equilaterally mounted decks of the lighter, climbed each mast in turn, rotating gimbaled spars into position and locking them perpendicular to the masts. The sails, the fine, almost monomolecular membranes that would catch the starwinds and carry the lighter onward, he left furled for the time being.

From the top of a mast he pushed himself gently, parallel with the deck of the lighter. He floated softly to the deck, landing with bent knees to absorb the light impact of his lean frame on the lighter's deck.

He opened the hatch and crawled into the cramped interior of the lighter to check the instruments and supplies he knew were there—the compact rations, the lighter's multiradiational telescope that he would bring with him to the deck and mount for use, the lighter's miniature guidance computer.

Instead, before even switching on the cabin light, he saw two brief reflections of the colored illumination of Yirrkalla—what he knew must be two eyes.

He flicked on his implanted radio and demanded to know the identity of the stowaway.

"Don't be angry, Jiritzu," her voice quivered, "I had to come along."

"Bidjiwara!" he cried.

She launched herself across the cabin, crossing it in an easy, gliding trajectory. She caught his hand in her two, brought it to her face, pressed his palm to the *maraiin*, the graceful scarifications on her cheek.

"Don't be angry with me," she repeated.

He felt himself slump to the deck of the cabin, sitting with his back to the bulkhead, the hatchway leading to the outer deck overhead, light pouring in. He shook himself, turned to look into the face of Bidjiwara, young Bidjiwara, she who was barely entering womanhood, whose voyage on *Djanggawul* was her first as a sky hero, her first offplanet, her first away from Yurakosi.

"Angry? Angry?" Jiritzu repeated stupidly. "No, Bidjiwara, my—my dear Bidjiwara." He brought his face close to hers, felt as she cupped his cheeks in the palms of her hands.

He shook his head. "I couldn't be angry with you. But do you understand? Do you know where this little ship is bound?"

Suddenly he pulled away from her grasp, sprang back to the deck of the lighter, sighted back in the direction of *Djang-*

gawul. Could he see her as a distant speck? Was that the great membrane ship—or a faint, remote star?

His radio was still on. He stood on the lighter's deck, shouted after *Djanggawul* and her crew. "Dua! Nurundere! Uraroju!"

There was no answer, only a faint, random crackling in his skull, the signals of cosmic radio emanations broadcast by colliding clouds of interstellar gas.

He dropped back through the hatch, into the cabin of the lighter.

He reached for Bidjiwara, took her extended hand, drew her with him back onto the deck of the lighter.

"You know why I am here," he said, half in question, half assertion.

She nodded, spoke softly a word in confirmation.

Still, he said, "I will die. I am here to die."

She made no answer, stood with her face to his sweater, her hands resting lightly against his shoulders. He looked down at her, saw how thin her body was, the contours of womanhood but barely emergent from the skinny, sticklike figure of the boisterous child his dead Miralaidj had loved as a little sister.

Jiritzu felt tears in his eyes.

"I could not go back to Yurakosi," he said. "I am a young man, my skin still fine and black, protecting me from the poison of the stars. I could not become a squirmer, alone in a world of children and ancients.

"I would have thrown myself with all my strength from the top of *Djanggawul*'s highest mast. I would have escaped the ship, fallen forever through space like the corpse of El-Kumarbis.

"Nurundere said no." Jiritzu stopped, looked down at Bidjiwara, at her glossy, midnight hair spilling from beneath her knitted cap, her black, rounded forehead. For a moment he bent and pressed his cheek against the top of her head, then raised his eyes again to the Rainbow Serpent and spoke.

"Nurundere gave me his own ship, his captain's lighter. 'Take the lighter, Jiritzu,' he said, 'I can unload at Port Bralku with the others, by shuttle. I need no glorious captain's barge. Sail on forever,' Nurundere said, 'a better fate than the one awaiting me.'

"You understand, Bidjiwara? I mean to sail the Rainbow Serpent, the tide that flows between the galaxies. I will sail as long as the rations aboard last. I will die on this little ship, my soul will return to the Dreamtime, my body will continue onward, borne by the Rainbow Serpent.

"I will never become a ground crawler. I will never return to Yurakosi. No world will know my tread—ever."

Bidjiwara turned her face, raising her eyes from Jiritzu's ribbed sweater to look directly into his eyes.

"Very well, Jiritzu. I will sail the Rainbow Serpent with you. Where else was there for me to go?"

Jiritzu laughed bitterly. "You are a child. You should have remained aboard *Djanggawul.* You had many years before you as a sky hero. Look at your skin," he said, raising her hand to hold it before them both. No power lights were burning on the little ship, but the colors of Yirrkalla glowed white, green-yellow, blood red.

"Black, Bidjiwara, black with the precious shield that only our people claim."

"And your own?" she responded.

"My own pigment—yes, I too would have had many more years to play at sky hero. But I killed Ham Tamdje. I broke the sacred trust. I could sail the great membrane ships no longer."

He dropped her hand and walked a few paces away. He stood, his back half-turned to her, and his words were carried to her by the tiny radios implanted in both their skulls.

"And Miralaidj," he almost whispered, "Miralaidj—in the Dreamtime. And her father Wuluwaid in the Dreamtime. No."

He turned and looked upward through naked spars to the glowing stars of Yirrkalla and the Rainbow Serpent. "We should set to work rigging sails," he said.

"I *will* stay with you then," she said. "You will not send me away, send me back."

"Dua knew you were hidden?"

She nodded yes.

"My closest friend, my half, kunapi to my aranda. Dua told me a lie."

"I begged him, Jiritzu."

For a moment he almost glared at her, anger filling his face. "Why do you wish to die?"

She shook her head. "I wish to be with you."

"You will die with me."

"I will return to the Dreamtime with you."

"You believe the old stories."

She shrugged. "We should set to work rigging sails." And scurried away, flung open lockers, drew out furled sheets of nearly monomolecular membrane, scampered up a mast and began fixing the sail to spars.

Jiritzu stood on the deck, watching. Then he crossed to another of the lighter's three equilateral decks and followed the example of Bidjiwara.

He worked until he had completed the rigging of the masts of the deck, then crossed again, to the third of the lighter's decks, opened a locker, drew membrane and clambered to the top of a mast. There he clung, knees gripping the vertical shaft, arms flung over the topmost spar, rigging the sail.

He completed the work, looked across to the farthermost mast, near the stern of the lighter. The Rainbow Serpent drew a gleaming polychromatic backdrop. The mast was silhouetted against the Serpent, and standing on the highest spar, one hand outstretched clinging to the mast, the other arm and leg extended parallel to the spar, was Bidjiwara.

Her envelope of close air shimmered with refraction of the colors of Yirrkalla. Jiritzu clung to the rigging where he had worked, struck still and silent by the beauty of the child. He wondered why she did not see him, then gradually realized, aided by the misty sidereal light of the region, that she stood with her back to him, her face raised to the great tide that flowed between the galaxies, her mind wholly unconcerned with her surroundings and unaware of his presence.

Jiritzu lowered himself silently through the spars and rigging of the lighter, through a hatchway and into the tiny cabin of the lighter. There he prepared a light meal and set it aside, lay down to rest and waited for the return of Bidjiwara.

He may have dozed and seen into the Dreamtime, for he saw the figures of Miralaidj and her father Wulawaid floating in a vague jumble of shapes and slow, wavering movement. He opened his eyes and saw Bidjiwara lower herself through the hatchway into the cabin, white rope-soled shoes first, white duck trousers clinging close to her long skinny legs and narrow hips, then her black ribbed sweater.

"Our ship has no name," she said.

He pondered for a moment, shrugged, said, "Does it need one?"

"It would be—somehow I think we would be more with our people," Bidjiwara replied.

"Well, if you wish. What shall we make her name?"

"You have no choice?"

"None."

"We will truly sail on the great tide? On the Rainbow Serpent?"

"We are already."

"Then I would call our ship after the sacred fish. Let it bear us to the Dreamtime."

"Baramundi."

"Yes."

"As you wish."

She came and sat by him, her hands folded in her lap. She sat silently.

"Food is ready," he said.

She looked at the tiny table that served in the lighter as work space, desk, and dining table. Jiritzu saw her smile, wondered at the mixture in her face of little child and wise woman. She looked somehow as he thought the Great Mother must look, if only he believed in the Great Mother.

Bidjiwara crossed the small distance and brought two thin slices of hot biscuit. She held them both to Jiritzu. He took one, pressed the other back upon her.

Silently they ate the biscuit.

Afterward she said, "Jiritzu, is there more to do now?"

He said, "We should check our position." He undogged the ship's telescope and carried it to the deck of *Baramundi*.

Bidjiwara helped him to mount it on the gimbaled base that stood waiting for it. Jiritzu sighted on the brightest star in Yirrkalla for reference—it was a gleaming crimson star that marked the end of a fang in the serpent face, that Yurakosi tradition called Blood of Hero.

On the barrel of the telescope where control squares were mounted he tapped all of the radiational sensors into life, to cycle through filters and permit the eyepiece to observe the Rainbow Serpent by turns under optical, radio, x-ray, gamma radiation.

He put his eye to the eyepiece and watched the Serpent as it seemed to move with life, its regions responding to the cycling sensitivity of the telescope.

He drew away and Bidjiwara put her eye to the telescope, standing transfixed for minutes until at last she too drew away and turned to Jiritzu.

"The Serpent truly lives," she said. "Is it—a real creature?"

Jiritzu shook his head. "The tides of the galaxies draw each other. The Serpent is a flow of matter. Stars, dust, gas. To ride with it would mean a journey of billions of years to reach the next of its kind. To sail the starwinds that fill the Rainbow Serpent, we will reach marvelous speed. As long as we can sail our craft, we can tack from wind to wind.

"And once we have gone to the Dreamtime, *Baramundi* will float on, on the tide, along the Rainbow Serpent. Someday she may beach on some distant shore."

He looked at Bidjiwara, smiled, repeated his statement.

Bidjiwara replied, "And if she does not?"

"Then she may be destroyed in some way, or simply—drift forever. Forever."

Jiritzu saw the girl stretch and yawn. She crossed the cabin and drew him down alongside the bulkhead, nestled up to him and went to sleep.

He lay with her in his arms, wondering at her trust, watching the play of sidereal light that reflected through the hatchway and illuminated her face dimly.

He extended one finger and gently, gently traced the *mara-iin* on her cheek, wondering at its meaning. He pressed his face to her head again, pulled away her knitted cap and let her hair tumble loose, feeling its softness with his own face, smelling the odor of her hair.

He too slept.

They awoke together, stirring and stretching, and looked into each other's face and laughed. They used the lighter's sanitary gear and nibbled a little breakfast and went on deck. Together they checked *Baramundi*'s rigging, took sightings with her multiradiational telescope, and fed information into her little computer.

The computer offered course settings in tiny, glowing display lights and Jiritzu and Bidjiwara reset *Baramundi*'s sails.

They sat on deck, bathed in the perpetual twilight of the Rainbow Serpent's softly glowing colors.

They spoke of their childhoods on Yurakosi, of their old people, their skins whited out by years of sailing the membrane ships, retired to the home planet to raise the children while all the race's vigorous adults crewed the great ships, sailed between the stars carrying freight and occasional passengers sealed inside their hulls, laughing at the clumsy craft and clumsy crews of all others than the aranda and the kunapi.

They climbed through the rigging of *Baramundi,* shinnying up masts lightly, balancing on spars, occasionally falling—or leaping—from the ship's heights, to drop gently, gently back onto her deck.

They ate and drank the smallest amounts they could of the lighter's provisions, tacitly stretching the supplies as far as they could be stretched, carefully recycling to add still more to the time they could continue.

They lay on *Baramundi*'s deck sometimes, when the rest time they had agreed upon came, Bidjiwara nestling against the taller Jiritzu, falling asleep as untroubledly as a young child, Jiritzu wondering over and over at this girl who had come to die with him, who asked few questions, who lived each hour as if it were the beginning of a long and joyous life rather than the final act of a tragedy.

Jiritzu felt very old.

He was nearly twenty by the ancient, arbitrary scale of age carried to the star worlds from O'Earth, the scale of the seasons and the years in old Arnhem Land in the great desert of their ancestral home. Six years older than Bidjiwara, he had traveled the star routes for five, had sailed the membrane ships across tens of billions of miles in that time.

And Bidjiwara asked little of him. They were more playmates than—than anything else, he thought.

"Tell me of El-Kumarbis," she said one day, perched high on a spar above *Baramundi*'s deck.

"You know all about him," Jiritzu replied.

"Where is he now?"

Jiritzu shrugged, exasperated. "Somewhere beyond Al-ghoul, no one knows where. He was buried in space."

"What if we find his body?" Bidjiwara shivered.

"Impossible."

"Why?"

"In infinite space? What chance that two objects moving at random will collide?"

"No?"

He shook his head.

"Could the computer find him?"

He shrugged. "If we knew exactly when he was buried, and where, and his trajectory and speed and momentum . . . No, it's still impossible."

"Dinner time," she said. "You wait here, I'll fix it."

She came back with the customary biscuits and a jar filled with dark fluid. Jiritzu took the jar, held it high against the ambient light—they seldom used any of *Baramundi*'s power lights.

"Wine," Bidjiwara said.

He looked amazed.

"I found a few capsules in the ship's supplies. You just put one in some water."

They ate and drank. The wine was warm, its flavor soft. They sprawled on the deck of *Baramundi* after the biscuits were gone, passing the jar back and forth, slowly drinking the wine.

When it was gone Bidjiwara nestled against Jiritzu; for once, instead of sleeping she lay looking into his face, holding her hands to the sides of his head.

She said his name softly, then flicked off her radio and pressed her lips close to his neck so their air envelopes were one, the sound carried directly from her lips to his ear, and whispered his name again.

"Bidjiwara," he said, "you never answered why you came on board *Baramundi.*"

"To be with Jiritzu," she said.

"Yes, but why? Why come to die with me?"

"Tall Jiritzu," she said, "strong Jiritzu. You saw me aboard *Djanggawul*, you were kind to me but as you are kind to children. Men never know, only women know love."

He laughed, not cruelly. "You're only—"

"A woman," she said.

"And you want—?"

Now she laughed at him. "You man, you mighty man. You don't understand that all men are the children of women."

She drew away from him, slid her black ribbed sweater over her head and dropped it to the deck. He put his hands onto her naked back, trembling, then slowly slid them around her, touching her little, half-developed breasts, fondling her soft nipples with his hands.

She buried her forehead in the side of his neck, whispered against his throat, "For this, Jiritzu, I came aboard *Baramundi* for this."

He ran his thumbs down her breastbone, to her navel, to her white duck trousers, and peeled them down, and took her.

And the next day they were nearly out of biscuit and they went on half rations to make their supplies last longer.

They played children's games, shouting and chasing each other up and down the lighter's masts.

They leaped and sailed from the decks, past the membrane sails, into the emptiness, then hung for a moment and fell back, gently, to *Baramundi.*

Jiritzu leaped too hard, too high, and feared that he had broken from the ship. He looked up—down—into the coils of the Rainbow Serpent. He felt himself revolving slowly, helplessly hanging in the emptiness, alone and unshielded except by the close air his generator made and the protection of the pigment he carried in his skin.

He thought to cry for help, then held back. If he was afloat, Bidjiwara could not help him. He turned slowly, facing toward *Baramundi,* her membranes bellied with stellar wind, her deck reflecting the lights of the Serpent; he could not see Bidjiwara.

He turned slowly, facing toward the Rainbow Serpent, feeling as if he could fall forever into its colored bands, its long coils stretching no lesser distance than the span between galaxies.

He turned slowly, revolving on the axis of his own body, feeling no motion himself but watching the stars and the Serpent and *Baramundi* the sacred fish revolve slowly around him, wheeling, wheeling, when his outflung arm struck an object as hard and cold as the ultimate ice of a deadstar world.

He recoiled, spun involuntarily, stared.

It was—yes.

He looked back toward *Baramundi,* revolved using his own limbs as counterweights, placed himself between the corpse and the lighter and pressed gently with the soles of his rope-soled shoes against the hard, frigid corpse.

Slowly he drifted back toward *Baramundi*—and, wheeling again as he drifted, saw the corpse drifting away, upward or downward into the lights of the Rainbow Serpent.

As he approached *Baramundi* he pondered whether or not

to tell Bidjiwara of his find. Finally he told her—the incredible happenstance had occurred.

Later they crept to the farthermost deck for their loving, then back into the tiny cabin to sleep.

And soon *Baramundi*'s supplies were exhausted, and still Jiritzu and Bidjiwara continued. Their water remained, and a few of the capsules. They had wine from time to time. They gave less effort to running the ship, ceased to play in the rigging, ceased to leap.

The wound in Jiritzu's leg resumed its throbbing intermittently. He would rub it, or Bidjiwara would rub it for him, and the pain would ease.

They made love, it seemed, with increasing frequency. The sensations of their couplings seemed to increase as lack of nourishment drew their bodies ever tighter, ever more acutely into awareness of each other.

They lay together most of the time, seldom dressing fully.

They drank water only, their wine capsules exhausted.

They slept increasingly.

In *Baramundi*'s cabin Jiritzu fed telescopic data into the lighter's computer, read the responses displayed on its little illuminated screen. After the acclimatization of his eyes to none but sidereal light, even the miniature display lights were dazzling: his eyes pulsed with afterimages for minutes following the exercise.

It was difficult to climb from the cabin back onto the deck.

Bidjiwara waited for him there, barefoot, sitting on the deck with her wrists clasped around her knees, wearing only her white trousers and black knitted cap. She smiled a welcome to him, asked a question wordlessly.

"Here," he said with a shrug. "Here is where we are. As we have been. Riding the Rainbow Serpent. Riding the tide. Sailing the starwinds."

He felt dizzy for a moment, reached out with one hand to steady himself against the telescope mount, then sank to a squat beside Bidjiwara.

She put her arms around him and he lay on the deck, his head in her lap. He looked up into her face. She was Bidjiwara the lovely child, Miralaidj her aranda half, she was Jiritzu's own mother on Yurakosi, the Great Mother.

He opened and closed his eyes, unable to tell which woman this was.

He reached and traced the *maraiin* on her cheek.

She nodded, began speaking softly, telling him the meaning of the scarifications.

When she had finished he took her hand, held it against his chest, and slowly told her the meaning of his own *maraiin*. He spoke with closed eyes, opened them when he felt a drop of wetness, saw her weeping softly, drew her face down to his own to kiss.

She lay down beside him and they embraced gently, then both slept.

After that they paid less attention to *Baramundi*'s needs. Jiritzu and Bidjiwara grew weaker. They slept more, confined their activity to occasional short walks on *Baramundi*'s decks. Both of them grew thinner, lighter. Their growing weakness seemed almost to be offset by the decreasing demands of the ship's artificial gravity.

They lay on deck for hours, watching the glow of the Rainbow Serpent. They were far beyond the Serpent's head now, the stars of Yirrkalla clustered now into a meaningless sparkler jumble far, far astern of *Baramundi*.

Jiritzu was awake, had taken a sparse sip of their little remaining water, left Bidjiwara to doze where she lay, her hair a mourning wreath circling her emaciated features. Jiritzu made his way unsteadily to the prow of *Baramundi*, bracing himself against masts and small stanchions as he walked.

He sighted through the ship's telescope, enjoying in a faint, detached manner the endless, kaleidoscopic changes of the Rainbow Serpent's multiradiational forms. At length he turned away from the scope and looked back toward Bidjiwara. He could not tell if she was breathing. He could not tell for a certainty who she was.

He returned to the telescope, tapped its power squares to cause it to superimpose its multiple images rather than run them in sequence. He gazed, rapt, at the Serpent for a time, then swung the scope overhead, sweeping back and forth across the sky above *Baramundi*.

He settled on a black speck that floated silhouetted against the glow of the Serpent. For a while he watched it grow larger.

He turned from the telescope back to the deck of the lighter. Bidjiwara had wakened and risen; she was walking slowly, slowly toward him.

In the glow of the Rainbow Serpent her emaciation was transformed to a fine perception that etched every line, every muscle beneath her skin. She wore sweater and trousers; Jiritzu could see her high breasts, the ribbed sweater conforming to their sharp grace, her nipples standing as points of reference for the beauty of her torso.

Her white trousers managed to retain their fit despite her starvation; Jiritzu discerned the lines of her thighs, the pubic swell over her crotch.

Her face, always thin, seemed all vertical planes now, forehead and temple, nostril and cheek. The ridges of her brows, the lines of her mouth were as if drawn on her face.

Her eyes seemed to have gained an intense brightness.

As she crossed the deck to Jiritzu she gained in strength and steadiness.

She held her hands toward him, smiling, and he felt his own strength returning to him. He took the steps needed to come to her, reached and took her two hands, clasped them in his. They embraced, calling each other's name.

The dark figure of Elyun El-Kumarbis dropped onto the deck of *Baramundi*. He strode to Jiritzu and Bidjiwara.

"Lovers!" he said. "Sky heroes!"

They turned to him, arms still around each other. Each extended a hand to him, felt his: cold, cold.

"All my years," the O'Earther said, "I wanted no thing but to sail a membrane ship. To be a sky hero."

"Yes," Jiritzu said, "you are known to all sky heroes, Elyun El-Kumarbis. Your fame spans the galaxy."

"And where do you sail, sky heroes?"

"We sail the tide, we sail the Rainbow Serpent."

"Aboard your ship?"

"Baramundi has brought us this far, but no farther. It is fit now for us to return to the Dreamtime."

Elyun El-Kumarbis nodded. "May I—may I greet you as brother and sister sky heroes?" he asked.

"Yes," answered Jiritzu.

"Yes," answered Bidjiwara.

Elyun El-Kumarbis kissed them each on the cheek, on the *maraiin* scarifications of each. And his kiss was cold, cold.

Full of strength Jiritzu and Bidjiwara sprang to the spars of *Baramundi*'s highest mast, scrambled up lines to the topmost spar of the lighter.

They looked back at Elyun El-Kumarbis, who stood wondering beside the ship's telescope.

They took each other's hands, dropped into place on the topmost spar, and together sprang with the full strength of their sky heroes' legs, toughened and muscled by years of training in the rigging of membrane ships.

They flew up from the spar, up from *Baramundi* the sacred fish, and looking back saw the fish flip his tail once in farewell.

They peered ahead of themselves, into the Rainbow Serpent, saw it writhe toward the far galaxies, heard its hissing voice urging, welcoming them.

They laughed loudly, loudly, feeling strength, warmth and joy. They plunged on and on, skimming the tide of the Rainbow Serpent, feeling the strength of the aranda, of all Yurakosi, of all sky heroes, mighty in their blood.

They threw their arms around each other, laughing for joy, and sped to the Rainbow Serpent, to the galaxies beyond the galaxies, to the Dreamtime forever.